D1357772

STEIN, STUNG

HAL ACKERMAN

A HARRY STEIN SOFT-BOILED MURDER MYSTERY

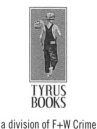

TYRUS
BOOKS

a division of F+W Crime

Published by
TYRUS BOOKS
an imprint of F+W Media, Inc.
10151 Carver Road
Suite 200
Blue Ash, Ohio 45242
www.tyrusbooks.com

ISBN 10: 1-4405-3307-5 (Hardcover)
ISBN 13: 978-1-4405-3307-5 (Hardcover)
ISBN 10: 1-4405-3306-7 (Paperback)
ISBN 13: 978-1-4405-3306-8 (Paperback)
eISBN 10: 1-4405-3205-2
eISBN 13: 978-1-4405-3205-4

Printed in the United States of America.

10   9   8   7   6   5   4   3   2   1

Library of Congress Cataloging-in-Publication Data
is available from the publisher.

This book is available at quantity discounts for bulk purchases.
For information, please call 1-800-289-0963.

Dedication

Love and gratitude to my fierce and lovely warrior, Barbara Poelle. I will never forget your telling me you were reading my manuscript on the subway and laughing out loud. Now look what you've gone and done.

Deep thanks and gratitude to Ben LeRoy and Alison Janssen Dasho for their ongoing belief and support.

Acknowledgments

To Orin and Patti Johnson, to the members of the California State Beekeepers Association who shared their stories; and to all the men and women who quietly go about the business of feeding the world.
This is a work of fiction. But Colony Collapse is real.

Four years after the bees are gone, humanity is gone.
~Albert Einstein

Prologue

Ned Peering had his family up and out of their motel room at seven thirty, marching them with good humor to their Range Rover for a day of family fun. He was a man who believed his irrepressible enthusiasm registered as infectious good cheer. Ned's goal for their Valentine's Day/MLK Day three-day weekend was to visit or pass through as many California parks and attractions as they possibly could.

His wife, Barb, a librarian in the Sacramento school district, had grown tolerant of Ned during their nineteen years together. Tolerant was not what she had hoped for when they married. She had wanted something powerful and unforeseen to change her life forever.

Sanford, their fifteen-year-old son, who was called Skip because he had skipped first and fifth grades, enjoyed family trips. That was not the only social aberration that kept him removed from his peers. He was a repository of answers to questions no one would ever think to ask. (According to the rules for the Olympic Walking Races what is the greatest number of feet a competitor can have off the ground at one time and still be walking?) Like his father, he was wearing a California Angels baseball cap and Bermuda shorts that exposed white hairless legs.

Sitting alongside Skipper in the back seat, or rather slouched into an impenetrable C-curve, was his sister, Sabrina, seventeen going on twenty. She wore spandex shorts over tights and a leotard. Her body was like a lush rolling meadow that was posted with signs warning that TRESPASSERS WILL BE DISDAINED.

Ned breezed his family through the redwoods, diagonally secanted across two points on the circumference of Yosemite so he could check that off his list, and began the climb up the eastern side of the Sierras that would carry them down into the San Joaquin Valley. Ned excelled at projecting ETAs, not only for a trip's final destinations but also for a series of interim checkpoints along the way. He hustled into the parking lot for Mountain Oaks Inn within ninety seconds of his morning projection, exceptional even for him. He glanced hopefully at his wife for a nod of approval, but she was using the side-view mirror to refresh her crimped blond hair.

There were vacant spots closer to the restaurant but Ned prudently parked in a shady spot under a stand of eucalyptus. His family would be comfortable when they came back to the car. It was one of the many anonymous good things he did for which he sought no acknowledgment.

The jukebox played country music as they were led to a semicircular booth under a window. The place had a rowdy western feel. Dark wood paneling. Large framed oil paintings of men on horseback in the days. As the Peerings ordered, an eighteen-wheeler maneuvered laboriously into the parking lot. Nothing about it was remarkable. There would have been no reason to notice the stiff-legged gait of the driver as he checked the security of his payload—neatly stacked white wooden boxes, all of uniform size, perhaps two feet by three feet—then made his way across the gravel-strewn parking lot to the café.

Skip noticed that the truck had South Dakota plates. His mind immediately skipped to its capital, Pierre (pronounced Peer); its exports, wheat and sunflower seeds; and the odd fact that South Dakota bees produced a higher yield of honey per colony than the bees of any other state, including Hawaii. Sabrina noticed the driver was tall with raw, bony shoulders atop a body that once had been leaner. That he walked like a bronco rider who had been thrown a few times too often, and probably gobbled down a handful of Advil in the morning with his black coffee and bourbon. A man who could teach things to a girl she'd regret.

Their food came, nestled up and down the length of their wait-ress's pudgy right arm. Skip was still hungry for breakfast and had ordered bacon and eggs and white toast. Barb felt lunchy and ordered a steak sandwich. Ned surprised everybody by forgoing his usual grilled cheese and tomato and ordering a banana split. Sabrina didn't care and disdained the cottage cheese and fruit her mother had ordered for her. She flipped through the ten pages of jukebox selections mounted above their table.

"See anything you like?" Ned asked.

Her father's interest instantly sapped hers. "It's all country," she said dismissively and stopped looking.

"Country can be good," he said, and backed up his claim by referring to the person who just happened at that moment to enter his visual frame. The driver they had seen out in the parking lot must have had gone directly into the bar through a separate entrance. He emerged now into the dining room with a drink in hand, perhaps a little tipsy, or maybe it was just the sudden contrast to the brightness of the room that startled him and made his first step look unsteady. He located his destination and serpen-tined his way among the bustling waitresses and noisy lunchtime crowd toward the men's room.

"I bet *this* guy likes country," Ned said in his wide-open, affable voice. "Am I right, Frank?" He read the name stitched above the pocket of the truck driver's shirt.

The driver cocked his head to one side and looked down at Ned from his six foot two inch natural height, enhanced by the heels of his engineer boots. "Do I know you?"

Ned ignored Barb's warning pressure on his left arm. He knew an invitation to conversation when he heard one. "My name is Ned. I was just telling my family that you probably liked country music."

"Is that right, *Ned*?" Frank looked down at each member of Ned's family. His gaze did not linger as long on the side of the banquette where the men sat as it did on the other, occupied by the mother and by the daughter, whose acetylene eyes burned behind their asbestos curtain.

"What makes you think I like country music, Ned, or are you just one clairvoyant sonofabitchin cowboy?"

"I'm certainly no cowboy," Ned chuckled, wishing that the fellow had just said yesirree Bob and kept moving. But now he had set his drink down on the leatherette bolster behind Skip's shoulder. There was a lull in the jukebox music so people at other tables looked around.

"What else do you know about me?" Frank asked. "That I cheat at cards? That I have a knife in my boot and a hunger for pretty women?"

Ned may have been the last person in the room to feel the undercurrent, but he felt it now and wanted to extricate with honor. "I certainly didn't intend to be rude," he assured him.

"Do you think I like to dance?"

"We really just want to finish our meals and get to Disneyland. I'm sorry if I gave any offense."

"You're absolutely right," the driver said, and clapped Ned's shoulder with a grip that nearly paralyzed his left side. "I do like to dance." He reached into the right side pocket of his tight blue jeans and spattered some change across the table in Skip's direction and told him to play E-9. Skip had already memorized the charts.

"E-9. 'If I Said You Have a Beautiful Body Would You Hold It Against Me?'"

Frank's eyes were drawn to the heat of the partially averted, young, ice blue gaze. But as the whine of the steel guitar penetrated the air it was not her hand that he reached for. "What about your wife, Ned? Does your wife like to dance?" He held all the Peerings in a hypnotic trance. He extended his hand and led Barb from the booth to the center of the floor and held her against his chest so the brim of his hat crested her face like a broken halo. He waltzed her into the middle of the room, elevated her feet onto the tops of his boots. Watching their bodies fold together, Skip thought of Africa and South America.

***

The stunned silence in the aftermath of what happened was as mesmerizing as the event itself had been. The bourbon Frank had poured into Ned's partially eaten banana split left its bitter reek over the entire booth. Technically, Ned had not been assaulted. He had not been struck. No bandages were needed to stanch the flow of blood. It was more that the bandages he habitually swathed himself in had been stripped away, revealing to the room full of strangers, who would forget soon enough, and to his wife and children, who would forever remember, his true nature. He had watched and done nothing while the stranger danced with his wife. He had silenced his children's questions with assurances that it was all right. When the music ended, she had walked, unsteadily at first, to the ladies' room.

Frank had bowed gallantly to her. He then returned to the bar for another drink before sauntering across the gravel-covered parking lot, his hands tucked into the back pockets of his straight-legged jeans. He didn't have to look back to know that Sabrina was watching through the window, fixated on his muscular haunches, imagining her hands tucked into his back pockets. He put on a show as if he were mounting his palomino: left foot on the bottom step, grasping the roof like it was a saddle horn and swinging his right leg into the cab. He slammed the door shut. The diesel engine gargled to life. He ground the gears with intent, two unyielding tectonic plates rasping across each other's surface. He crunched gravel across the lot and blew his air horn as he drove onto the road.

Only after the last vestige of sounds had receded did Barbara Peering return, her slender body recomposed, her jacket back in place.

"Are you all right?" Ned asked, daring to seek out her eyes.

"Am I all right," she repeated.

They delayed their departure over the semblance of coffee, giving the driver enough time and distance to avoid another encounter. In the parking lot, the sun had shifted position and the anticipated shade from the eucalyptus trees was gone. The interior of their Rover was a kiln. Sabrina complained that they needed the air conditioner.

"Not going uphill," her mother said, keeping in place their rules of the road even if everything else had been shattered.

"It's okay," Ned murmured. He reached for the dial. His fingers briefly met hers at the dashboard, where he let them linger to assess whether the current in her hand carried solace or repulsion. Reaching the summit of the eastern crest, an ovation of sunlight bathed the expanse of the San Joaquin Valley below them.

"San Joaquin was the father of the Virgin Mary," Skip informed everyone.

The vista of farms under cultivation was marred only by a mysterious dark, palpitating cloud that gyrated and changed shape below and ahead. From their angle and altitude, perspective played tricks with the eye. The phenomenon could have been small and nearby or a distant monumental cataclysm. Skip grasped the back of his mother's seat for leverage and pulled himself forward for a better look. The dark cloud hovered in place, then thinned into a long chain, rose up, gained altitude, broadened, flattened, expanded into a long streak of black lightning, then disappeared, as if the entire elaborate display had been a stage effect or hallucination.

Ned took each of the next three hairpin turns with emboldened speed, bearing into the turns like he had a sports car under him rather than a top-heavy vehicle with a propensity for rollovers. "Evel Knievel," said Barb. She had not looked at Ned since the incident.

He murmured a mild protest about being behind schedule, but he slowed down to an obedient twenty. Sabrina slumped deeper into her seat, sensing that the diminished speed meant more time spent with these people. It was from this angle that she glimpsed down through the tree line to where the road emerged below after its next curve. "Shit!" she exclaimed.

The Rover skidded to a long sliding stop thirty feet from what looked like a felled brontosaurus splayed across the road. Twin geysers of diesel smoke billowed up from the eighteen-wheeler's engine and exhaust. The four hundred white boxes that had been tied down and packed with such precision now lay strewn and broken across the road. The four doors of the family's Range Rover opened in cautious unison. The rear guard advanced first. Ned cautioned the children about going any closer but his authority was gone. They went forward, outflanking their father's extended arms.

The truck's cab had separated from the rig and was bent over on its side as though felled by a ferocious beast. Out of the open window, resting on its lower frame, ready to be guillotined, the neck of the driver hung at an impossible angle. The expression on his face, which had been so fiendishly cocky when he summoned Ned's wife, was now distended beyond recognition. His cheeks were four times their normal size. His forehead bulged off its cranium. His eyes were ghastly, and open.

It was the ice queen who lost her cool. Sabrina watched with grossed-out disgust as an orange and black striped body crawled feebly out of Frank's open mouth. "Eeewww. It's a bee," she said, and drew back.

"Honey bee," her brother verified. "*Apis mellifera.*"

It beat its wings twice, toppled in a vain attempt to fly, tried one more time, and fell motionless on Frank's cheek, corpse on corpse. An electronic hum began to fill the air. So transfixed were the foursome that it took several moments of the sound's approach before they noticed and looked up. At first nothing was visible. It sounded as though police helicopters were approaching from just over the other side of the mountain. And then the sky darkened.

Ned stampeded his family to the car. Sabrina stumbled and slipped to the hard ground. Her brother did not stop to help. Her father lifted her to her feet and carried her to safety. He remained a sentry until his wife and children were safely inside. The shadow descended from the sky like a pterodactyl, then partitioned into a hundred parts, a horrifically beautiful still life of hanging clusters.

Before he could reach his door, the first swarm settled on Ned's back. He felt its vibrating weight like a rear-mounted engine. The next one wound itself slowly around his right leg. He stood without moving. Inside the car his horrified family watched the spectacle. His other leg was now covered as well. Excruciatingly slowly he reached out his arm, indicating for them to shut the one remaining open door. His outstretched arm was surrounded. Then the other. Sabrina whimpered. "What are they doing to Daddy?"

"Bees go crazy for bananas," Skip replied. "He had that banana split."

The soft scarf of organic life revolved itself upward now around Ned's chest, then higher until it covered his throat, his mouth, his eyes, and totally encased him. Inside the whirling darkness the buzzing filled his senses. It went beyond hearing. His body became a tuning fork in sympathetic vibration with the universe. He felt an eerie nostalgic ecstasy, as though he had been here before. And then nothing.

Chapter One

Bliss.

Stein scrunched his hips deeper into the lush foam pad cushion of Lila's chaise to catch the full warmth of the sun. Through the glorious heydays of his youth, Stein and his merry band of miscreants dedicated their lives to the disruption of the lives of the privileged and contented. But experiencing it firsthand was a whole other deal. While February acted out its Napoleon complex on the rest of the world, making up for being the shortest month by punishing it with marrow-crunching cold, it was seventy-seven degrees with clear skies here in Beverly Hills.

Maybe it was getting past fifty, as none of Stein's male antecedents had done. Maybe it was having security for the first time in his life. Maybe it was the mellow Santa Anas blowing off the desert, not hot and crazy like they did in October, but with a warm glow so it felt like you were having your five-minute audience with God and he'd grant you any reasonable request.

Look where he was! Lord of the Lila manor, the two-story home her husband had left to her, in what she called the "slums" of Beverly Hills, south of Wilshire. Three thousand square feet. The pool that she kept heated all year long. The Jacuzzi. Her Guamese housekeeper, Mercedes. For him, the luxury was still more an amusing novelty than anything he really cared about or needed. He still refused air-conditioning and microwave ovens and his car had crank windows. The selling point was that Stein's sixteen-year-old daughter Angie was happy here. It was not only that her room was twice the size of her room at Stein's old apartment and she was exempted from a fair number of upkeep chores. There was stability. During the six years of joint custody spending equal time with both parents, Angie always referred to Stein's apartment as "Dad's place." After six months at Lila's house, she was calling it home.

Lila was great with her. Lila never had children of her own, though she had raised her husband's from ages six and eight into their early adolescence when he got pulled down by cancer. Angie was like a new electronic gadget to Lila, a crazy, delightful, unmanageable surprise every time she pressed a button.

She popped from the kitchen onto the patio, bent over Stein's reclined head and kissed him lightly near the lips. She was taking Angie today for her first mani-pedi. Her wide-brimmed straw hat momentarily shaded the sun from Stein's bare chest. She smelled good. She was dressed in a swanky silk blouse and white slacks with a tasteful gold necklace. Her cosmetician had taught her well how to soften the sharp bone structure and enhance the vibrancy of her dark eyes.

"For a second I thought I was being kissed by Winona Ryder's mother," Stein said.

"You should be so lucky."

"See ya, Pops." Angie popped her head out to say goodbye. Stein roused himself and turned around. She had let her hair go back from its mélange of colors to its natural copper blond. Her eyes had the pixyish wisdom that Stein felt was his genetic contribution.

"I can't believe you're going over to the other side," he said, affecting profound dismay. "Getting your nails done at a Beverly Hills salon. What would Ani DiFranco say?"

"Probably that geezers should learn to pronounce pop stars' names before they try to make cultural references." She grabbed Lila's elbow and herded her away toward the gate that led to the driveway where Lila's brand-new 2001 white Lexus coupe sat waiting. Stein closed his eyes, basking in spongy security. The timer clicked on for the Jacuzzi heater. The mechanism engaged or attempted to engage, and instead gasped and clunked and gnashed its gears, hissed . . . and then nothing.

He had been so sure he'd be able to fix the busted heating coil. No event in his life had ever offered the slightest foundation to support that belief. Yet, he expected that since he lived here now, somehow he would have osmotically absorbed a oneness with the appliances and the intuitive ability to make right whatever was wrong. He bore the same delusion about his power, that his continued presence in it would gather a critical mass and return things to the way they were in the sixties.

His effort to replace the heating gasket and thermostat, which in the proper hands would have been a thirty-two-dollar operation, had resulted in the entire Jacuzzi having to be dug up, along with the main plumbing line that supplied the house and a sizable chunk of what had formerly been Lila's backyard. At a cost of fourteen thousand dollars. So far.

Lila had been upset, of course. But amazingly, not *that* upset. He had been pilloried (or, in the case of his ex-wife, Hillaried) far worse for far less. Once the love of your life has died of cancer you see life in a new perspective and a few broken pipes aren't that big a deal.

The contractors had left a gaping maw of oozing, oily muck that was coming from a subterranean channel connected to the La Brea Tar Pits—or so Stein extrapolated from the few cognates he got from the foreman's combination of English and Tagalog. He took it as his penance to wait for them, as he had done each day for the week they had promised to return.

He kept a secret from Lila. He never stayed here alone. Soon after the girls had departed for their beauty venture, Stein was in his Toyota Camry heading east on Olympic. As soon as he crossed the border out of Beverly Hills the socio-ethnographics began to change. Landscaping was less lush, the sun less shaded. A mile east of Fairfax he took a left at Hauser. A casual observer might think he was driving just to clear his head, to think, to drift. But he had driven this route so many times it had become ingrained in the engine's DNA.

On the other side of Third Street sat an enclave of single-story private homes and cool funky duplexes, including the one where Stein had resided since the separation and divorce from Hillary, with his now deceased dog, Watson, and on alternate weekends with Angie. He parked out front and sat in the car for a few moments. The unkempt pine welcomed his arrival by dropping a few dusty sprigs of greenery on his hood. He fished through the random clutter in the glove compartment (funny that it was still called a *glove* compartment) for the small metal box that had originally held licorice pastilles. He opened the lid and let the apartment key drop into his open palm.

His was the second unit in the little horseshoe-shaped courtyard. There was a cluster of mail stuck in the slot. Penelope Kim, his irrepressible twenty-year-old Korean bisexual neighbor, was away this week, having been named Miss Long Bed Trailer 2001 and flown to Bent Fruit, Virginia, to preside over the annual Truck Pull. The rubber tree that commanded the courtyard made it seem like New Orleans. The six duplexes all had wood-hewn balconies built out from their second-floor French doors. The bougainvillea grew up along the balustrades and carpeted the walkway below them in purple blossoms on windy days.

He used his key and went inside. He still half expected to hear Watson's excited bark at his arrival. He had been the archetypal sixties dog, a complete optimist. He always expected the next thing to happen would be good. Stein hadn't taken a lot of his stuff with him to Lila's. His pinball machine, his rows of standing orange gym lockers and mismatched easy chairs purchased at different garage sales did not exactly complement her décor.

He went upstairs, stopping first at the room that had once been Angie's. Random remnants of her former tenancy lay fossilizing in corners. A baseball glove and a poster of Ani DiFranco, the dresser she had put together, refusing help, its emptied drawers splayed open, listing to one side on uneven legs like an ancient relative you have to help to the bathroom.

His bed was still here, the box spring and Serta. The framed picture taken on his twenty-fourth birthday with him grinning between John and Yoko still hung on the wall above his old dresser. Stein's beard in the photograph was longer than his hair was now. He sat on the floor with his back propped up against the stucco wall and stretched his legs and sifted through the mail: solicitations from all the causes he supported. Veterans Against The War, Doctors Without Borders, ACLU, Special Olympics, SDS, NARAL. Those, amid the colossal mountain of penny savers and brochures, catalogs and throwaways. All the ink and paper it took to manufacture this crap. Waste had become America's chief manufactured product.

From the apartment next door, the unmistakable sounds of copulation began. The wall he leaned against was the common boundary between the adjacent apartments. The gasps of female pleasure rose and quickened. He had never met the girl who lived there. She had moved in after Stein had moved out. She was gloriously uninhibited. Her middle alto register yowled her chant to Dionysius. After a goodly aria, the thumping recessed into a gentle rocking sound, the descending glissando of an ingénue expiring of the vapors, and then silence. Stein had a fierce impulse to knock on the wall and hail a congratulatory, "Well fucked, young man," but he resisted.

***

A familiar white limo of astonishing length was idling in Lila's driveway when Stein returned. The first time he had seen that white whale he dubbed it Moby Dick and thought of himself as Ahab until he remembered the end of the story. The tinted driver's-side window receded, revealing an impeccably dressed Asian man in his early twenties.

"Andrew, is that you?"

"Yes, sir, Mr. Stein. That's right."

"Did you just happen to be driving by?"

"Mrs. Pope-Lassiter wants to chat with you."

"She doesn't believe in phones?"

"One of you doesn't," he said with a circumspect formality. No matter what Andrew did, his suits never creased.

"Point taken." Stein assured Andrew that he would definitely call her back, but he couldn't come right now as he was waiting for contractors.

"Mrs. Pope-Lassiter was pretty confident the contractors wouldn't be here today."

"How the hell would *she* know?" And then painful recognition. "Oh, don't tell me."

"You know Mrs. Pope-Lassiter."

Indeed he did know Millicent Pope-Lassiter and the Re-insurance company of Lassiter and Frank that bore her name. He had known her since she was twenty-two-year-old Millie Pope, hair down to her gorgeous round ass, eyes that were half awake and half in a dream, glistening mango lips. She could suck ice cream out of both ends of a cone and catch the drippings out of midair with a snap of her chameleon tongue. She had thickened and Republicanized, gone from Lady Godiva to Lady Bracknell. For years, through an intricate loan-out arrangement where Stein's services were commoditized and monetized, a majority of Stein's income had come by way of that arrangement.

"Ten minutes is all I'm giving her," Stein declared as he got into the limo.

"My business is just getting you there."

Andrew's Class II nuclear destroyer drove west on Little Santa Monica Boulevard and veered down into the parking lot beneath the most elegant of the Century City smog scrapers. Andrew left the car with the valet and conducted Stein through the atrium into the private elevator, which rose to the penthouse suite occupied by the product liability firm of Lassiter and Frank.

"Ah," Millicent Pope-Lassiter said upon seeing Stein.

Her voice was an instrument strung more for power than inflection. Her office had the scope of a planetarium, floor-to-ceiling windows with a 270-degree view from Santa Monica to San Bernardino. "Sit," she invited, in a tone a Great Dane would obey. Stein declined the command, which felt idiotic to him because he had been about to sit on his own volition before she told him to.

She glanced up at him for a moment as if he had just walked in. "Do you know anything about honey and bees?"

"You want to know if *I* know anything about honey and bees?

"Yes, Harry. Who else would I be asking?" Only she and Hillary called him Harry. Probably for the same reason.

"I know they make honey and they were put on Earth to be my mortal enemies. Why have you abducted me?"

"Just once I hoped you would know more about a subject than I did."

"You know I don't work for you anymore, right? Even when I was technically *doing work* for you, I wasn't *employed* by you. You understand that. I was an independent contractor."

"I admit. Some of your past assignments were a bit on the dry side. That's why I have this one to make up for them."

He regarded her with a skeptical tilt of the head. "You do not represent an old hippie from Ojai."

"Did you read about that humorous little incident yesterday up around Fresno? Some citizen became encased in a swarm of bees?"

"Sorry. I canceled my subscription to the *Enquirer*."

"Some of those bees apparently belong to, or more to the point, *belonged to* a beekeeper named Karma Moonblossom. He claims a dozen of his colonies were stolen from him. I simply want you to confirm that his claim is accurate. He's one of your people. An old hippie living in the hills outside of Ojai."

"First of all, Moonblossom?"

"I'm guessing there was a name change somewhere along the line."

"And second of all, *no*! You know my history with bees."

"You're not listening, Harry. I said his bees have been *stolen*. Which means there would be *no bees.*"

"You said his bees had *apparently* been stolen."

"Does exhaustion always have to be the cost of doing business with you?"

"How would you even *steal bees* anyway? Lasso them with little ropes?"

"You see? You're immediately asking the right questions."

He rose from the chair, told her it had been nice seeing her again

"Harry." The command in her voice was like bolas that wrapped around his psyche. "This is for you. Your mind is getting as soft as your body."

"You give altruism a bad name."

"You could pay Lila back some of what your little Jacuzzi peccadillo has cost her."

"How do you know about that?"

She gestured benignly to the scope of her airy roost. "Knowledge is power, Harry."

"God, do you remember when you had a social conscience and a benevolent world view?"

"And now I have a penthouse with an ocean view. And you still keep your apartment in the Fairfax district you're still paying fourteen hundred and seventy-five dollars rent every month."

"What is this, blackmail?"

"I'm giving you five thousand dollars to take a nice drive to Ojai this weekend. Talk to Mr. Moonblossom. Use those great gut instincts of yours. Tell me if he's lying."

"That's all you want?"

"That's all."

"Fine but I want the money in cash." He knew that would never happen. The next moment, a stack of hundred dollar bills was in his hand and the moment after that, Andrew was driving him home.

So much for bliss.

Chapter Two

The girls gave it to Stein relentlessly over breakfast. Angie kept referring to the caper as honeybee "wrestling" no matter how many times he said no, it was *rustling*. And Lila chimed in, "What do they do, turn them over and brand them with tiny little branding irons?" Angie had a greater affinity for humor than Lila. She was younger, hipper, quicker, and never had to worry about her father breaking up with her if she stepped over the line.

Lila was still insecure about the jump from friend-girl to girl-friend. They had been lovers for a brief time years earlier, then "flovers," friends who had once been lovers. She knew that Stein loved her but was not *in love* with her, and that living here would change that. For the better, she hoped. Though she knew the odds favored the other outcome. They had a quickie before breakfast in Lila's elevated platform bed. A skiing injury to Lila's sacrum in her thirties and a repressed childhood had limited her repertoire of comfortable sexual positions. Given Stein's more worldly experiences she was apprehensive that he expected a more adventurous sexual partner. She was pleased that he was a sexual middle-of-the-roader as well. He had grown less self-centered, less performance-oriented. He had come to understand, as some men do when they get older, that the instrument he wields is a baton, not a hammer.

***

Lila practically foisted the Lexus upon him. It was a long trip, she insisted, why risk snapping a fan belt or throwing a rod? (Whatever those things were.) So Stein found himself cruising westbound on the Ventura Freeway on a sunny Saturday afternoon, leaning back in the contoured leather seat of a brand-new 2001 Lexus sport coupe with less than six thousand miles on it, with a vintage Dylan CD playing on the quadraphonic speakers, and a cell phone that he had no idea how to use. The car held the road like it had talons but flew when he just tapped the pedal. He had to admit, it took the stress out of driving.

As the 101 hit Oxnard and bent around to the north to follow the coastline, the only slight cloud on the emotional horizon was the prospect of bees. Despite Millicent Pope-Lassiter's assurance that the theft of her client's colonies had rendered his environment bee-*free*, Stein had arranged to meet Karma Moonblossom at a neutral location.

Off Route 33 into the coastal range, then three turnoffs onto smaller and smaller byways, with road signs giving the mileage to towns Stein had never heard of, there was an old ramshackle taverna called Scooter's. The place had originally belonged to a guy named Scooter, a biker dude. Its three wooden steps looked like a junkie's dental work. The porch slanted downhill, then up, as if someone had just stopped building at some point and called it done. The joint had recently been purchased by a consortium of transcendental lawyers who had renamed it Incarnation and were remodeling it. There were signs for both names. People called it what it was named when they first started coming.

"Don't tell me. You're Stein." The voice and the solid handshake belonged to the stunningly handsome, sandy-haired college-football-hero-looking guy wearing a short-sleeved tan work shirt and khaki shorts. His mountaineer's calves had a virile dusting of hair and great, thick, ropey veins that Stein envied. He could have been a male model except for two things: his squinty smile that would drive photographers nuts, and that modeling would be the last thing on earth Karma Moonblossom would ever do.

"What makes you think I'm Stein?" Stein joked.

"I'm pretty good at identifying foreign species." Karma squinted up toward the woods and sky, and in that small gesture Stein reckoned that he knew the mating and migration habits, the songs and nesting places of most of the winged creatures that habituated the canyon. He pointed toward an empty table out on the unkempt lawn. They were slabs of solid oak, cut and shellacked. The benches were split pine logs held on triangular crotches.

"I appreciate your meeting me here," said Stein. "I hope you didn't have to come too far."

"Nah, I'm just a little ways up." Karma shook the back of his hand toward the adjacent hills.

"I have a kind of adversarial history with bees."

"Probably you have some past-life issues with them to work through. Bees are very psychic creatures."

"Funny. That's what the ER doctor said."

"Very hip doctor."

The waitress wore a body apron over her T-shirt and tight jeans. She had twenty-year-old skin made out of sunlight and ivory. She described the components of each of several batches of flavored sun teas and their specific palliative powers.

"How's the organic Diet Coke?" Stein deadpanned. She had not learned irony. Beauty never has to.

"Bring a couple of mulled lemonades for me and my humorous friend," Karma said.

She, even she, lingered an extra moment inside Karma's aura.

"So," Stein said, after the waitress had pried herself away and they were alone, "*Karma*? Long for 'Car'?"

"Short for Carmichael."

"Carmichael fits you so perfectly."

"You know how it is with names. You grow into them or you molt them."

"And Moonblossom?"

"Just for the honey jars. Sounds better than Mundschein."

Stein opened the blue file folder that Millicent Pope-Lassiter had messengered to Lila's house and riffled through some of the papers. "I've been reading through these reports . . ."

"No, you haven't," Karma laughed.

"No," Stein confessed. "I haven't." He tucked the folder away. In its place was his own bemused curiosity. "How the heck do bees get *rustled*? You don't lasso them, right? And part two of the question, if you found them, how would you know they were *yours*? They all look alike, don't they? Or was that some horribly racist remark?"

Karma squinted a long penetrating gaze into Stein's face. When he realized the question was sincere and not meant to show him up, he answered in the polite nonjudgmental way you'd talk to an undergifted child. "No offense meant, but why would they send a man up here who knew absolutely nothing about the subject?"

"It probably has to do with the high regard in which both of us are held by the Establishment."

On that note they bonded and Karma educated Stein on the basics of beekeeping and bee pilfering. Thieves did not steal individual bees. Usually the thieves were beekeepers themselves. They took entire colonies. Those white boxes on the side of the road were commercial hives, each holding forty thousand bees.

"Did you say forty *thousand*?"

Karma nodded.

"That's a fuck of a lot of bees!"

The waitress returned with their mulled lemonades. Her apron strap brushed against the back of Stein's neck as she set his glass down, setting off a whole sequence of unrealistic fantasies. He managed to return his attention to Karma after she departed. All right, so he kind of vaguely understood how. He was still miles away from why.

"Do you know where almonds come from?" Karma asked.

"From those cute little blue cans."

"And before that."

"I'm guessing trees?"

"Excellent. You're a wise and intuitive man. But did you know—and no offense, I'm guessing you did not—that ninety percent of the world's supply of almonds are grown a couple hundred miles from here in the San Joaquin Valley?"

"I'll definitely try to remember that next time I'm on *Jeopardy!*"

"It's a multibillion-dollar industry."

"Did you say *billion*?"

"Every single blossom has to be cross-pollinated to produce a nut. This is such a vast and complex job, only bees can do it. It is the largest pollination event on the planet. And it has to be done in the two weeks that the trees are in blossom."

"I'm understanding that I want to stay as far away from this place as possible. But I still don't see where the money comes in."

"There aren't near enough bees up there do the job, so beekeepers all over the country ship their colonies in on flatbeds. Six trillion bees'll be working those orchards."

"Did you say *trillion*?" The thought made Stein's skin shrivel. He took a healthy swig of his lemonade, which Karma mentioned in passing wouldn't exist without bees to pollinate the lemons and sweeten it with honey.

"A healthy colony can rent out for a hundred and fifty dollars a month."

"Oh," Stein deflated. "I thought you were going to say ten thousand a month. No offense, but a hundred and fifty is chump change."

"For one, yes. Even for my dozen. But a commercial operation may run one or two thousand colonies. Suppose they were stolen and rented out for a hundred and fifty each. Do the math."

That's exactly what he was doing.

"Now suppose you educate me. Why do they send you?"

"They want me to help get your property back."

"No, they don't." Moonblossom's tone was a lot more derogatory this time.

"No." Stein admitted. "They don't."

"They want to know if I'm telling the truth about losing them."

"Yes," said Stein. "That's exactly what they want to know. And are you?"

***

Karma said that he was telling the truth and Stein believed him. So that was that. Job well done. As he retraced his route through winding roads back up toward the summit and over Lake Casitas, one thought kept grating at him. Karma was claiming a big thousand dollars for his loss. Why would Lassiter and Frank pay Stein five grand to verify a claim one-fifth the size? It just didn't add up.

He pulled over to the side of the road and sifted once again through the details of the accident that had killed Frank Monahan. This time when he read that the overturned trailer had been carrying four hundred colonies, he had a greater understanding of the scope of the incident. Two *million* bees had been turned loose. He remembered the time that one bee that had flown into his ear. It had buzzed against his eardrum for three hours, like a sawmill had been set up in his brain, so he thought he'd be driven crazy and die. Or that it would crawl into his brain and sting him and he would die. Or that the bee would become exhausted and die and the noxious fumes of its decaying body would poison him and he would die.

He noticed a detail in the photographs that had not registered before. The overturned truck had North Dakota license plates. Alarm sirens began to go off in his brain as Karma's story unraveled. If his bees indeed had been stolen, what the hell would they be doing on a truck coming *into* California from North Dakota? Fuck. He pounded the steering wheel. The man just lied to his face. He must have heard about the accident, figured why not make a claim? A thousand bucks was a small enough amount to pass under the radar. The company probably spent more every month on air freshener. Stein had a mini-ethical crisis of his own to face. If the little man was striking a tiny gnat's blow against the beast, more power to him. Why should only kings plunder? And yet. Stein's Achilles' heel had always been that he could not let one hand wash the other. They both always came out dirty.

By the time he got back to Scooter's Incarnation, Karma was long gone. His local honey stand was well known, and people were fine about giving Stein the vague directions to his place. He followed the bends in the paved section of the back road, careful to avoid overhanging branches and mud puddles. He had done enough damage to Lila's expensive toys.

There were a goodly number of rutty dirt paths that could equally have fit the directions he'd been given. He tried several. Each of them ultimately dead-ended so that he had to back his way up to the main rut. His neck was killing him from all the looking back over his shoulder, and he was ready to bag the entire venture when he noticed a turnoff to the left that looked more promising than the others. He locked the car and set out on foot. The air felt sweet and fresh, the late-day exhalation of rosemary and sage.

After a short distance, the path doglegged to the left and then to the right, where it opened up into a semi-paved asphalt road. He briefly considered going back for the car, but less than a hundred yards ahead he saw a house. A rustic A-frame. The woman who answered the door told him Karma was out in the orchard supering his stock. Stein wondered what that meant and speculated on what the woman's relationship to Karma might be. She looked to be in her forties, a little bit dykey in the shoulders, so probably not his girlfriend. Too young to be his mother. She hadn't referred to him as *Mister*, so probably not his housekeeper. Not that Karma would be likely to have one.

With his mind thus preoccupied, Stein did not take notice of a more significant factor until he was in the midst of it. Karma was kneeling beside a stack of white wooden boxes while thousands, perhaps tens of thousands of bees flew about him in chaotic profusion. When Stein saw where he was, he froze as though he had been dipped into liquid nitrogen.

"Well, howdy there. What a nice surprise," Karma's voice sang out. He gave a couple of puffs with his smoker tool, sending wafts of white cloud across the colony, then pried open the top of a wooden box with a small, sharp tool, and withdrew one of eight wooden frames that hung like file folders. It was covered completely by blankets of active bees crawling over a loom of perfect, symmetrical six-sided cells.

"Brood," Karma explained. "Honeybee nursery."

He worked without fear or haste, extracting a second then a third densely populated frame while explaining to the stock-still statue of Stein that he was attempting to regenerate his lost stock by starting new colonies, placing these frames into new, empty boxes. Each of them was branded with the design that Stein now vaguely remembered Millicent Pope-Lassiter had described: circles inside triangles inside circles. Karma's face was right up close to the frame as he gently pushed his index finger through their mass. "There she is. Do you see her?" He proffered the frame toward Stein. "That's the queen we're going to move to the new hive. See how much bigger she is?"

"I'll take your word for it." Stein drew back and made his voice sound pleasantly innocuous. "Can we go somewhere else to talk?"

"No need to worry. As long as you come with a pure heart and no malice intent they won't bother you."

Stein had a feeling he was being fucked with, but wasn't ready to put it to the test.

"Would you like to go inside?" Karma asked.

"I would like that very much."

Inside meant a high-roofed ramshackle barn out behind the A-frame. It housed tubs and barrels and basins and machines so unlike anything Stein had ever seen that he gave up trying to fathom their purpose. There were a couple of folding chairs that had seen better days and a sofa that had seen better centuries.

Karma ambled toward a fifty-gallon drum filled nearly to the top with a rich, amber, viscous liquid. He dipped a beveled tool with a spiral groove into the contents of the barrel then let a few golden drops dribble onto his visitor's tongue. Stein's jaw hung as if he had tasted divine revelation.

"I raise my bees organically. No pesticides. No antibiotics. This is how they express their appreciation." He reached up to a shelf above him and handed Stein a couple of jars, labeled with his MOONBLOS-SOM logo. "Take some home to your family. I assume that's why you came back."

He sensed that Karma knew that wasn't the reason. "This is my boss's idea, not mine. But I'll be honest, once she brought it up it made me wonder about it too. How would your bees wind up on a truck coming *into* California from North Dakota?"

"You're thinking I'm trying to cheat the insurance company?" A few stray bees strafed around Stein's periphery, making him very uneasy.

Karma chided him. "Do you know what happens when a bee stings a human? The barb stays rooted inside the flesh so when they fly away it tears open their abdomen and they die. Quite frankly, their life here is too good to throw away on you."

Stein leaned forward with his elbows on the wooden barrel that served as a table. "I want to believe you. Convince me that your bees could be coming in from North Dakota."

"You said the *truck* was from North Dakota. Do you know how long it had been in state?"

Stein had to admit he did not.

"North Dakota raises very healthy bees. Nobody uses pesticides. They winter them in empty potato silos. It's a perfect environment. Truck could have brought down a load from ND and still had some room for mine. Maybe others."

Even if the guy was completely full of shit, Stein dug his style and was ready to go to bat for him. "Here's the thing though, man," Stein said. "I know Lassiter and Frank. Before they'll part with a cent they'll want to see proof that your equipment was on that truck." Stein had remembered seeing the word "equipment" on the report and waited to be praised for using it correctly.

Instead, what Karma said was that he had never filed a claim with Lassiter and Frank.

"Excuse me?"

"Yeah, that's the odd part. I'm not insured with Lassiter and Frank. I never heard of Millicent Pope-Lassiter until she contacted me."

"She contacted you? Why would she contact you?"

"If I had to guess, I'd say she's insuring someone a whole lot bigger than me and wants to stay under the radar."

It made such perfect sense it embarrassed Stein not to have seen it. "We should switch jobs," he said. Then a couple of bees flew low-level recon over his forehead and he thought, *maybe not.*

Chapter Three

Lila was standing on the balustrade outside her second-story bedroom window wearing one of her wacky getups—an oversized straw beach bonnet, black culottes, sunglasses, and a polka-dot blouse—when Stein drove in. She waved down to get his attention and mouthed, *They're here!* Stein had grasped that the contractors were there when he saw three trucks blocking the driveway. He followed the sound of a compressor and the trail of an insulated electrical extension cable and a thick pipe down the full length of the driveway and into the backyard.

Four bare-chested Filipino bantamweights were cursing in Tagalog and wrestling mightily with the clogged hose. The compressor sputtered, roared to life, then died. The hose went into death throes like a python choking on the warthog it had swallowed whole. A few gulps of putrid muck and tar dribbled out, then receded back into the open pit that had so recently been a swimming pool.

The foreman, who was wearing a Florida Marlins baseball cap, made a series of contorted physical gestures that could either have meant they would need to return yet again with still heavier machinery or that he had a terrible case of hemorrhoids. In either case, the operation was kaput for the day.

"When?" Stein gestured urgently at his watch.

He couldn't tell if the foreman's answer meant *today* or in *two days* or *next Tuesday.* And each version of the translation that Stein proposed for confirmation was answered with an enthusiastic "yes."

In the wake of their departure, Stein lingered at the wrought-iron fence. Bubbles of methane popped sporadically to the surface.

The scope of the damage he had inflicted made the five grand he just earned seem paltry. He heard Lila in the kitchen directing Mercedes in the preparation of a tuna salad sandwich for Stein, and he ambled inside.

"Coffee, Señor Estine?"

"Thanks, Mercedes." He asked Lila where Angie was.

"They're probably still at the mall."

"They?" Stein's sentries came to attention at the sound of the plural pronoun. "Is her mother here?"

"Matthew came down for a visit from Berkeley."

Stein couldn't immediately place the name.

"Matt," Lila clarified. "My stepson. He likes to be called Matthew now."

Stein's paternal anti-boycraft guns raised out of their silos. "You drove them to the mall and left them there?"

She laughed at his anxiety. "Stein, he has his own car. He's eighteen."

"Wasn't he just fourteen?"

"Weren't we all?" She offered him her cordless phone. "Her cell is on speed dial. Number three. If you have the overpowering urge to chaperone."

"Sorry. I get protective."

"Maybe just a little."

Lila dispatched Mercedes to the living room, where she said the plants looked dry and ought to be watered, and slid alongside Stein on the banquette. She was dying to know what happened on his trip.

"I wish I could tell you," he said, in an offhand manner that she took completely the wrong way. She slid away from him as if she'd been shoved. He caught hold of her receding shoulder. "I don't mean that I can't tell *you*." He explained his mystification about why Millicent Pope-Lassiter had wanted him to go up there. He couldn't discern any useful purpose to the trip. The intimacy mollified Lila.

She wanted to be part of a team. A repository of disclosure. Stein exhumed the wad of hundreds he had been paid and pushed them into Lila's hand to put it toward the damage and repair.

She felt embarrassed, as if he had interpreted her upset as dunning for upkeep and pushed the money back at him.

"We should talk about our financial arrangement," Stein said. "I'm feeling a little bit like a squatter."

"Or," Lila countered, "Mercedes put fresh sheets on the bed. We could try them out."

"Hold that thought till I come out of the shower." He kissed her in the center of her furrowed brow and headed up the red tile circular staircase. Lila rinsed out the coffee cup and then trailed him up the stairs. Mercedes glanced up from her watering to give Lila an arch look. She had been with her ten years and had become the source of church lady advice. The shower was running full force when Lila slid into the bathroom, dropped her clothes and opened the glass door. The torrent sounded like an ovation.

***

Stein knew it was irrational but it upset him when he didn't know where Angie was. On the alternate weeks when Hillary had custody, he rarely fretted for her safety. But the closer she was, the closer he needed her to be. Following the shower and its amorous aftermath, Stein knocked on Angie's bedroom door. When there was no reply he asked Lila for her phone and pressed numeral three on the speed dial. The ten-digit melody of Angie's phone number sang in his ear. A telephone somewhere downstairs began to ring in perfect synchronicity with the sound of the outgoing tone in Stein's ear.

He handed the phone back to Lila, saying she gave him the wrong speed dial number.

"Maybe you pressed the wrong number," she suggested.

"Maybe I didn't." He hung up. The ringing stopped. He redialed. It started. "Okay?"

"It's Angie's number," Lila insisted.

Holding the handset in front of him like a dowser rod, Stein followed the sound of the ringing down the stairs, through the dining room and into the kitchen, where its source lay on the counter, nestled in a sweater. It was not Lila's other line but Angie's orange-colored flip-top, the kind all the kids at school had. He hit the kill button and again the ringing stopped. "Angie?" he called her name like she was lost in the wilderness.

"Dad! Come out here. You've got to see this!"

She was ankle deep in the primordial soup that filled Lila's pool. Her jeans were rolled up to her knees. Afternoon sun haloed around her newly styled burnt Sienna coif. It almost overwhelmed him how beautiful she was. She was holding, as if an offering to a god who liked bizarre offerings, an object covered in the birth placenta of the tarry muck from which it had emerged. Its gently curved shape and solid heft gave a clue to its identity.

"We think it's a tusk!" Angie said as she slogged toward her father.

"We?"

A full baritone voice sang out of the adjacent garage to the second story, asking Lila where she kept kerosene. Following some metallic clanging, the same voice called out again, "Never mind. I found it." Lila's stepson emerged from the pool house, a gallon can metronoming from his dangling right arm. He was shirtless, wearing a pair of brightly colored surfer shorts, sunglasses pushed up over his dark spiky hair and darker gypsy eyes, where both immortality and the specter of early death lay visible.

"Hello, Mr. Stein. Good to see you again." Matthew offered his hand, but quickly withdrew it when he saw it was still covered in oily residue. The lad's show of respect was mitigated somewhat when Stein perceived the print of that same hand lithographed on the right shoulder of Angie's shirt. The boy beckoned to Angie to give him the tusk. Their offhand familiarity made it seem like they had known each other forever.

"You're going to get tetanus," Stein mothered. "Get out of there."

On the patio just adjacent to the pool Matt had spread newspapers out and was dousing rags in kerosene, vigorously scouring the petrochemical glop off their find. It did not take long for the tapered end to reveal the glinting, ivory tip of an elephant's tusk. Their exultant voices braided around each like strands of DNA. Lila came out to see what all the hubbub was about and Matt told her she might have a prehistoric mastodon buried in her yard.

"That's no way to talk about Angie's father," Lila cracked.

Matt turned quickly to Stein. "I wasn't talking about you, sir."

"Thanks for thinking you had to clear that up."

Angie summarily dismissed the notion of the tusk belonging to a prehistoric mastodon, declaring it was too small.

"And you know this," Matt said, "from your junior high school biology?"

"I'm a junior in high school. Not in junior high."

"Oh, well then. You've studied paleontology in great depth."

"It doesn't take a doctor to know when something's too small."

"You girls are so into size," Matt muttered, but it was loud enough for Stein to hear, upon which he summarily stepped in like a referee ending a bout.

"Dad, we're having a serious paleontological disagreement. Matt thinks that it's a prehistoric mammoth and I say it is not."

"What I'm *saying*," Matt said, contrasting her agitation with his own cool self-control, "is that none of us really *knows* what it is."

"That doesn't stop *one* of us," she exaggerated his pontifical syntax, "from being *sure* that it is."

"Or *some other of us* from being sure that it *isn't*."

"This may be one of those times where people have to agree to disagree." Stein said. "Angie, I think you should go inside now and—"

Lila emitted an involuntary shriek of horror at those tarry feet headed for her Italian tile kitchen floor. She wheeled Angie around by the shoulders, back to where Matt was crouched on his haunches cleaning the tusk. She plunked Angie down on a beach chair and extended one of her tarry soles in Matt's direction. Angie sat perfectly still, affecting an expression of ecstatic detachment as Matthew poured the kerosene over her feet and ran the cloth back and forth through the notches of her toes. A bubble of methane gurgled up from the depths of the pool and popped into the surface.

"Earth fart," Angie called out. Stein was grateful to see the twelve-year-old still briefly alive inside her.

Lila recalled that she had brought her third-grade classes to the La Brea Tar Pits, and that they had scientists there who identified bones people brought in.

"Perfect," said Angie and withdrew her leg with exquisite control. "The truth shall set us free."

"I'll go with you," Stein called after them. "We can make it an outing."

"You ought to spend more time with Lila, Dad. She's chafing."

***

The Wilshire Boulevard Miracle Mile was an unlikely place for a relic of the Pleistocene Age. Especially in Los Angeles, where a historical monument meant that it had been there since last week. The La Brea Tar Pits and Page Museum were set on well-kept grassy knolls with paved walkways for lunch-hour strolling and benches for reading and flirting. The focal point was the Lake Pit, which appeared to be a lake, two hundred feet long and forty feet wide. A tall fence protected onlookers from meeting the same fate that befell the mammoths and mastodons, depicted in life-sized statues watching with terrified awe, their mates being sucked down into the depths.

Muriel Rabinowitz was eighty-eight years old, still as strong-willed and charismatic as she had been during her fifty years teaching in the New York City school system. A troop of fifteen wide-eyed Brownies pressed up against the observation platform that overlooked the Lake Pit, all caught up in her magnetic spiel. She made slow, mesmerizing eye contact.

"I want you to picture how this all looked forty thousand years ago. There were no tall buildings. No streets. No traffic lights. No cars. All around you was a teeming jungle. Wild wolves and saber-toothed tigers roared at every turn. Gigantic birds of prey flocked down and grabbed up animals even bigger than you are in their talons. Was there a fence around the lake to protect them?"

"No," they chanted in unison.

"That's right. Now imagine with me that it's early one morning. A wooly mammoth comes out for a drink. He looks around warily to be sure there are no predators." Her body took on the ponderous, swaying gait of the wooly mammoth. Even Matt and Angie, who came striding through the main gate filled with a single shared purpose, were diverted by the power of Muriel's presentation.

"Suddenly from the trees, a saber-toothed tiger leaps on its back." Her body dramatically changed from lumbering *Loxodonta* to ferocious feline. The children gasped and recoiled.

"They struggle fiercely. The tiger snarls and sinks its fangs into the unprotected underside of the mammoth's body. The beast rises up, bellowing in pain and in fury and fear. It lowers its head and thrusts its massive tusks. It hurls the tiger backwards into a boulder. The tiger is wounded. Its shoulder has been broken. And now he is the victim. But he doesn't run. No! He hurls himself at the charging mammoth and latches onto its face, going for his eyes. The mammoth bats him away with his powerful trunk. But the tiger holds on. His flesh is impaled by the razor-sharp tusks, while his own saber teeth are imbedded in the mastodon. They stumble this way and that, knee deep in the lake. But it isn't a lake, is it girls? *Is it?*"

"No!" they chanted. All of them scared to death.

"What is it?"

"Tarrrr."

"Yes, it's tar. But they don't know that. They are fighting so ferociously they don't even realize until it's too late. They struggle to break free but the pull of the tar is too strong. Down they go under their own weight. But wait! As they're going down a vulture in the sky sees a meal."

Muriel's body shape-shifted to a flying creature.

"It swoops down from the sky and lands on the mammoth's head. *Ha ha*, the vulture thinks. *Those two fools were fighting for their life, and they both lose. I win!* And she gets into position to rip the flesh off the dying animals. But what happens? The tips of her wings get caught in the tar. She tries to flap the tar off, but once it's on you it's on you. Her wings are too heavy to fly. And she gets sucked down into the lake too."

Muriel locked into the eye sockets of each little girl. "Predator, prey, or scavenger, the justice of the pits makes no distinction." When she had brought them half a gasp away from fainting, she called out, "Okay, lunch."

Angie and Matt headed across the promenade to the low-slung, white, circular building that was the Page Museum. Matthew strode with strong unhurried purpose, tossing and catching the tusk confidently behind his back. Angie made a stink at the entrance gate at having to pay to get inside. The guard was about to toss them when Matthew pulled out his Amex Gold card and paid for the tickets.

"Was that supposed to impress me?"

"You know what makes you such good company? You don't even take yes for an answer."

Inside, the museum walls were covered with mural-sized displays chronicling the evolution of Los Angeles from a sleepy campo, through its mad conversion into an oil town in the 1920s, to its contemporary incarnation. None of this interested them now. Their target was the glass partition in the center of the lobby, behind which white-coated paleontologists worked with intent concentration, meticulously cleaning and cataloguing finds from ongoing excavations in the pits.

Dr. Brian Watanabe was a thin, impatient man in his forties with a bristly brush cut and severe spectacles. He would rather be doing just about anything else. "What have we here?" he said as the tusk was placed on the viewing table before him.

"I was hoping that's what you would tell us," Angie said.

He muttered a phrase in Japanese to a nearby colleague that roughly translated as: *Another smartass American. How refreshing.*

Yet something about this find, not the usual leg of a pet cat or discarded barbecue spare rib, interested him slightly. "Where you find?"

Matt stepped in. "In my aunt Lila's swimming pool."

"Where?" The doctor was dissatisfied by the stupidity of the answer, and thrust a detailed map of the Los Angeles basin onto the table. Matt made a circle with his index finger around the area where Lila lived. Watanabe shook his head knowledgeably. He placed atop that map a transparent plastic sheet of the exact same size, a geological map of the intricate underground system of faults and crevasses. From the Lake pit, where many wide and narrow tributaries branched out—rivers and veins that flowed out from the lake's auricles and ventricles—a significant artery went right under Lila's abode.

"Connected," Watanabe explained. "Bones from here. . . ." He made a flowing motion with his right arm. "Go there."

"So this *is* a tusk from a prehistoric mastodon?" Matt managed to constrain 80 percent of his glee. With the other 20, he looked around toward Angie. She had conveniently glided away to the wall display of saber-toothed tiger skulls, feigning indifference to their conversation.

"How old is it?"

"Hard to say absolutely. Neighborhood of seventy-five. Perhaps eighty."

"Eighty thousand years!"

"Not thousand. Eighty years. From the 1920s. Maybe a circus animal."

Angie waltzed back in, having heard it all, not saying a word, just grinning as bright as a comet.

***

She asked Matthew when he dropped her back off at Lila's why he called his stepmother Aunt Lila when she always called him her stepson.

"It's complicated. My mother is a little bit—"

"Crazy? Yeah, I heard."

"I was going to say possessive."

"Sorry."

"It was hard enough when my father left her. And then died. She didn't want to lose the title."

Angie laid a sweet goofy understanding smile on him and punched his shoulder lightly.

"I'll try to get back later on if I can," he said.

It was uncharacteristically quiet at Chez Lila. Angie called out to her dad, to Lila, peered in through the unlocked kitchen door and called "Hello?" Her voice echoed across the tile and stucco interior. She went up to her room, which was down the hall from the master bedroom. A thought too distasteful to bear made her body recoil. She listened with dread for the sounds of intercourse. Thank God there were none.

She returned to the patio after she had changed into grunge clothes, resigned to do her good deed for the day and clean up the mess. She doused a rag in turpentine, knelt and scrubbed a blotch of tar from colorful tile. It did not come up easily. She had to put all her weight to it. A loud belch of methane startled her. An object caught her eye that seemed to be floating at the spot where the methane bubble had erupted. Not so much *floating* as *protruding* through the surface. It was large. She could see that. The protruding end was as wide as her fist. She did not feature wading into the muck to fish it out. It was out of reach, though, even if she were to lie out on the side of the pool and stretch as far as she could.

She went into the pool house looking for an implement. It was haphazardly loaded with all the junk Lila had no use for inside. A chandelier. A microwave oven still in the box someone had probably given her as a gift. There was a net on a long aluminum pole that was likely used for skimming leaves out of the pool in summer. She tucked the pole under her armpit and looked like a jouster coming back to the yard. The object had risen a few inches higher out of the ooze. She was able to lie along the edge of the pool and net the thing like a butterfly. She turned it carefully to gain a grip and then tugged. The tar held tight. She lost her balance and had to plunge her hand down to catch herself. Her fingers slid off the top step and her body weight followed. The side of her face was an inch above the sludge. With the hypnotic voice of the docent in her ear describing the predator and prey and scavenger being pulled down into the pits, Angie strained and tugged to keep herself elevated. Her body bent like a birch but her slim, strong trunk held firm. Her quarry rose from the deep: a long, straight, solid bone.

***

When Lila returned from shopping, recostumed in a pink sleeveless blouse, toreador pants, gold earrings, and a silk scarf, Angie was so immersed in her finds that she did not hear the car pull into the driveway, or the back gate, or even Lila's voice calling out Angie and Matt's names. When Lila saw tar dripping all over the Italian tile tessellated patio, it took all her years of training not to grab Angie by the throat and scream, *What have you done?* Instead she forced a smile and said, "Well, I see you've been busy."

Angie heard only the trumpets and not the bassoon. She was a downed power line of writhing enthusiasm. "I think Matthew may be right," she said. "There may be a prehistoric mastodon buried in your pool."

Lila was still biting hard on her tongue.

"Don't worry. We'll clean it all up."

She patted Lila's furrowed shoulders with the sweet affection Lila never got from her stepdaughter, Matthew's sister Rhonda.

"Is my dad here?" Angie was anxious to show him the new find.

Lila was surprised Stein hadn't called Angie to tell her. He got a call from that woman he works for. "He had to go back up to some place called Las Viejas and wrestle some more bees."

Chapter Four

Stein's second mistake was driving up in his own car. He had put a good deal of thought into the decision, weighing the comfort and dependability of Lila's Lexus against the man-of-the-people look of his Camry. Not that he loved the Camry. The last vehicle he loved was the '69 VW bus. He missed the road trips with Van Goze and Shmooie the Buddhist and the whole cluster of them driving off to incite some urban guerrilla theatrical event, to puncture the bubble of comfort that protected the rich and privileged, with Terrier pooch Watson leaning out the passenger-side window, his muzzle blowing in the breeze. His first mistake was going at all. Stein didn't know who the hell Ned Peering was or why it mattered so much to Millicent Pope-Lassiter that he had emerged from his coma. She was paying Stein another nice chunk of change to drive up to the hospital where Ned was recovering to ascertain whether he or any of the family had spoken to the driver before he died or had any information regarding the source and/ or destination of his cargo of bees. It was never the money that got to Stein. It was Millicent's maddening ability of linking the money to issues that meant a great deal to Stein; in this case the possibility of retrieving the few salvaged colonies of Karma Moonshine's pilfered bees and at least finding some sweetness to come out the adversity.

The back-and-forth exhausted them both and in exasperation she finally asked Stein if he knew what a "derivative" was. It was less a surrender than her way of illustrating to him how much he would have to learn merely to reach the starting line.

"It's a . . . well, something that is essentially derived from something else."

"Basically they are loans backed by commodities whose value has been leveraged to fifty or a hundred times their inherent value. Think of Atlas holding up the Earth plus Jupiter, Mars, and Venus."

"Okay, I get it."

She emitted a laughter-like sound. "You don't even come close to getting it. These loans are then bundled together as a brand-new commodity and traded as a financial instrument."

"Okay, so you're selling something that doesn't exist?"

"No, that would be too tangible! I'm *insuring the value* of something that doesn't exist. Yes, we're out there on the cutting edge of theoretical physics. But mark my words, Harry. Derivatives will be the salvation of the global economic system in the next decade."

"And this relates to Ned Peering coming out of his coma how?"

"Since the collateralizing commodities don't actually exist, I'm a bit concerned that these missing bees could become a trigger point that could expose the entire company to significant loss. To help avert that disaster, I am asking you please, in your own inimitable, charming way, to find out everything you can about the cargo Frank Monahan's truck was carrying, whether those colonies of bees were salvageable, if so who got them, if not, who replaced them. Can I possibly be any clearer?"

***

Two hundred miles north of Los Angeles, on a straight, level road, cruising at a steady sixty-five, Stein felt a clank, then a whoosh then a gasp, then a rapid deceleration akin to a jet fighter getting netted on a carrier deck. His head thrust forward. His body accordioned at the waist. Then came a tremendous shudder and a great wrenching, as if the abdomen had been ripped out of the chassis. He sensed this was not good.

With the power steering out, it felt like pulling a tank through deep mud to get across three lanes. Pumping the gas and brake were nothing more than aerobic exercises. Still he managed to tack and weave and ultimately pilot the disabled craft off to the shoulder. Trailing vehicles swerved to avoid the rolling hunk of aluminum that had dropped from his chassis and rolled end-over-end like a wildebeest giving birth on the run. This object was soon to be identified by the driver of the sixty-thousand-dollar BMW that it had sideswiped—chipping a wedge of paint off her left-side wheel guard—as Stein's transmission.

The girl was nineteen, blonde, wearing a short skirt, a silk blouse, and an expensive gold necklace, and was taking pictures of the damage on her brand-new gadget that was a cell phone and also a camera, and making sure that Stein heard her telling whoever she was talking to, "Why do they let old people on the road? Shouldn't there be special handicap lanes for them so they don't have to drive where regular people go?"

Stein had thought this species had been confined to the Beverly Hills/Brentwood/Encino corridor, but seeing her so far north, he feared the spore had breached containment. Stein told her cordially after she hung up that it wasn't his transmission.

She backed off like old age was contagious. "Your car doesn't have a transmission. There is a transmission on the road."

"Crazy coincidence."

"We'll see what *he* says." She gestured to the local deputy sheriff, who was now arriving on the scene.

Deputy Gresham was a strapping varsity athlete, three years out of high school. He took their information with meticulous care to be objective. He asked the victim to estimate the extent of the damage, and when she had no idea, he subtly guided her toward an astronomical number. "Those cars have special paint and they have to take the whole side panel off to strip it down." To Stein he said, "I hope you have good insurance." He had one final pro forma question for her to complete the paperwork. "When you made contact with the obstacle in the road, ma'am, was it at rest or in motion?"

With the deputy's back to him, Stein caught the girl's eye, and in an obsequious gesture *implored* her to say the thing was moving.

"It was still," the girl said.

The officer's pen froze above his pad. "You're sure about that?"

Stein again cajoled her in pantomime to say it was moving.

"Yes," she said. "Absolutely still." She signed the statement imagining it was a scalpel and the paper was Stein's forehead.

"That's . . . very honest of you to admit," the officer said. "If it was moving, technically it would still be part of the car and the driver would be responsible. Once it stops, it's road hazard and he's not at fault."

"Why didn't you tell me that?" She bent over to pick her cell phone off the grass, flashing Deputy Gresham a tidbit of what he had squandered.

***

Sig Kroll, the surgeon general of the auto repair shop where Stein's car had been towed, wore scrubs over his striped mechanic's jumpsuit. He carried a clipboard in hand and bore a device around his neck that resembled a stethoscope. His bedside manner sucked. When Stein asked him what the verdict was, Kroll asked him if he'd ever seen a man's kidneys and liver and heart go out all at once. "That's what you've got here. Timing belt, water pump, and trannie. The grand trifecta."

The tow truck driver still had Stein's Camry on the hoist and asked what he should do with it. Kroll gestured for the kid to set it down. "But what you should do with it is drive it off a pier. Buy American," he lectured Stein, "they last forever, not like these foreign pieces of shit."

The local car rental place was caught in an inventory pinch and all they had was a new brand just arrived from Korea. Which is why, three hours later, Stein pulled into the parking lot of the Las Verdes Hospice Care Center behind the wheel of a generically copied lightweight piece of aluminum and composite plastic called a Kia Sephia. The rental guy had joked about its name, that it came from IKEA and that there was "some assembly required."

The rehab center was a two-story building with some landscaping out front that probably looked exactly like the watercolor drawing the architect had first made. The nurse at reception was cordial to begin with, and when Stein told her he was there to see Ned Peering, her eyes absolutely lit. "Isn't his recovery a wonder?" she gushed. "Isn't God just the greatest thing?"

"Unrivaled," Stein agreed.

She provided Stein with instructions for finding room 207 that included locating the elevator (within eyeshot) and noting several times that this floor was considered the *first* floor, not the ground floor, so two was just one floor above them. If she had been cuter, Stein would have asked if she missed her high school baton twirling days, making her blush when she realized she'd been gyrating her pencil over and under the three fingers of her free hand, a habit none of the men she had slept with had ever noticed.

From the looks of the tableaux in Room 207, Stein had gotten there just in time. Ned was sitting on the edge of his bed, looking vacant and spiffy in a blue and white seersucker sport jacket, his overnight satchel sitting packed and ready for departure. Barbara Peering was on the other side of the room, one hand resting composedly atop the backrest of the Naugahyde visitor's chair, looking toward her husband but not specifically at him. Skip had gone for a soda. Sabrina was at the window, her back to her parents, impenetrable as a screensaver, gazing out at the bland agricultural non-scape.

All the car drama had taken up so much of Stein's mental energy that he hadn't given much thought or planning to how he would question a man just emerging from a coma. That was fine, though. He didn't want to break the spontaneity by over-preparing. He had skimmed the material Millicent had foisted upon him to register the names and faces of the Peering family, and to grasp the basic details of their encounter with the overturned truck and its driver, which were practically nonexistent.

Stein introduced himself and attempted to break the ice by telling a self-deprecating tale of his own apian misadventure. His ex-wife had given him a pair of Rollerblades for his fortieth birthday. He had never bladed and found himself going down a steep hill. He didn't know how to stop or turn so he threw himself onto a lawn and landed face first on a cluster of clover. He was immediately stung on the upper lip—the bee got stuck in his mustache and kept pumping more and more venom until his whole face blew up to the size of a cabbage. The emergency room doctor took one look at him and blurted out the three words you never want to hear a doctor say: "*Oh, my God.*"

Stein turned theatrically toward Ned. "And *this* man gets stung a thousand times and walks away. Amazing."

"He wasn't stung," Barbara Peering informed him. "Ned was covered with males. Drones have no stingers. Or so our son tells us, and he's rarely misinformed. The coma was from suffocation."

"Well." Stein tried to keep the artificially inflated revelry going. "Aren't we glad males are harmless? It's our most endearing trait."

He was bombing. Sabrina leaned back against the window frame. "What is he doing here?" she asked.

"Sabrina," her mother reprimanded, though she was wondering the same thing.

"No, it's a legitimate question," Stein encouraged her. "I appreciate the trauma you've all gone through. The report says none of you spoke to him—the driver of the semi. But sometimes an image imprints on your retina that's too brilliant to see it right away. If you can remember any trivial detail it might help."

Ned Peering's throat was still quivery with the damage it had incurred. But his statement was definitive. "He was dead when we got there. Nobody saw or heard him say anything." He looked toward his daughter, then his wife for corroboration. There was no disagreement.

"Just one more question and I'll be out of your hair. Do you remember anything about the white bee boxes that were strewn on the road? Any particular brand you might have seen etched into the sides. Circles inside triangle inside circles?"

Barbara Peering practically sprang at him. "My husband saved his family and was swarmed by murderous insects. Do you think anyone gave a thought to anything else?" Stein apologized once again for the intrusion and was two-thirds out the door when Skip returned with an armload of cold soda cans pressed to his breasty chest.

"Ah, young master Sanford. I presume that the truck driver never spoke to you either?"

"He gave me money and told me to play E-9. The Bellamy Brothers. 'If I Said You Have a Beautiful Body Would You Hold It Against Me?' Then he slow-danced with my mother." Skip handed out the sodas in cheerful oblivion. "Of course they stole the line from the Marx Brothers, but everybody knows that."

A Social Service nurse bustled in from the hall with a sheaf of discharge papers to be signed, and intricate instructions for after-care. Stein beckoned Barbara Peering to step outside the room with him.

The hallway was neat, a little musty. White Spanish stucco. Something out of 1930s Hemingway.

"Yes," she said, "I danced with him."

"I don't mean to make you uncomfortable. I'm just trying to put together the circumstances around this truck driver's death."

"You don't have to call him 'this truck driver.' He has a name. His name is Frank."

"Actually, it was Aloysius," Stein said.

"He told me to call him Frank."

"He told the state of California something else." Stein showed her a Xerox of a driver's license, part of the packet of information Millicent Pope-Lassiter had supplied. He watched her study the face on the photograph. He was surprised she made a point of humanizing the man. But when was the last time he knew anything about women?

"I don't want to bring up any uncomfortable memories, Mrs. Peering. It's just that the people I work for think it's very important to know. . . . Did he say anything else? Anything at all about where he was going? Who he was delivering his cargo to? Where he loaded on? Anything like that?"

"Is that what you talk about when you dance with a woman?"

He replied with care. "I wasn't under the impression it was a reciprocal arrangement."

This would be the moment in a forties film when Veronica Lake's perfectly coiffed hair would fall over one eye. She would reach into her purse for a silver cigarette case and light one in her long manicured fingers, exhaling a semaphore of skywriting through her nostrils.

"He sang to me," Barbara Peering said, barely above a whisper.

"He *sang* to you."

"In my ear. To the song." Her upper lip twitched but her chin stayed high. "At first I knew, I knew he was dancing with me to humiliate my husband. Ned thinks strangers take to him more than they do. But something else happened. Something changed in the way he was holding me. It stopped being for display. He lifted me up. He pushed my shoes off with his toes and set me down on the tops of his boots."

"Jesus."

"He held me so softly I thought I'd grown wings. He covered my ear with his ear and said he was listening to my thoughts. It was like a curtain came down around us. We were invisible. I had no husband. No children. No will of my own. Then the song ended. He lifted me off his boots and placed me back on the floor. Everyone in the entire café was looking at us. Except for Ned. Of course. I couldn't bear the weight of his shame. I locked myself in the ladies' room until I heard the sound of his truck pulling away."

She would have taken another drag off a cigarette if she had one.

"The next time I saw him his truck was overturned. He was bloated and dead. Do you have any idea what I felt?"

"Relief?" Stein guessed.

It was not at all what she meant. But upon further consideration, she admitted, "Maybe."

An orderly clattered down the hallway pushing a wheelchair to Ned's room. Stein and Barbara Peering jumped apart as if they'd been caught naked. Inside the room, Ned had signed all the forms and now rebelled against being pushed out in a wheelchair. The orderly, whose nametag read KINSHASA, had heard it all before and assured Ned, "The oniest way peoples leave here is sitting on they butts or flat on they backs."

"Please, Mrs. Peering." Stein detained her one more second before she went back into her husband's room. "You wanted someone to know that something important happened to you. You've told me, and it stays our secret. Is there anything else? Anything else at all you can tell me?"

The way she balked, he was sure there was. The look of bittersweet resignation in her eyes as she went in to rejoin her family gave Stein the crazy impulse to kiss her, which he resisted.

***

It took one well-placed phone call to Ben Tagasunta, Stein's effetely gay racetrack cohort and recently promoted vice president at the Bank of Hank, to have faxed to him the records of Aloysius

(Frank) Monahan's credit card activity for the past three months. Frank used a lot of gas. That was no surprise. He lost money at several Internet gambling sites. That was interesting. On the road, he stayed at inexpensive motels. Not particularly stunning. One of them was the Sleep 'n' Stay just fifteen miles from Ojai on the day before Karma's bees were reported stolen. That was electrifying. From Ojai, he drove a circuitous route two thousand miles north and east through Vegas (where he made three cash withdrawals), Salt Lake, Bozeman, and Billings, out into the Little Missouri National Grasslands of North Dakota, where he stayed overnight in the towns of Batteneau and Williston. He drove on to Meaguery, Wishek, and Gackle, before heading back down to California by way of Rapid City and Reno (where he gambled, and lost, again), through the Angeles National Forest and into Groveland, where the overturn occurred and where Stein would be headed once he grabbed some lunch.

***

He wasn't sure how he'd locate the precise accident site. As he got closer he asked some locals if they knew where it happened, though as it turned out, he could have found it with Braille. There was a gash in the side of the road where a copse of trees had been flattened. Ruts and skid marks and debris still remained. A volunteer from the local highway maintenance branch of the Kiwanis Club was stationed there to keep gawkers away.

Stein flashed some bogus piece of paper that allegedly identified him as someone who belonged. Clay Potter was all gangle and belt buckle. He was wearing a shirt that read, "My Lover is Gay But I'm Not." He looked like Huck Finn's less sophisticated cousin. Stein had never seen such phenomenal range of neck motion outside of a parrot. He could swivel his head nearly all the way around. "One hell of a royal mess, let me tell you," Clay indemnified.

"I can see that," said Stein.

"You're looking at the wrong side of the road. The whole load got throwed off that way." Clay pointed around 180 degrees to the other side. "Bees flying around overhead like a million bad ideas."

"Sounds like a lot of bees."

"Picture an oil spill," Clay said. "But up."

"I'm wondering about those wooden boxes. Do you know if any of them had a design burned into them?"

"You'd have to ask the bee boys about that."

"The bee boys?"

"Whenever something like this happens, we call the local bee-keeper's association and they put the word out to their people." Clay beckoned Stein to the other side of the road, where it dropped off down toward the valley. There were signs of fire. A cleared-out patch with the remnants of charred wood, a lot of it.

"Did the truck catch fire?" Stein asked.

"You're not following. Truck goes one way. Hives go t'other. The bee boys came in and set the unbroken boxes upright, load them onto their flatbeds. Bees fly in calm as their mama had called them in for dinner. If I didn't see something like it a couple of times every year I'd say I never saw anything like it. The boxes that was too broke to fix they piled up and burned. That's what you're looking at."

"So if I wanted to talk to one person? Who's the head bee boy?"

"Doc Moody's the medical examiner. He keeps some bees too. He might could tell you something."

Stein jotted the name down.

"Likely be at the morgue. Be a piece of work trying to make that driver look human. Ain't nuthin' nice what those bees did to him."

"Bad?"

"Bad don't begin to tell it."

***

54

Stein wasn't queasy about death. He had been to the LA County morgue where they hung bodies from meat hooks and scrubbed them down like plate glass windows. The scrubbers laughed and joked, smoked cigarettes and feigned performing lewd acts on them, the more disfigured and maimed the corpse, the better. They had nicknames for the different types of death. Crispy critters for the burn victims. Road kill for the gangland drive-bys left dead on the street.

The Groveland morgue was different. Stein was met at the door and conducted inside by Doc Renn Moody and his wife, Jarlene. By the looks of them, they had run the place since the end of the Civil War. Forty-seven years of close proximity had eroded them into looking like littermates. Doc's full mop of white hair was straight and combed to the right; Jarlene's was thick and coarse. Both wore dark framed glasses and white smocks with their name stitched across the breast pockets. Their bodies looked like sections of a stone fence that had remained standing where nearby pieces had crumbled.

Stein looked down at Aloysius Frank Monahan, resting eternally on the metal slab. He searched the dead eyes for any remnant of what had mesmerized Ned Peering's wife. Whatever people call it—soul essence, life force—the place where memories and pain transformed into character, a look in the eye, a key to the heart. Whatever it was it was all gone. He remembered when he had taken Watson to that last sad visit to the vet from which there was no return. He remembered asking as the needle went in how long it would take to work, and from the vet's expression, realizing that it already had. As Shmooie the Buddhist used to say, what a short a distance it was from just barely here to just barely not.

Stein gave kudos to the embalmer's skills. The swelling and horrendous distortion that Clay Potter had so graphically described had been eradicated. "Thanks to Jarlene for that." Renn bowed to his bride with surprising agility. "She does all the cosmetics."

Jarlene curtsied back. "Doc's my biggest fan."

The woman had a gift for neorealism. Also a capacity for white wine. She poured herself a flagon of the local Chardonnay, clearly not her first of the day, judging from the redolent aroma of fermented grape seeping from her pores. And yet there was something in the dead man's face that could not be eradicated. Some residual echo of terror that resided in the ganglia of nerve cells.

Doc Moody was as proud of his medical degree today as he was the day he earned it in 1964. He handed Stein a copy of his toxicology report, which after a game attempt at deciphering, Stein set aside. "I'm guessing it says he died of multiple bee stings," Stein ventured.

"And that would be a helluva good first guess," said Moody. "Obviously the first thing we tested was levels of apitoxin in his system." He waited a polite moment for a gleam of recognition from his listener, then filled in the blank. "That's the venom from a bee's stinger."

"You're describing my nightmare death," Stein said. "I'm allergic as hell."

"You've been stung?"

"Oh, yes."

"Ask him if he swelled up," Jarlene chimed in from the corner of the office where she was putting away her brushes and paints.

"Like a Pillsbury doughboy," Stein answered her.

Jarlene grinned a knowing smile at her husband. "Tell him he's not allergic."

"You aren't allergic," Doc corroborated.

"What would I have to do to prove it to you? Die?" Stein gestured toward the corpse for emphasis.

"He wasn't allergic either," said Doc Moody.

"He looks about as dead as I ever want to be."

"Oh, he's dead all right," Doc agreed.

"Only not of a bee sting," Jarlene added. It was hard to tell if she thought her husband had run out of ideas or run out of breath.

Stein was sure he had read that Monahan had died of multiple bee stings.

"I sense some incredulity on his part," said Jarlene. "Do you sense incredulity?"

Renn opened his own neatly typed report, replaced one pair of glasses for another and read through the results to corroborate. "Nope. No indication of anaphylaxis. And barely a trace of apitoxin in his blood."

"That means his breathing passages were open," Jarlene footnoted.

"I know what anaphylaxis is."

"The other anomaly," Moody continued, "is that if a person were morbidly allergic, he'd swell up a whole lot *less* than our boy here did. It's a good sign when a body swells. That person almost never dies. So it wasn't the bees that killed him."

"Then what *was* the cause of death?"

"He sounds miffed," Jarlene giggled.

"You'll have to excuse my wife. She's grown to have more affection for the dead than the living."

"Not a single corpse ever concealed the truth of himself from me. Can you say that about the living?"

"She's got a point there." Renn glowed whenever he spoke about Jarlene. "It's his heart valve that was shut. Cause of death was morbid atherosclerosis. Eighty-five percent occluded arteries. Any stimulation could have triggered it. Methamphetamine usually, but I didn't find any. Blood alcohol content point-O-six."

"Lightweight," Jarlene scoffed.

"Maybe he found a truck stop that offered some female stimulation," Moody discretely suggested. "There was recent ejaculate in his shorts. And then of course there's this." He lifted Frank's left arm and indicated bruising around a sizable puncture mark.

"Did he get stung by a queen bee?"

Both of the Moodys chuckled. "A bite that size she'd have to be the queen of Russia," said Jarlene.

"With a stinger the size of a hypodermic needle," Renn concluded, "capable of injecting a one-milliliter dose of epinephrine. Something kind of like this." He pulled from the evidence bag a single-use needle. He could see Stein was having trouble keeping up. "Suppose you were driving a truck with two million bees, and you're pretty sure you're allergic. And let's say you get stung. Maybe by one of the bees you were carrying. Maybe one just passing through. You feel yourself swelling up. You fear it might shut your breathing down. Your chest gets tight. Your heart races. That's what anxiety does."

Stein felt his own chest tightening, his heart starting to race.

"Of course you'd carry an anti-venom kit. You reach in. You find the syringe." Renn clenched his right fist as if it were grasping a needle and jammed it powerfully into his left arm. "But instead of alleviating the problem, you've exacerbated it. Your heart races faster. Your calcified arteries can't handle the load. Pop goes the weasel."

"Are you saying that's what killed him?"

"Fear of death is often the cause of death," Jarlene said in a sing-song voice. "And now, if you boys are done gabbing, we've got a long drive over the mountain."

"Please. Just one more quick question. Do you know if there was any equipment found from the deceased's truck branded with a circle inside a triangle?" He tried to say "equipment" like he'd been using the term for years. "A friend of mine had some colonies stolen."

Jarlene was already at the front door. "Tell him if he's interested in hearing stories about stolen bees he should come to the meeting tonight in Las Viejas."

Renn slung his arm around his wife's ample shoulder. They walked to the door like a two-headed squid, with Stein swimming behind them through a dark pool of ink.

Chapter Five

New clusters of bones had been plopping to the surface of the pool all day. While the dredging machine had failed to clear the Jacuzzi line, it had succeeded in puncturing a previously obstructed subterranean artery, a geological aneurysm, through which the buried remains were flowing. With cloth and brush, turpentine and rags, Matthew and Angie had become bone-cleaning machines. They had covered the patio with a secondhand bed sheet from a garage sale and were attempting to form the skeletal shape of an elephant with each new bone they processed.

Lila could barely look without getting severe stomach cramps. Unruliness upset her. She had no license, no authority to discipline Angie. Of course Matthew was a co-conspirator, but the enterprise was Angie's initiative. Boys were easier. Men accommodate more readily to dominant and submissive roles. Maybe because they're bred to run in packs. With women, there could only be one queen to a hive.

The problem the kids were having was there were too many bones of one length and not enough of others to make anything that plausibly resembled an elephant. He'd place a bone, she'd pull it away. "Something big can't come out of something small," she growled at him. It fueled her frustration that she was no closer than Matt to cracking the code. She studied the mélange from all angles but could not find its organizing principle.

Angie idly picked up an armload of bones they had designated as elephant toes and moved them, setting them down in the thoracic area as opposing ribs. They actually looked pretty good in that alignment. Matt brought a few more from a pile of as yet unplaced bones. Their shape and dimensions matched. The work took over and the two labored in silent tandem. Bones were doused in kerosene, wiped clean, handed over, placed. They worked smoothly at it. The skeletal outline of a mammalian chest began to manifest.

"This may not be an elephant." Matthew said.

She had begun to think the same thing.

Matthew realigned a chain of bones from their four-legged position and tried to make arms out of them. "How many bones are in an arm?" He cocked his left arm into a weightlifter's flex under her chin. Angie was not prepared for the sensual assault of sweat and turpentine and whatever oil he used on his skin.

***

Stein had written down Renn and Jarlene's driving directions in his crappy shorthand that he always thought he'd be able to read afterward and never could. They had each given Stein slightly different landmarks and places to turn in order to find the meeting hall in Las Viejas, so he was on the lookout for everything. Plus trying to digest the new information that Frank Monahan had died from cardiac arrest and not anaphylactic shock. This seemed gigantically significant and Stein expected the revelation should generate an avalanche of *eurekas* and *ahaaas*, but no such fireworks of enlightenment exploded. Monahan was dead. That didn't change. Whatever he knew about the stolen bees went with him. Had he stolen them himself? Was he an unwitting accomplice? Where was he taking all those bees? Was there a buyer? A receiver? And what the hell was a derivative? In his state of mental preoccupation, Stein whipped past the turnoff he meant to take onto Route 53.

Had he been more familiar with the territory he might have acted with more aplomb. But he didn't know how far it was to the next exit or whether he could get back on in the opposite direction.

As Stein's role model, Tom Paine, prophetically wrote, "Desperate times require desperate measures." He eased over to the left lane, studying the flat, level fifteen-foot median that separated the two directions of vehicular traffic. He scanned the rearview mirror. Traffic was light. As if anticipating his bad intentions, prominently placed signs read DO NOT CROSS DOUBLE YELLOW LINES. While to some people these directions would leave little room for interpretation, Stein rationalized that local traffic regulations were pitched to the driving acumen of the local inhabitants. Farmers. Country people. Whereas a cosmopolite like himself, one with a more highly developed skill level and sense of judgment . . .

The maneuver was so outrageously blatant that Highway Patrol Captain Anthony Caravaggio, observing the action take place right in front of his nose, did not pull its perpetrator over immediately, but rather trailed along behind him to see what other antics he might perform. The big man had been in law enforcement twenty-two years and had been disappointed of late in the poverty of imagination most miscreants displayed. The typical violations fell within the boring parameters of speeding, expired tags, and the occasional FOR SALE sign displayed in a nonmoving vehicle parked more than two hundred feet from its registered address, a misdemeanor. But this looked like fun.

The exceptionally mild February weather had continued to prevail, and as Stein was now headed west into the sun, the car became unpleasantly warm. He cranked his window down. He had always disdained air-conditioning as an indulgence of the rich to glide through life in perfect comfort. Power windows were another peeve. Was the effort *so* burdensome to rotate one's *entire wrist* that the operation had to be reduced to the use of one finger? What was next? TV in the car? Automatic pilot? Was the ultimate goal to make ourselves extraneous to our own lives?

Gusts of wind buffeted the lightweight Kia. Stein vaguely recalled seeing a warning about GUSTY WINDS but he had immediately filed it in the category of *gratuitous information you can do nothing about.* Like BEWARE OF LOW FLYING PLANES. What precautions can a person take against a low-flying plane? Drive at a different altitude? Jesus!

He leaned across the seat to crank the passenger side window down, to give the incoming wind a place to exit. For the moment that he was stretched across the front seat he lost peripheral vision on his left side, and was startled by the blast of an air horn from a sixteen-wheeler that blew past him. He instinctively shot back to upright and grabbed the wheel in both hands, a reflex that proved to be life saving. The powerful wake generated by the truck propelled him nearly off the road into the shoulder. Once unleashed, the full repertoire of Newton's Laws of Motion and Aerodynamics got to perform. A partial vacuum was created in the volume of space that the truck had just vacated, and into that emptiness, Stein's plastic and carbon composite vehicle was pulled; all the way across from right shoulder to the left lane before Stein regained control and was able to swerve back into the right lane where he had started.

The wind currents through the front seat billowed the driving instructions tucked into a crease in the passenger's seat. He flailed at the elusive butterflies with his right hand, keeping a tight grasp on the wheel with his left. The papers flew to the open space above the partially lowered window. He lunged for them, the motion causing the car to swerve nearly off the road once again.

Up to this point Captain Caravaggio had been fascinated more than disturbed by the unorthodox driving patterns. He had even radioed in to see if such a brand name as Kia truly existed. But now, as he observed the driver's head dart down and out of sight, he had seen enough. He flashed his lights, sounded the siren, revved his four hundred horses till he was right on the Kia's tail, and jerked his thumb to the right.

Stein pulled off onto the shoulder, fumbled to find the ignition switch and shut off the engine. The specter of the three-hundred-pound body in uniform bearing down on Stein threw him into a bit of a sweat. He saw an outcropping of soft flesh that overhung yet a second helping of pulchritude, which thrust upward under the pressure of his brown equipment belt. It reminded him of a time right after the "Sergeant Pepper" album had come out and he was walking in Greenwich Village wearing a full-dress West Point jacket with tails over his jeans and T-shirt and a cop who looked like this one threw him against a wall with his fat mug in Stein's face and said, "Where's your fuckin' drum?"

Now he was indecisive about whether to remain in the car or to make the more hospitable gesture of greeting. Only a few area codes from home, he felt like he was in a foreign land whose customs he had read about but never yet practiced. He decided that a show of goodwill would be appreciated and stepped jauntily out to offer a hello.

"I need you to get back into your vehicle."

The strength of Caravaggio's unamplified voice was startling and Stein retreated like he had hit an invisible electronic fence. The officer's bulk filled his side window. "Registration and pilot's license please."

"Pilot's license?"

"Weren't you trying to do loop-the-loops back there?"

Stein was buoyed by the deadpan humor. So when Caravaggio said, "Do you know why I pulled you over?" Stein was tempted to quip that he hoped it wasn't about that bank robbery in Chowchilla the other day. But he wisely sensed that would be pushing it.

"I know it must have looked like I was weaving across lanes," Stein volunteered.

"Have you been drinking?"

"I don't blame you for thinking so. The truth is—"

"You were bending over that seat. Do you mind if I look what you've got down there?"

"Would it matter if I minded?"

"Not the slightest little bit."

Caravaggio betrayed only small disappointment at finding nothing more incriminating than of a bag of roasted almonds and a jar of flavored iced tea that Stein had purchased an hour earlier at a roadside fruit stand.

"I was trying to open the window."

"I'm going to ask you to stop talking and to breathe into this." He held the nozzle of the Breathalyzer toward Stein's face.

"I absolutely will," Stein said. "Just let me say this is a rental car. It's the first time I ever traversed this road and I was not prepared for how gusty it was through the pass. The car I usually drive hugs the road."

"Traversed?" Caravaggio repeated. "This was the first time you ever *traversed* this road?"

"I'm sorry. I just meant it was the first time I've ever *driven* here and I'm unfamiliar with—"

"I know what the word means." Calories burned into heat at an alarming rate behind Caravaggio's eyes.

"I'll show you what I was looking for. It's nothing dire." He reached into the front seat of his car.

"Freeze!" Caravaggio's weapon was drawn and pointed at the back of Stein's head.

"Oh, come on. You know I'm not going to hurt anyone." Still bent across the front seat, Stein extended his arm back toward Caravaggio like a crippled crab. Caravaggio took the paper from Stein as if he were using calipers to extract a hair from a bar of soap. Then he noticed the name and address imprinted at the top of the memo paper. "You know Doc Moody? Why didn't you say so?"

"Can I stand up?"

"Yeah, yeah." Caravaggio stepped back and allowed Stein to return to upright. He continued to scowl at the illegible scrawling. "I can't read a goddamn word of this. You write Greek?"

"I know. I have crappy handwriting. I'm trying to get to a meeting of the Central Valley Beekeepers Association in a town called Las Viejas."

Caravaggio scrutinized him in a new more benign way. "You one of the eastern professors doing the research on colony collapse?"

"No . . ." Stein tried to recall where he had heard that term used before. Colony collapse.

"I know you're not a beekeeper. You're too soft and indoorsy."

"Thank you for noticing."

"You want to get to Las Viejas?" He pointed Stein in the direction he'd been going before he had pulled him over, as if he were now doing him a big favor. There was an exit 4.6 miles down this road that would take him onto the road that would bring him down to the 202, and that would get him close enough where it would be obvious.

Stein thanked him, both for the directions and for sticking a gun in his face. "That hardly happens often enough."

"Don't forget this," Caravaggio said before Stein closed his car door. He handed Stein the ticket for multiple lane violations.

"This still stands?"

"Have I given you any reason to doubt it?"

***

Four point six miles later, Stein came uneventfully down off Route 53 onto the turnoff Caravaggio had instructed him to take. The long narrow road ran along the perimeter of fields that were plowed or ready to be plowed or already growing a winter crop. It made him just a little bit nostalgic for the horticultural time of his life, when he had been the Johnny Appleseed of hemp. The Burpee of boo. The maestro of Mary Jane. Some of his heirloom hybrids were still in cultivation today.

Heavy-bladed guillotines of agricultural machinery lay idle on the sides of the road like resting Panzer Divisions. Cattle plopped down on hillocks of muddy cow shit. Flat out in the middle of nowhere, also plopped down at a completely arbitrary locale, was some misguided soul's brilliantly wrong idea: a condo development. It was like a meteorite had fallen out of nowhere into nowhere. A gravel road led up to a cluster of brand-new urban boxy structures from which GRAND OPENING buntings snapped noisily in the breeze. Not an occupant or a prospective occupant's car was parked anywhere nearby. And then there was farmland again for three more miles before the town of Las Viejas appeared.

Stein wove slowly through the deserted streets of downtown in search of The Old Basque Inn, or a person he could ask. His was the only car on Main Street. It felt post-apocalyptic, after a neutron bomb had annihilated all human life but left the buildings. There was a patron or two in the Eight Ball Tavern just across the street from His Outstretched Hands, which Stein at first thought was a massage parlor, but turned out to be an evangelical ministry. Capillio's Video Shop was shuttered and for lease. Lois's Beauty was open but empty. Fantasia Tapes and Videos was gone. There was a handwritten sign taped to the front window of Vornado's Floor Covering that read GONE TO THE DOCTOR. BACK TOMORROW. Stein wondered how long that sign had been hanging there.

Making a right turn on Seventh, Torvaald's Numismatics was advertising metal detectors—"The Hobby That Pays for Itself." The Valentine's Day sale at DINNETTS AND THINGS was not drawing a crowd. Nor were they lining up to get into Carla's Fashions, "Where Women Can Dress Their Best for Way Less." He came to the end of town without finding the restaurant and made a last desperation right turn onto a street that did not look at all promising, and there it was: The Old Basque Restaurant and Tavern. He parked around the corner. Three adolescent skateboarders took turns thrashing the four-inch curb in front of the post office. None of them made it.

There were three steps up to the entryway to the restaurant. Two plaques hung over the lintel. One told of the restaurant's history as a safe haven for migrants and refugees fleeing European tyranny. The other was too faded to read. Stein paid his registration fee at the door and went inside. He expected the Beekeeper Association Convention to be comprised of three or four snoozing patrons, but no! Activity at the bar was buzzing. Men with white hair and minor injuries, men with bulk, men who worked out of doors, men who knew each other's business. They were unpracticed at false civility, uncomfortable with public gatherings. Their faces archived many weather reports predicting harsh wind and sun. They were outdoor guys. Guys who had or still worked on telephone lines or road gangs. There was talk of wintering locales for their bees. Of pesticides and pollen patties. Stein felt like he was in a foreign country catching occasional cognates but not enough of them to grok their meaning.

Dinner was already being splayed out in the next room. Sixty or seventy people sat at long wooden tables on wide chairs in a rathskeller-style room with low ceilings. They long-armed for bowls of potato salad and baked beans and heavily dressed iceberg lettuce plopped down by harried waitresses calling out storm warnings. The men were not young. The few who were young looked older. The wives were hardworking pioneer women who might have thought differently forty years ago if they knew that beekeeping would become their husbands' lives. With doughty, ironic cheer they had become absolute necessities: bookkeepers, honey extractors, sales and purchasing agents, social secretaries, cooks, Jills of all trades.

Stein scanned the crowd for a familiar face. He spied Renn Moody sitting across the table from a lean, rawboned young man wearing a cowboy hat. The plaintive look etched into the contours of his face made him look like a man perpetually struggling to clamber over a wall too high for him. He was seeking solace from Renn, or advice. He had been kicked down the list from March to April by the company that sent out new queens. He'd have to wait an extra month before supering his colonies. Supering. Stein had heard that word before, too. He cast a net back into his recent memory. Karma had been "supering" his hives. What the hell did that mean, again?

Renn placated the younger fellow's fears. May queens, he said, were always better than those bred and shipped earlier in spring. The egg-laying patterns of early queens were messed up, he said. They lay two and three eggs per comb and they set too much drone brood. Whatever that all meant. The extraordinary thing Stein noticed was that Renn's pupil actually listened to him. Not to ridicule or demean, as the modern generation did to their elders, but to acquire knowledge he valued. Renn enjoyed the hell out of his role of teacher and elder statesman.

Dick Jupe came up to one of the middle tables and tapped a beer bottle against a stanchion. When there was enough quiet he introduced himself as the president of the organization and called the meeting to order. Order here was a relative concept. There was no mike or podium. No Roberts Rules. The president didn't wear a suit. He was just one of the men who'd gotten boondoggled into saying he'd do it for a year, which was the way George Washington envisioned the American presidency. The folks in the room were people who shopped in his hardware store and met him for coffee every week, so it was slightly awkward shushing them down. The women handled that job and the room became quiet except for the clanking of dishes in the kitchen.

Jupe stood up on a bench so people in the back could see him. There was important business to be done. First, there was a report on the newest government regulations around trucking. The topic was roundly booed. They were Libertarians all, when it came to Washington. Finally he introduced their special guest. "A friend to beekeepers, who has been traveling all over the state talking to local groups like this one, Captain Anthony Caravaggio of the California Highway Patrol."

Stein's nemesis from earlier that day edged his bulk into the center spot. He was out of uniform now. The amount of shirt material necessary to gird his waist could have made two mattresses. "Guys," he began, "you're a vital force to the agriculture of this state. I only wish Washington understood that better. All kinds of changes have been made to existing regulations. You're not going to like all of them."

"Are we going to like *any* of them?" somebody hectored.

"Probably not."

Caravaggio outlined the complex minutiae around trucking regulations and allowable hours per month of road use and maximum load weight, new strapping requirements, which, he parenthetically mentioned, would have saved the life of the driver whose truck had tipped over not far from here.

All this information had to be written in logbooks. People groused that the government was making them bookkeepers instead of beekeepers.

Dick thanked Caravaggio, asked for and got a round of appreciative applause for him, and plowed ahead to the next topic, which was honey. Last year was a pretty decent year, he acknowledged. There was a lot of moisture into late spring and production was up across the board. This year figured to be off just a little but not too bad. The good news was pollination fees. Eight frame boxes were going for a hundred and fifty dollars.

The expression on his face became more solemn as he came to the topic of colony collapse. "We all know that something's going on out there. Some of us have been hit and some of us not. Healthy bees are disappearing. Just dying. Hives are being abandoned. Not from disease. A lot of us here, we've had twenty, thirty percent depletion. Our friend Jack Dellingham from up there in Worshington, who came down and talked to us last year, he lost eighty percent of his bees. These were healthy bees."

Stein felt a current pass through the room. Murmurs of assent and concern followed. People who were not used to speaking aloud in public places testified of their own losses. Others, long in the habit of interruption, did so without reprimand. There was a lot of anger under the skin of these principled, mainly Mormon and Seventh Day Adventist, 4H club, law-abiding anarchists. No one had been untouched by the blight. One man in overalls at the back table had the worst story. He had twelve hundred healthy hives one day. The next morning he came out and not a single bee was to be found. His hives were empty. There was plenty of honey, so it had not been bears or predators, or mud wasps. There were no dead bees around the hive. The boxes were still there, so the bees had not been pilfered. They had just flat out vanished. Listening to their tales, Stein thought of the ride through the deserted streets of Las Viejas and realized that colony collapse affected more than just bees.

The tenor of the room became more abrasive. Everyone had a theory around what was causing the problem. People blamed the nosema virus carried by the varroa mite. People blamed the Australians on whose bees the virus entered the country. People blamed the government for not keeping the Australian bees out. They blamed the government for cutting sweetheart deals with the Russians, letting their beekeepers come in and ruin things, and with the Chinese, letting their inferior honey undercut prices.

They blamed the pesticide manufacturers—fifty-three different toxic chemicals had been found in dead bees. They blamed the growers for removing all the natural sources of nutrition, which weakened the bees' systems and rendered them susceptible to the pesticides and varroa mites. They blamed Sacramento for screwing the farmer, for diverting their water to LA. That brought on a whole new chorus of anger. Water needed to stay here. City people needed to understand how food got put on a table. Somebody blamed the Africanized bees for taking over European hives.

The one black man in the room stood up. "Yeah, I was waiting for someone to say that," he said. He had a military bearing.

Jupe smoothed it over before anyone's neck got pulled out of joint. He informed the group that their dues had been put to hiring a lobbyist who would help the government understand the beekeepers' concern. Anybody wanting to contribute more could sign up for a 2 percent levy on the honey they sold. He asked if there was any other business. Before chaos and disorganization descended, Stein stood up.

He said that a friend of his had some of his colonies stolen and that he was hoping to get them back, or at least get his equipment back, and that if anyone had any information or had any of their stuff pilfered, he'd be happy to buy them a beer. He tried to sound as affable and unthreatening as any outsider prying into peoples' private lives could sound. A male voice from somewhere in the room yelled out, "I *wish* someone would steal my bees. Put me out of my misery." A female voice right alongside him yelled out, "Put *me* out of his misery too." That got lots of laughs from the women.

***

The bar filled quickly. Stein tried to make himself conspicuous to anybody wanting to find him. He was ignored and vaguely invisible. He thought he saw a woman in the periphery make surreptitious eye contact with him but she retracted into the crowd before he could be sure.

The only two guys in the room who were wearing suits had found each other. One kept talking about "management techniques" and "vectors of service-oriented revenue" that were overtaking the "production-oriented" sector of his business. The other had just come from seeing his in-laws in Spokane.

The heavy hand of Anthony Caravaggio dropped onto Stein's shoulder. "Well, look who's here. My favorite airline pilot. Harry

Stein. Of 237 Sycamore Alley, West Hollywood, California. Born December 8, 1950. Height five-foot nine, weight one-seventy. But I'd say closer to one-ninety."

Not to be outdone, Stein answered coolly, "You have an excellent memory, Captain Anthony Caravaggio, badge number 38336, driving California Issue Highway Patrol Vehicle number 797."

"Impressive," Caravaggio said. "Too bad you weren't even close with my badge number."

"That's because you don't know my transposition code."

Caravaggio pressed Stein very subtly away from the nucleus of the crowd. "Why don't we go outside for a cup of coffee?"

"A little late for caffeine, but thanks."

"You wouldn't mind telling me again, a little bit more specifically this time, why you're here?"

"I just don't see how it's any of your business."

"Really? You don't?" Caravaggio pressed closer.

"I'm just going to this meeting. It's no crime."

"You'd be surprised what's a crime and what isn't."

Stein put his drink down so he could express his childlike innocence with two open hands. "I'm just looking for stories."

"No one's going to be telling you any stories. People around here like to settle disputes among themselves. We don't go whining to the media."

"I'm not media. I'm just some guy."

Caravaggio nodded to a cluster of four men at the end of the bar. "See the Chamber of Commerce over there? They run fifteen hundred hives each." He weather-vaned Stein a few degrees east. "Renn Moody over there? Three thousand. Your friend, Moonblossom, how many? Ten?"

He slung his yoke of an arm around Stein's shoulders and guided him outside; for all the world to see, a couple of old drinking buddies. "It's a beautiful night for a drive to LA," Caravaggio said. "If you leave right now and drive at a reasonable rate of speed, you should be tucked in your own bed by two, three at the latest."

"Are you running me out of town?"

"Nothing of the sort. I'm simply a source of information. By the way, did you check *all* the signs around the corner where you parked? I'd hate to see you get booted."

"Maybe I better double-check." Stein walked unhurriedly down the three steps from the restaurant doorway to the sidewalk. He paused there for a moment and turned right.

"You parked in the other direction."

Stein guessed that Caravaggio was watching him but didn't want to obviously check. Throwing an arm up in gratitude, never looking back, Stein spun around and headed in the proper direction. Just before he reached the corner, a bandy-winged arm darted out from behind a nonworking street light and plucked at Stein's sleeve.

A voiced hissed, "My husband had some bees stolen."

It was the elusive woman from inside.

"Does he want to talk to me?"

"Billy Bob!" She stage-whispered into the dark alley behind her. Her husband appeared. He was the young man Stein had watched conversing with Renn Moody. "I'm sorry for your loss," Stein said.

"Excuse me?"

"Your pilferage. Your bees being stolen."

"Oh. Right. Funny way to put it."

"Do I call you Billy? Or Bob? Or Billy Bob?"

He had to laugh. "She does that. My name is Hollister Greenway. The wife is Ruth Ann."

"I better take my own car and follow you."

Ruth Ann took the keys from Hollister and slid in behind the wheel of the Ford Bronco. "Billy Bob's medication don't like him to drive at night," she said.

"I don't take medication," Hollister clarified. "And she doesn't talk like that. She just likes to drive trucks."

***

Stein tooted his horn and waved a conspicuous farewell to Caravaggio as he drove past the entrance to the restaurant. He drove down Seventh Street, obeying every traffic law possible. At the corner of G he made rendezvous with the idling 1977 Ford Bronco and followed the fleeting taillights back through town. It felt even more desolate than it had earlier. The Bronco busted a red and swung around a corner. Stein waited dutifully for the light to change. When he made the turn he found himself looking into utter blackness. His own thin beams illuminated the two-lane blacktop that went right or left right in front of him, but there were no red tail lights in either direction. A tremor of paranoia swept through him. Images of ambush, hijack, vigilantes, *Mississippi Burning.*

Suddenly a pair of Solaris Xenon ultra-brights exploded out of the utter darkness right at his windshield punctuated by the blast of a horn. Stein recoiled and threw his arms up in front of his face as the vehicle blasted at him, head on. At the last instant the Bronco veered off and skidded to a stop. Hollister leaned from out the passenger-side window. "Don't mind Ruth Ann."

The little woman set out along the two-lane at a nice, straight-faced rate of speed that Stein could easily follow. He had no sense of where they were, and after a few miles paranoia kicked in again. He was relieved when he saw an oasis of light in the distance. As they got closer Stein recognized that they were heading for the deserted condo development he had seen earlier.

He followed the truck onto a gravel side road under the banners that hung still in the windless nighttime air. The Bronco parked in the spot designated TENANTS ONLY. Ruth Ann's hand reached out the driver's-side window and directed Stein to the spot right behind her, reserved for VISITORS. She hopped down from the cab and strode like a long-legged woman up the walkway to the first unit and let them inside.

"You live here?" Stein asked, trying to make the prospect sound admirable.

"Hollister can be a little impetuous with his financials," she said. "But where there's love, any house becomes a home." She hostessed Stein inside.

The lights had all been left blazing and Stein figured that utilities must be included with the purchase price. The furniture looked straight out of DINNETTS AND THINGS. Stein took a seat on one of the polyester easy chairs that matched the plaid pullout sofa. Ruth Ann moved two of the formal place settings off the laminated dining table placed under a chandelier of hanging glass globettes.

"Can I get you something to drink?" She opened the kitchen fridge, displaying a bounteous array of foodstuffs. "We've got fake milk, fake apple juice, fake diet Coke . . ."

"We don't really live here," Hollister subtitled. "This is the model home. Ruth Ann works as the booking agent. Our place is on the other side of the hill just past the Paulsen Reservoir."

Stein's interest in the theatrics was diminishing. "I've got to get back to LA tonight. You say you had some bees stolen . . . ?"

Their story itself was unspectacular. Two years prior, a coworker of Hollister's at the Sunkist plant named Boyd Weber, whom everyone called Spider, got a promotion to Southeast Regional Area supervisor and was transferred to Baton Rouge. Hollister said he'd take care of Spider's bees while he was gone—he had no experience, but it looked easy enough. The bees did all the work. All you had to do was gather the honey.

Who knew they had to be moved to a winter location? Who knew they had to be fed pollen patties and a mixture of nectar and sugar? Who knew about disease and pesticides and mite control and how to replace a queen? Who knew about all the time it took out of your life? He lost half of Spider's bees in the first year. Those that survived were ragged and unproductive. His healthy eight-frame boxes had depleted down to two, maybe three decent frames of bees.

It was about that time that Renn Moody paid a visit. When he saw what things had come to he volunteered to take the bees. Hollister had been so embarrassed of his negligence that he made a bold proclamation: If Renn would teach him, he would work as hard as any man ever could to learn. True to his word, Hollister became a dedicated pupil. Sometimes his dedication exceeded his abilities, but he was resilient and learned by his mistakes. By the end of the following summer he had brought his twenty-four colonies back to good health.

"One night a month ago, they were gone," Ruth Ann abruptly concluded, as if the whole long tale had been a set up for her to jump the ending.

"How?" Stein asked them.

"How is the easy part," Hollister shrugged. "All you need is a flatbed and a forklift."

"And the will to do evil," Ruth Ann amended.

Stein spoke from lofty experience that it was never that easy.

"Come on. We'll show you." Ruth Ann bolted up out of her chair.

"What do you mean, you'll show me?"

"Let's go commit a felony."

***

Moments later Stein found himself trailing Hollister out the door. "Boy, did I have a wrong first impression of your wife," Stein wheezed.

"Tell me about it," said Hollister, who himself was trying to keep up with Ruth Ann.

Stein followed them back over Route 53 in his rented Kia. The landscape looked spooky at night with bare witchy branches groping at him from the sides of the road. He followed the truck into a nearly blind driveway just past the Paulsen Reservoir siding.

"This is us," said Hollister, who had hopped out of the truck. He pointed to a place for Stein to park in their gravel driveway under an overhanging scraggly oak and alongside a spiffy red Camaro convertible with Massachusetts plates.

"Out of state visitors?" Stein asked.

"Mine," said Ruth Ann. "Imagine how happy my parents were that after I graduated Harvard Business School and came west for a Venture Capitalist job, I married a hillbilly named Billy Bob."

"That's not *exactly* how it happened," Hollister explained to Stein.

"Yeah. Somehow I had a feeling."

Hollister lowered the Bronco's tailgate and wheeled his forklift out from the garage and onto the flatbed.

"Let's skedaddle," Ruth Ann whooped.

The three of them wedged into the cab.

"See why I love it here?" Ruth Ann grinned. "You never get to say *skedaddle* at a business meeting."

They did not go very far. The place she stopped to pull over seemed arbitrary. There was no barbed wire or fencing of any sort. Rows of trees twenty feet tall stood like silent regiments in the harsh underlighting of the headlights and the soft blush of the quarter moon. The trees were not the point of interest, but rather the stack of white wooden boxes whose purpose Stein now had been educated to recognize. With her elbow out the window, the sleeve of her flannel shirt rolled up over her bony arm, Ruth Ann backed the truck to the lip of the row and cut the engine. While Stein watched in wonderment, Ruth Ann and Hollister lowered the tailgate and wheeled the forklift up to the neatly stacked boxes.

"In five minutes I could lift this pallet onto my truck and those bees'd be mine."

"If he had the will to do evil," Ruth Ann amended.

"That's how mine got boosted. Just that easy."

A small detail had caught Stein's attention. Everything else faded to white noise.

"Who do these boxes belong to?" Stein asked. There was an authority and directness in his voice that had not been there before.

"Don't worry, we weren't going to take them." Ruth Ann laughed. "You just went all sheriff on me."

Stein beckoned for Hollister to hand him his flashlight and began tiptoeing closer. "Are there bees in those boxes?" Before he got the answer, which he knew would be yes, he edged closer. Just an arm's length away now, he shone the light across the top plane of the two boxes. Someone had made a crude attempt to hack it away, but the owner's brand was etched too deeply into the wood frame to be obliterated: three circles inside a triangle, each with a triangle inside of it.

"These hives are stolen property," he said. "I need to know who they belong to."

Ruth Ann went berserk. "What is this, Stein, a *sting*?" She turned her rant on Hollister. "Damn it, Billy Bob, I knew the minute I looked at him he was the law!"

"The law? You've got to be kidding." Stein still expected people to see him as the subversive warrior with his shoulder-length mane tied up in a bandana made of a ripped U.S. flag. Not the "before" picture in an ad for exercise equipment. "I'm here to bring these back to their rightful owner."

"Their rightful owner is Renn Moody and he's giving these boxes to my husband. He's coming over in the morning to split some of his hives. You can ask him yourself."

Stein glanced down at his watch. The drive back to LA would have to wait.

Chapter Six

While Hollister and Ruth Ann Greenway were setting up the roll-out cot for Stein to bunk in overnight, it was Lila's night to host her book club, which meant that Mercedes had been up to her maracas all day making hors d'oeuvres and salads and those little fancy pastries the girls loved.

Stein called them the Trust Fund Girls. The eight women had an average net worth of seven million. Like Lila, they were in their late forties, Beverly Hills High School gals, sevens and eights on the male Universal ratings system for faces and bodies. Most went to college for the proverbial MRS. Money they made on their own was in real estate and stocks. One of them, with her husband, owned a gigantically successful chain of burger shacks. One was married to a heart surgeon. Connie, the one who had never been married, had the best genetically engineered body of them all, and was the major nutcase.

Although their pampered lives represented everything Stein believed wrong with the world, he was never unkind to them. Except once, to Connie, who had plunked herself down in front of him while he was trying to watch a Lakers game and initiated a conversation about why he thought the dermatologist she'd been going to for six years had never asked her out. She had been wearing a daringly low cut blouse, exposing a good bit of enhanced pulchritude. Frustrated at his lack of response she had accused him of staring at her breasts, to which he had laconically replied that he was more interested in the wonders of nature than the wonders of science.

During much of the afternoon, Angie had noticed Lila peering out the kitchen window with increasing levels of anxiety. After Matthew had gone for an obligatory evening with his mother, Angie knocked on Lila's bedroom door. She found her reading the book that was up for discussion that night, *The House of Sand and Fog*, which had put her to sleep by page thirteen the previous four times she had tried. *Who Moved My Cheese?* and *The Millionaire Mind* had been suggested but the consensus was they should read fiction. After that discussion, the Trust Fund Girls had decided to found a second book club, dedicated to finance and current events. Lila hadn't read that book, either, and they'd meet tomorrow.

Angie held onto both sides of the doorframe and let her body twist inside so her face was almost buried in her arm. She wanted Lila to know she appreciated all she did to make her feel welcome. She liked Lila and her father together. She had encouraged her dad to see past Lila's middle-of-the-road politics and the other incongruities of their lives. And when Stein had tiptoed around the subject of possibly moving in with Lila, Angie had been thoughtful and mature and considerate and enthusiastic.

Angie returned to the patio with the unequivocal intention of fulfilling her promise to cover the pool with the blue plastic tarp Lila had bought for that purpose and to move all the accumulated bones to the pool house. Except. As Zimmerman's Law states with such unerring accuracy: Whatever you think is going to happen next, it will almost always be something else.

That event in question had already happened. The pits had yielded up a new treasure. It was sizable and manifest, and sat partially above the surface of the muck. It looked to Angie at first like an elephant's ear, but she knew elephant ears did not have a solid bone structure and that the false ID was just her brain doing what it does—identifying the unknown as the closest thing it has on file. Exactly the way God came to exist, she had long believed.

Angie knew she was here to clean up and that what she was now irresistibly compelled to do would delay that chore. But the winner in any battle between obedience and curiosity in Angie's psyche was a foregone conclusion. The object was situated near enough to the shallow end that Angie was sure she could reach it from the second step.

She was wearing her Nikes and her good jeans on the possibility that Matt might come by following his command performance *avec mama*. To be on the safe side, she slipped her shoes off and stepped out of her jeans. The muck level seemed to have receded slightly. Her bare legs extended into a long V. Her body bowed into a graceful arc. Her arm extended while at her anchor point her toes grasped for stability and balance. She reached the object. It was solid and palpable. She girded herself and tugged. The unanchored object came up with such surprising ease it nearly staggered her. She wavered for a moment but never lost her center of gravity. She took a step backward up onto solid ground and sat on the new grass to examine her find.

It was about a foot and a half wide, shaped like two ears, not one, and it tapered down to a narrower width at the bottom. As she gave it a superficial cleaning, the covering ooze plopped back into the pool and one of her hands encountered a circular opening that her closed fist could pass through. Her other hand found a symmetrical opening on the other side. She held it up in front of her, her hands through the openings. Chills surged down her body. She knew what she had found. If this hip joint belonged to an elephant, it was the Jane Fonda of pachyderms.

A loud blast like a rifle shot startled her. She whirled around to face the pool. A methane eruption had opened a small crater from whose caldera now arose a round, smooth protuberance, which was thrust higher by a second expulsion of gas. It had two symmetrical marble-sized sockets a few inches apart, another opening below and centered between them, and beneath that, a wider, jack-o-lantern opening. Without taking her eyes from the hypnotic apparition, she speed dialed a number on her phone. She could barely form words.

"Matthew," she breathed. "You have to come over here now. Make some excuse to your mother. This is no wooly mammoth we found. This dude is a dude!"

***

Stein awoke to the aroma of frying bacon. No bouquet quite fills a house like the scent of punished pig. He rolled carefully out of the guest bed, testing the effects on his back from a night away from Lila's Sacropedic mattress. It came as a pleasant surprise when he propped himself into sitting position and felt relatively pain free.

Ruth Ann, framed in the kitchen doorway, noted ironically that he was up early. Through the sliding panel glass door that led to the back-yard, Stein saw two figures encased in white bee suits, bent to industrial labor. Boxes were being pried open, frames removed, studied at close range, and their living seething contents scraped off into new homes.

"I wish somebody would have gotten me up earlier," Stein grunted as he threw himself into his pants, shirt, and shoes. He had slept in his underwear.

"The staff is deeply apologetic. The night concierge did not communicate all your special instructions."

"I didn't mean it that way."

The kitchen was large and open. The style of the house was hard to categorize. Early sixties suburban ranch crossed with real ranch. Stein looked longingly at the pile of eggs and bacon and toast sitting on a sideboard. "I should really get out there and help them, I suppose," he said, fervently hoping for dissuasion.

"Aren't you the brave little worker bee."

He couldn't tell if she was mocking or praising him, which had been his historical problem with women.

"Billy Bob put this out for you."

Stein hoped she meant the food, but she was gesturing toward a white HAZMAT body suit that lay draped over the back of a kitchen chair. "Okay," he said, and intoned the mantra of the gladiators. "We who are about to die salute you."

"Oh, stop being a little baby. They're just supering new hives." Ruth Ann slapped him gently with a sleeve of the bee suit.

It was made of thick canvas, stiff and unwieldy, difficult to put on. Ruth Ann instructed and assisted him. Legs first. She grasped his left calf, guided his leg down into the opening while holding the right side taut. When he got stuck, she reached her arm way down into the suit down to bend his ankle. Then once it was secure, she tugged it up tight around the thigh. The proximity was hard to ignore. She helped fit his arms inside and then knelt before him and zippered up the front, crotch to throat. She made sure the Velcro stays were secure at his wrists and ankles. "Don't want those suckers crawling in there, do we?"

Outside, Renn Moody was instructing Hollister, pointing out a necessary detail of how the work needed to be done. Hollister listened carefully, lifted a frame of bees out of the box and checked with his mentor that he was doing it properly. Ruth Ann read Stein's thoughts. "Renn and Jarlene's only son died in the war. Hollister's dad croaked early. What can you say? Nature's eternal law of compensation."

She topped Stein's head with a safari hat. "They can sting through canvas. I'd hate to see you get any more of a swelled head. Now go. Before the job is all finished and I don't get to watch you in action." She turned him toward the door and gave him a goodly shove.

Stein walked robotically to the door, slid it open, and went EVA, as the astronauts say. The air all around the men was a chaotic solar system of flying bees. Their wildly erratic mass was not as thick as a swarm, not as dense as a cloud, more like windblown ash from a swirling forest fire. He had once gone down in a diving suit and hated the encasement. This was all that plus the incessant buzz. Yet he could not help marvel that with all those thousands of bees, darting around each other in chaotic proximity, there were no mid-air collisions. How did they do that? If they were all planes there'd be carnage.

Renn made a broad gesture of welcome when he saw Stein come out. So easy and familiar was the beekeeping coroner with his work that he had set his veil and headgear aside and was scraping off a frame containing ten thousand bees as if they were breadcrumbs. "Know what we're doing here?" he called cheerily to Stein.

Stein's throat felt too dry to have a speaking voice. "Supering some new colonies?"

"Very good." Renn elbowed Hollister. "Hear that? The man's a learner."

Among the boxes into which Renn was scraping his own healthy bees, one was branded with Karma Moonblossom's insignia. "Hollister tells me of your interest in this particular piece of equipment right here."

"Sorry if it's a little awkward."

"Awkward's relative. I once had to embalm a baby girl who'd been impaled by a hunting arrow. Hollister will finish up. Why don't we go inside?"

Back in the house, Stein stripped out of his gear. The house sounded empty. Ruth Ann had probably left for work. Stein hoped some of the food had been left out but she was a tidy housekeeper.

"So you like bees," Stein said.

"Being around death all day, it's good to be surrounded by life."

"How do you manage the balance with work?"

"We have a deal. Nobody dies during pollination season."

"I guess the news didn't get to Frank Monahan."

"There's always someone who doesn't go along with the game plan. Then look what happens. Hollister says you think maybe these boxes were stolen?"

"I didn't say I think maybe. I said they are. They were. I'd be grateful to know where you got the boxes from."

"If you're sure you want to dig this deep into the hive, Hollister needs an extractor. I'm going to be taking him up to Butch and Burleigh Branston when we're done here. Those are the boys I got these boxes from. I feel like I'm feeding the poor boy to the wolves. But if you want to watch a feeding frenzy, you're welcome to come along."

"Thanks, that'll be helpful."

"You haven't met the Branston boys. I'd lower my expectations a notch."

***

They went together in Doc Moody's luxury truck, a well-appointed vehicle of Japanese ancestry. He had parked it at the L of the driveway, alongside a stand of maguey plants that divided Hollister and Ruth Ann Greenway's property from their neighbor's. The long-spiked shoots that burst up out of the center were almost wide enough to be rolled into narrow canoes. Each had a sharp-tipped talon at the end an inch or two long. He could never see one of these magueys without getting sick to his stomach, remembering the point of one sticking clear through Angie's big toe. She had stepped on the plant growing on their hillside property the day he and Hillary told her they were getting divorced.

Whatever Renn Moody's chronological age was, behind the wheel he was sixteen. Traffic signals and lane demarcations were merely suggestions of possible behavior. He was good though, skillful enough so that Stein never felt endangered. Also, now that he was aware of what he was looking at, Stein fathomed the immensity of the orchards. Last night in the dark he could only see the first rows of trees the headlights penetrated. There were a fuck of a lot of trees. "They all almonds?" Stein asked.

"Mostly almonds," Renn confirmed. Like everyone else up here, he pronounced it *amands*. "Some pistachios too. Some oranges. Hear a couple of folks are trying pomegranates."

Hollister chuckled at the mention of pomegranates, like they might as well be trying to grow trout.

The road jogged to the right and elevated up an easy grade. A fully loaded flatbed was laboring about fifty yards ahead of them, chugging in one of its lower gears. The driver was looking for signs at each small turnoff into the orchards that bounded both sides of the road. "Yep," Renn said. "He'll be making his drops at ol' Jim Bottomly's."

As predicted, the driver came upon the turnout he was looking for and began making his left. Lanes had been laid wide enough to accommodate trucks this size but the driver was not experienced and overshot, leaving his load jackknifed at an angle that blocked the road. He needed to back up, and doing so now blocked lanes going in both directions. The kid had a busted front tooth and a brush cut. He yelled out his window, "Sorry, man," and commenced a laborious effort to put the truck into the angle to make the turn. Renn shut off his engine. They were going to be here for a while.

"Too early in the day to be unloading, isn't it?" asked Hollister.

"Not by the time he makes that turn."

Stein recognized the cargo of white boxes neatly stacked and loaded on the back of the semi. He felt protected enough to be curious. "How does this work? People just bring their bees in and turn them loose? How do they get paid?"

Moody let his seat recline and closed his eyes. "I told you I'd give you a ride, not an education."

"Seemed to me you like teaching."

"I teach Hollister because, God willing, he'll learn enough to take over my operation when I retire."

Hollister had likely hoped for that announcement before, and resisted the urge to ask Renn to repeat what he'd said.

The kid in the truck was making little headway. Each maneuver got him in deeper. With Renn feigning a nap, Stein turned his questions toward Hollister about how the whole bee-renting thing worked. The pupil waited deferentially for Renn to answer. When there was silence, both out of politeness and to validate Renn's faith in him, Hollister gave Stein a decent enough overview of the business. That it cost two hundred dollars to keep a healthy hive alive for a year and they could make nearly all that in one month's rental fee. That left honey and wax and pollinating other crops to make a profit. Some went north to Oregon and Washington for blueberries and cherries.

The conversation flourished with Renn excluded, a position he could not abide. He jumped in at an unguarded intersection and took it hostage. "In a few days the call of 'Bloom's Up' is gonna go out, and this whole valley is going to look like Cinderella at the ball. Half a million acres of almond trees in blossom all at once, every blossom needing to be cross-pollinated from another species. Hell, in the old days they were happy to pull down eight hundred pound per acre. Now they cry poverty if they don't get four thousand. Back in the day there were plenty of local bees. There were forty different kinds of flowering plants for them to feed on and stay healthy. Look around. Do you see anything else growing? Don't bother looking. The answer is no. They spray till they kill off everything that drains water, soil nutrients away from their trees. There's no pollen for them to forage. You see those yellow patties on top of the bee boxes, look like little pumpkin cheeseburgers? They're pollen patties. We have to *feed* them pollen. That's like putting out dishes of blood for mosquitoes."

"He's right," Hollister concurred.

"That's not *farming,*" Renn spat. "It's manufacturing. They've killed off the environment that supports the bees but they need ten times more." He nodded toward the laboring truck. "They get shipped in from Worshington, Oregon, the Dakotas, Florida. We had a guy last year ship in from Maine; I think he's coming back."

"I heard that he was," Hollister said.

"Doesn't it get expensive shipping them across country?"

"Hell, yes! Cheaper to steal 'em."

Stein waited a moment and then asked quietly, "If that's what Frank Monahan was doing, how would I find out where he was delivering his shipment?"

Before Hollister understood that Renn did not want to get into the whole matter, the young protégé volunteered that Stein should probably check with Henny Spector. Henny was the local contractor that put together most of the independent and especially the last-minute deals.

"Doesn't matter who's taking the shipment," Renn growled. "Growers don't give a damn where their bees come from. Half of them never had their hands in dirt. They're not farmers. They're agricultural *management practitioners*."

"Or Russians," Hollister added.

"Don't get me started on the Russians."

The truck ahead of them finally made it into the orchard lane. The kid waved back a sincere apology. Stein was still working to connect all the dots. "So the bees that were on Monahan's truck . . . somebody had contracted for them. And since they didn't get delivered, that owner still needs that same number of bees, right? So how do they get replaced?"

"Well *now* you have asked your first intelligent question," said Renn, and he restarted the engine.

***

Butch and Burleigh Branston were forty-one-year-old identical twins, star linebackers on their high school football team twenty-five years ago. They went through life with two basic thoughts: About any man they saw, *Could I take him in a fight?* About any woman, *What are my chances of fucking her?* They could be told apart only by the legs on which they wore their knee brace. Butch blew out his right meniscus in a post-game dare involving a flatbed truck going sixty. Burleigh blew his left jumping off the same flatbed, even though by then it had slowed down to forty-five. He had never lived down the stigma of being outdone by his younger brother.

Scraggy wild blackberry bushes grew alongside the busted wood fence that bounded their rain-gullied driveway. It widened out to a level area in front of the house that with a woman's touch (or really with the touch of anyone remotely sane) would have been a yard of some sort, a place for grass or trees. Instead it looked like a hoarder's closet. Stein counted ten industrial-sized sewing machines, half a dozen refrigerators with and without doors, the skeletons of two rusted Oldsmobiles interlaced in a perpetual embrace, and the promise from beneath unseen piles of much much more.

The brothers greeted Doc Moody with respect. Their quarry would never be anyone who knew more than they did. When Renn presented Hollister as "the young fella I told you might be looking for equipment," their expressions turned herpetological. Renn was cryptic in his introduction of Stein, just saying he had driven up from Los Angeles in a brand of car nobody had ever heard of. Burleigh gimped over to the brothers' red pickup truck and fished a creel of Coors out of the cooler. He tossed one to Renn, who snatched it one-handed, and offered one to Hollister, who declined, laughing that he ought to keep his wits about him.

"In other words, Ruth Ann don't let him drink in the daytime," Renn chuckled.

"It's not her." There was something sweet in the way Hollister smiled when he talked about Ruth Ann.

"Does your friend who drove from Los Angeles like an adult beverage?" Burleigh asked.

"Thanks," Stein said. He readied his hand for the can to be tossed to him. Instead Burleigh popped it open and handed him the brew. Stein wasn't sure whether to read the gesture as sarcasm or as hospitality.

"Cheers," he said, and took a guzzle.

"Why don't you show Hollister what you've got," Renn suggested. "He may be in the market for a honey extractor."

"Sure. Just tell us which arm and which leg he's willing to pay." Butch punctuated his humor with the slinging of his python left arm around Hollister's shoulders. "Come on around back. We'll see what we got."

"Mind if I tag along?" Stein asked. "There's some equipment I might be interested in too."

Surreptitious looks passed between the twins and Renn Moody.

"We wouldn't want to have two buyers going against each other and us take unfair advantage," said Burleigh.

"That matches my first impression of you," Stein said. "My needs are pretty specific, though. Equipment branded with three circles inside a triangle. Like ones you found for Dr. Moody."

"Hellfuck if I ever look. But I tell you what. My brother's gonna take Hollister to find that extractor. You come around with me to the back of the house, and we'll see what we turn up. Truth to tell though, you're likely to be disappointed."

"First time for everything," Stein said amiably.

Hollister had already disappeared with Butch. Burleigh limped ahead. His gimp made every other step look like he had just come up with a great idea he couldn't hold in. "Coming, Hollywood?"

"Buyer Beware," Renn chuckled. "Burleigh's crazier than a two-dick dog, and he's the sane one."

Stein was led around a circuitous path through an archipelago of junk that made Stein think of a losing army's battlefield piled high with body parts. A piece of a tractor. Vacuum cleaners. A stack of tires. Some bicycle frames. Stein thought about archaeologists a thousand years from now unearthing this site and trying to piece together a picture of twentieth-century civilization.

"You're Butch, right?"

"Burleigh. But you can call me Butch. A lot of people do." He hauled a croquet mallet out of a pile. He took a few practice swings.

Stein looked askance at the pile of rubble. He wasn't going to look through all this crap. He repeated again that he was only interested in more of the boxes they sold to Dr. Moody.

"Some doctor," Burleigh scoffed. "Nobody he ever treated came away feeling any better."

"Can you tell me how the boxes came into your possession?"

Something small scurried out from under a pile. Burleigh took a whack at it with the mallet—made good, solid contact that sent it flying. He held his follow-through and watched the full parabola of its flight. "Ever play possum golf?"

Stein slapped his own hand down hard on Burleigh's shoulder. "Don't make the mistake of thinking I came up here on my own. Big people are interested. You know what happens to the little man when he plays against the house?" Stein didn't crack or blink as he let that settle in through the strata of Burleigh's brain tissue. "I'm not looking to hurt you boys. I just need to talk to whoever got you those boxes."

Burleigh's attitude became all helpful and verbose. "Well, hell-fuck, Hollywood. Why didn't you say so before? Those boxes came here from a guy."

"And suppose I wanted to talk to this guy? How would I find him?"

"Why'nt you just leave that up to Henny Spector? He wants you to find him, he'll find you."

Henny Spector again.

Butch's knee suddenly buckled and he grabbed onto Stein's shoulder for support. "Damn other knee's going bad. Know where they want to take a ligament? From my brother. Only his is going bad too. Know where they want to get a new one for him? From me."

Linked at the hip, they returned to where they had begun. Hollister was happily loading a trove of new acquisitions into the back of Renn Moody's truck: some decent-looking frames and a box/

tub apparatus. Upon seeing Stein, Hollister proudly proffered a white box, worse for wear. Its roof was cracked in and it looked usable only as spare wood, but its frame bore Karma Moonblossom's brand.

"How do ya like that?" Burleigh said. "Looks like everyone leaves happier than they came."

"What about the bees that came in it?" Stein asked.

"Pssssss," Butch flicked his wrist up toward the sky. Stein tried to look dubious but didn't have a leg of knowledge to stand on. Even Renn confirmed this information. "They might find another home if they had a queen, or try to join another colony. But you'll never see them again."

***

True to Burleigh's diagnosis, everyone was relatively happy on the drive back. Hollister was happy with his honey extractor even though he knew he had paid too much for it. Renn had brought the young man along another small step. Stein could sense him extrapolating whether there was enough time for his protégé to learn enough to take over his bees. And Stein at least had a box or two he could ceremoniously return to Karma. But he wasn't happy. It didn't compute that here were two people, Renn and Hollister, whose equipment had been stolen and who didn't seem motivated in getting it back.

"Who's Henny Spector?" Stein asked, as they pulled into Hollister's driveway. Stein's Kia had gotten doused in sap and white-crusted bird shit. "He seems to be in the middle of everything. I should talk to him."

"My advice," said Renn, "And I'm a doctor. Take two aspirin and call me in the morning."

"Meaning?"

"Take your stuff and go home."

He popped the back so Stein could get out and remove his boxes. Even with Hollister's help it was an awkward fit trying to wedge them into the trunk of his own car. The lid wouldn't shut no matter how many different angles he tried. He gave up and decided to find room in the car's interior. He pushed the passenger seat forward and wedged the box into the rear. Hollister clambered in through the driver's side and reached over the flattened seat back to pull while Stein pushed. The box became inverted during the effort, spewing a minor avalanche of fine dirt and pine needles onto the back seat and floor.

Hollister apologized profusely. Stein told him not to worry about it.

"I'll just get the car vac from inside."

"It doesn't matter. It's a rental."

Hollister was already hustling toward the house. Renn slung himself out of the cab and watched his eager, young protégé. "He ain't the world's fastest learner but he's a good boy."

Stein empathized. A psychic had once told him his daughter would do great things. But after he was dead.

He still couldn't let the other thing go. "I had a feeling from Ruth Ann the other night that you all know who the bee thief is."

Renn took Stein firmly to task. "I don't know how it is where you were brought up, but here we don't talk personally about another man's wife."

Hollister returned chagrinned, with a whiskbroom and dustpan. "Ruth Ann must've taken the vac to work." Despite Stein's protestations he fell to the task of cleaning the mess.

"Hollister." Stein grabbed hold of his whisk-brooming hand. "You know who's taking the bees around here, don't you? Why won't you say?"

Something else had gotten Hollister's attention. "Look at this," he said and held out the dustpan toward Stein and Renn.

"If it's a condom it's not mine."

"No, it's these pine needles and these white oak leaves." He sifted more carefully, rubbed some soil between his thumb and two fingers and watched it float. "See how thin this soil is?"

"Hollister, I'm sure Mr. Stein needs to started heading back and doesn't care about thin soil."

"He would be if he wanted to know where the box has been. White oak grows in fine soil around twenty-five hundred feet elevation."

"Hollister."

There was a strong storm warning in those three syllables, but Hollister sailed on. "Doc," he said, "I appreciate your helping me get back on my feet, but I'd feel a lot better getting back what was mine."

"What do you think the city boy can *do*?"

"Something, maybe."

"You boys know who who's doing all the pilfering, don't you!"

"Knowing's not all it's cracked up to be," Moody scowled.

Stein pressed them to know what the damn problem was.

Almost on cue, the county sheriff's car drove past. "There's the damn problem," Moody grumbled. "Sheriff Slodaney. If he wasn't wearing a badge he'd be wearing stripes."

"There's two problems," Hollister amended.

Alongside the sheriff was none other than the ubiquitous Captain Anthony Caravaggio. Stein's eyes got wider than a vegan baby's at his first taste of sugar. "You boys were going to deprive me of the chance of having some fun? Shame on you!"

Chapter Seven

"Stein!" Lila's voice rang out with the gusto of the two glasses of Beaujolais she had quaffed that afternoon while trying to finish *The O'Reilly Factor* for her second reading group. Stein's phone call was a welcome respite.

"How are things going there?" Stein asked. He was standing in Hollister's kitchen not long after Caravaggio and the sheriff had driven past.

"We can talk about it when you get home. I'm putting dinner on." She covered the receiver with one hand and with the other pointed out a series of tasks for Mercedes to do, indicating dishes, refrigerator, microwave. She glanced at the clock. It was five. Then back to the phone, and Stein. "Things actually have gotten a little strange."

"Oh, shit. Don't tell me. I'm too young to be a grandfather."

"I'll tell you all about it when you're home. And you're not."

"What?"

"Too young to be a grandfather. But that's not it."

"Listen, it's gotten a little complicated up here."

"Did you meet somebody?"

"Lila . . . ? Jeez. There's something I have to do here that I can't do until tomorrow." Silence. "I have to stay over another night."

Lila's anger, long since dammed by her own emotional Army Corps of Engineers, registered as stony silence.

"I understand it's an imposition. On the other hand, you said you wanted to be more directly involved. This is what that looks like."

All the right words were rattling in her head. Words like: *To me, it looks like you indulging your quirky unpredictability because you know you have a dependable safety valve.* But what she said was nothing.

"Okay. I get it," Stein said. "I'll see you as soon as I see you."

"Stein! I didn't mean that—"

"You're absolutely right. I took you for granted. I had no right. She's my daughter, she's my responsibility, not yours. I will be home as soon as humanly possible."

"Stein. It's fine. Do what you need to do. Everything is fine."

"You said before there was some weird stuff."

"It's just about those bones." She was gesturing disappointedly for Mercedes to take the food out of the microwave and put it back in the fridge. Mercedes narrowed her eyes at the cause of this disruption, the man on the phone. Lila gestured back at her that she had benevolent feelings to this man. "They found a body in my pool."

"A *body*?"

"I didn't mean a body." His being upset flustered her. "A skeleton."

"I already know that. They think they found a wooly mammoth."

"Okay, well. It turns out it's not an elephant. It's a person."

"Jesus. What are you doing down there?"

"It's not my fault it's not an elephant. I'm going to need to sand-blast the whole patio."

"Oh, Jesus. Look. Tell her I don't want her going near that pool. I will be back as soon as I possibly can. Lila, you're really great."

"I know."

"They really found a person?"

***

"This is my mom. Mom, this is Angie Stein." Judy Cooper-man was five feet seven inches tall, 106 pounds. If at her morning weigh-in she was 106 and a half she did an immediate herbal colonic cleanse. She spent three hours each day with her personal trainer, spinning, Tae Bo, power yoga; forty-five minutes at the tanning salon; one day each week at the cosmetician where layers of dead skin were exfoliated and new layers were infused with jojoba and aloe vera oils. She had had the lining of her vagina replaced after the birth of her second child. When she climaxed, which took an inexplicably long grueling time now even with the vibrator turned to high, she squirted like a busted shower nozzle.

She knew somebody that had something to do with the financing or the advertising campaign of the movie *Hidden, Slouching Something*, hence she had invited (read *coerced*) Matthew to a private screening of a rough cut. She was not gigantically pleased to see that her son had brought his little friend along, even less so when she understood the friend was the spawn of the man who was now the new boyfriend of the woman who (in her mind) had destroyed her life.

After the third aerial fight scene Angie pleaded altitude sickness, not to mention character deprivation, and scooted herself past the rapt investors and crew people and made her escape. She waited in the lobby for Matthew, who soon joined her there.

"My mother is not going to be happy about this," he warned.

"Your mother is not going to be happy about anything."

He had never heard it put that succinctly but he had to concede the point. They found refuge at a nearby Johnny Rockets, pretty confident they would not likely bump into Matthew's mother here in a fifties retro diner. He looked so easily delicious in anything he wore. He had on a loose-fitting white shirt with a dark sport jacket over it. His sandy blond hair that fell over his forehead when he leaned down toward her could be flicked back into shape by the smallest movement of his neck.

The waiter whose nametag said RAY RAY could not take his eyes off Matthew and nearly sliced his finger cutting a piece of apple pie. The waitress spilled coffee. Johnny Mathis crooned "Chances Are" on the juke. Angie twirled her scarf twice around her neck to avoid dunking the fringe in fruit filling. "So what are we?" she ventured. "Friends? Archaeological paleontologists on a break?"

"You and me? Isn't it obvious?"

"I don't think so."

"We're stepbrother and stepsister."

"We are?"

"Yeah. Aren't we? In a kind of way. Our fathers are both Lila's lovers."

She hadn't thought of it in that way. Her mood plunged through five levels of emotional geology, from bemused to embarrassed to sadly ironic.

"It's a little weird, don't you think? If your dad hadn't died, my dad would never have met her. We wouldn't be sitting here."

"I wonder if that's true. I wonder if we'd be here anyway."

"You mean Fate?"

"Or who knows if they would have stayed together. My dad wasn't the most—"

"Yeah, neither is mine."

"I was going to say dependable," said Matt.

"I was going to say a fan of commitment."

Matthew nodded a thoughtful yes and took a sip of his coffee.

"Are you saying yes, you can see that my dad is not a fan of commitment?"

"No. Just that it's hard."

They drifted into private nostalgic thoughts for a moment.

"Why can't people just find the person they're meant to be with and stay with them forever?" Angie complained. "That would make life so much easier."

"I think it has something to do with mortality."

"It was a rhetorical question. You didn't have to answer."

"Anybody ever mention that you weren't easy?"

"So?"

"That was also a rhetorical question."

He picked up the check, which Angie allowed him to do with minimal protest. She did get a little irked though when he opened the car door for her. "I'm capable, you know."

"It's just a courtesy."

"Fine." She went around to the driver's side and opened his.

Okay, he thought, this was going to be interesting. They agreed on one major point, though, during the drive back to Lila's. Mortality completely sucked. It made them wonder about whose body it was that had floated up into Lila's pool.

Lila was gone to her O'Reilly book club when they got back to the house. Angie asked Matt to give her a hand removing the tarp cover from the pool. He put the outside lights on and they scanned the surface. "Are you hoping to find his wallet and driver's license?" he asked her.

"Maybe."

The pits had yielded up no new secrets. She beckoned him to the garage where she had stowed their trove of findings. They carried everything to the patio and rebuilt the skeleton. He was nearly complete. Most of his spine, both legs, parts of both arms, ribs, hips, skull. Not everything, but enough to see what they had, which was a six-foot-two-inch male. They figured maybe there was a cemetery somewhere nearby and the tar had eroded the coffin. Or maybe some not-too-bright tourist had fallen into the lake pit and his body had been carried along in the sludgy subterranean current. The vexing question was not about the pieces that were missing, but about the one extra piece. How in hell did a tusk fit in?

None of their brilliant ideas stood up under scrutiny. Matt thought maybe there was a whole elephant still down there that hadn't come up. They speculated about gravity and surface tensile strength, and various other topics of which they knew next to nothing. Or maybe someone was riding the elephant and they both fell in and he grabbed the tusk to hold on and . . . the idea trailed away.

They heard Lila's car arrive.

"I guess I'll say goodbye to her and take off," Matt said.

"You're not going to stay?"

"My mother expects me to stay at her place when I come down."

As Angie jumped up from kneeling alongside the skeleton, the fringe of her long, Indian scarf caught on a jagged edge of one of the bones. She had to stop and kneel and carefully unhook the delicate material from the snag it had caught on. Something about the snag arrested her attention. She bent close to the rib bone and smoothed away a bit of residual dirt. There was a V-shaped wedge in the bottom half of the middle rib bone on the left side of the chest.

As she carefully extracted the delicate fabric, she noticed a matching gash in the top half of the rib bone just below it. Her scalp began to tingle.

"Matt!" She was breathless. "Hand me the tusk."

He did. She held it in her two hands and slowly inserted its pointed end into the space between the two ribs. She pressed the ivory deeper into the chest cavity. It encountered no resistance until it was fully imbedded down to the hilt. Only then did the twin notches in the ribs form a perfect seal. The point of the tusk was buried deep into the body's hollow infrastructure, right where his heart would be, if he still had one.

She turned around and looked up into her stepbrother's face. "Matt, this dude didn't just die. I think he was stabbed to death with this tusk. I think he was murdered."

At that moment, Lila came back. She was delighted to see them. "Your dad called," she chirped. "He'll be home tomorrow. He wants you to stay away from the pool."

***

"No, Harry, I will absolutely not authorize you to rent a helicopter."

"And a pilot."

"This conversation is concluded."

Despite all the grandiose schemes of Stein's that Millicent Pope-Lassiter had shot down over the years, he was still surprised when she said no to this one without giving it a moment's serious consideration.

It was nine o'clock in the morning. Stein was standing in the office of the one helicopter rental place within thirty miles of Las Viejes, convinced once again that if he could summon just the right words he could penetrate to the marrow of an unreachable woman. Indeed, using the company phone to make this call.

"Millie, let me explain to you what you are not grasping."

"Harry, I have grasped your proposal around the neck and choked the life out of it. You want to scour an area of rough country at an altitude of twenty-five hundred feet, where you are certain you will find a hoard of stolen merchandise, some of which belongs to Karma Moonblossom. The rental fee with pilot is two thousand dollars for half a day. Have I missed any of the salient details?"

"Plus how important it is to me."

"Of course, Harry. Whatever is important to you is always of paramount importance to me."

"You wanted collateral for your derivatives. For two thousand bucks I'm going to find it."

There was the half a moment's lethal break in rhythm that is always followed by unexpected bad news. "We've divested our holding in those financial instruments. We no longer risk exposure."

Stein subtly turned his back for a little privacy. The proprietor of the establishment and owner of the neat and manly desk was Major S. Wilson (Ret.). He was a black man with a trim military body, youthful eyes, and just a hint of grey at the temples. He could have been forty or seventy. The office was as tidy and robust, clear-eyed and direct as the man.

"Okay, but I think I can get some of Karma Moonblossom's bee boxes back for him." There was dead air. "Millie?" He plunked the phone down disgustedly back into its cradle.

"Sounds like you convinced her," Wilson said.

Framed photographs of fixed-wing and rotary aircraft, and of huge industrial farm equipment, all hung at eye level, equidistant from each other, creating a feeling of perfect confidence.

"God, I mean, some people. You just can't budge them with a crowbar and dynamite."

"I see her side of it. The cost of recovery exceeds the recovery value. The economics make no sense."

"Really. I thought you'd see it differently," Stein said.

"Because I'm black? Power to the people and all?" He gave a sarcastic closed-fist salute.

"What's wrong with that?"

"Nothing, except have you met any people lately you'd want to give power to?"

"I keep expecting them to change back."

"Into what?"

"When people cared about people."

"Sorry, I couldn't make it to Woodstock. I was flying F-16s over Hanoi."

Something in the cadence of the man's voice clicked. "The Africanized bee comment the other night. That was you."

"And look how proud you are it only took you ten minutes. I had you the moment you walked in."

"I'm distinctive. What can I say?"

Wilson chuckled and offered his hand. "Spade Wilson. U.S. Air Force wing commander. Retired."

"Spade?"

"My mother had a thing about farm equipment. She called my sister Hoe."

"No, she didn't."

"No . . . she didn't. I don't have a sister."

"So you're a beekeeper?"

"Not like they are. I train bees for the military."

"Bee bombs?

"Bees are inherently peaceful creatures. They don't attack unless provoked. We use them to detect land mines."

"No, you don't."

Wilson smiled enigmatically.

"You are either one weird guy or an amazing bullshitter." Stein waved a parting salute that impishly turned into a peace sign as he cruised out the door. In the same motion he wheeled around and one-eightied back in. "I just have to ask you about those pictures." He gestured to the array of photographs on the wall of huge pieces of farm machinery. The one closest to Stein looked like a crouching demon from hell: a tractor of sorts with four vise-like extensions.

"That's a shaker," said Wilson.

Stein awaited further information.

"You think almonds are handpicked?"

"I never really . . ."

"Of course you didn't. You city boys think oranges grow in crates. These babies grab on to a trunk and shake the bejeezus out of them." His arms suddenly tensed and assumed the ferocious strength of the machine. Stein was sure he felt the entire room vibrate.

"Seems a little mechanized."

"If you want to feed the world, you need a big shovel. Now tell me. Why are you so interested in retrieving this Karma Draft-dodger's honeybees?"

"You say you'll do something, you try to do it. Wouldn't you do the same?"

"Don't try to get into my head, son. That's not a place you want to be. Give me one good reason why I should accept the deal you proposed."

"Huh?"

"You said, or at least I thought I heard you say, you'd give me all the money you had in your pocket right now to take you up in my helicopter and find your friend's equipment."

Stein caught on that Wilson was making an offer. He dug into the righthand pocket of his Levis and put his full wad on the table. It came to about ninety. "A little under," he said.

"Dang," he said. "You Jewish peoples are hard bargainers."

***

Two hours later, liftoff was smooth as a dish of frozen yogurt. The Wing Commander knew what he was doing at the stick. Stein had once flown in a police helicopter, an impressive bird that held seven or eight. But this was like a flying warehouse. It could swallow a dozen of those plastic bubbles the TV weather guys get. It was all high-tech, with radar and something Wilson called GPS that displayed the terrain below them on a monitor and made it look like they were right there.

"How's your gas mileage on this baby?" Stein asked.

"Better than on your Toyota Camry."

"Bullshit."

"Doesn't use gas. Atomic pellets, baby."

"Bullshit. Really?"

"We're at thirty-one hundred feet looking down," Wilson said as they crossed into the pine belt and looked down on third-growth conifers. "What are we looking for?"

"That's why I brought Hollister."

"And that would be the gentleman curled into the corner in the fetal position turning white in catatonic shock?"

"How ya doin' there, Hollister?" Stein gave him an encouraging grin.

"I shouldn't have had bacon and eggs this morning."

"You shouldn't have bacon and eggs *ever*," Wilson ordained. "You're injecting plaque right into your ventricle." Wilson spoke in declarative sentences with no mitigation. He told Hollister he'd feel a lot better coming up there alongside him.

"Moving doesn't seem like too good an idea."

"You've chucked your cheese twice sitting still," Stein pointed out. "Moving can't be worse."

Wilson swiveled around to the quivering mass. "Son. You're needed here." Hollister pushed himself up and staggered to the co-pilot's chair. He kept his hands over his eyes, and resisted when Wilson tried to pry them off. "Your eyes will get used to the motion if you let them. And your kishkas will fall right in line."

"Where did you learn about kishkas?" Stein laughed.

"You don't think there are Jews in the CIA?"

"I didn't. No."

"Well, good. That's one secret we kept."

For the next forty-five minutes they skimmed along the wood line, dipped down into gullies and coverts, rifts and ravines. The detail of imagery that the surveillance equipment produced was shocking to anyone who believed in the First and Fourth Amendments. Wilson could bring up a cow's eyelashes when she blinked.

Stein sensed that he was getting impatient when the first shots were fired.

Branches ripped out of the green carpet below them. Wilson instinctively veered their bird into an angular attitude to the ground. He vectored his heat-seeking infrared camera and GPS and made visual contact with the course of the gunfire. "Meat!" he roared, and spiraled up high out of range, training his guns. "We caught a regiment of Sandinistas out in the open like this, washing out their coffee pots in a little stream after breakfast. Ugliest-looking naked bodies you ever saw!"

The quarry below them now was wearing camouflage gear. A brace of geese was slung over his shoulder.

The helicopter hovered over the break in the trees. The wind from the whirling blades crushed the foliage below it. The hunter took an offensive supine position on the ground and steadied his gun on a rock. Wilson lined him up in his sights. "This was El Salvador, he'd be liquefied."

"Don't you mean vaporized?" Stein asked.

"We didn't have the technology yet to vaporize. All we could do was liquefy."

On the ground, the emboldened hunter rose to his knees and took aim with his shotgun. Wilson flipped on the external broadcast mode and bellowed down to him. "Make my day, sucker."

The hunter held the braces of birds out at arm's length and yelled something that without an amplification system came out like a pantomime of defiance.

"That's the game warden," Hollister said. He was looking at a magnified image of the man on the console monitor.

"The game warden is poaching geese? Does everyone else not find that hilarious?"

Hollister had a faraway look in his eye. Like he was about to do something bigger than his own normal life would have predicted.

"He's the one," said Hollister. "He's the one who's been stealing everyone's bees."

A small break in the pine forest two hundred rugged yards away revealed a clearing. In the clearing stood a ramshackle barn. Outside the barn was a pickup truck. Alongside the truck was a forklift. On the forklift was a pallet of bee boxes. The barn doors were open and even from this altitude Stein could see it was a warehouse.

"I think perhaps we found what we're looking for," Wilson deadpanned. He began to descend into the very tiny opening between the stands of monumental trees. Down to treetop level, the huge rotors came within inches of the extended evergreen arms. No one spoke or breathed until the wheels touched the planet. Then the release of nervous laughter. "You've done this before," Stein hoped.

"Venezuela, we were landing between a booby-trapped helipad and the edge of a cliff."

"Weren't the Sandinistas in Nicaragua?" Hollister asked.

"People like to think so," Wilson answered darkly. They hit ground, bounced just a little and nestled. Wilson cut the engines and jumped down.

"I should point out," Stein said, "that we're not a paramilitary operation. We're just three guys."

Wilson ordered silence, and duck-walked commando style toward the barn. After three steps he got a terrible cramp in his left quad. Hollister helped him up and rotated his leg to shake it out.

"That's better. Thanks."

"You weren't in El Salvador," Hollister suggested.

"Desk job in Tacoma."

"I'm afraid to ask if you have a pilot's license," Stein added.

"Hey. Did I get you here?" Wilson commando'd ahead to the warehouse and pounded a closed fist on the partially open door. "I've got a warrantless search order to investigate the premises. Any objection to my coming in?"

Before an answer could be given, even if there were someone within earshot to give it, Major S. Wilson, now retired, moved through the open door and stood gaping at the contents of the warehouse. There was every kind of beekeeping equipment imaginable, and not psychotically scattered like Butch and Burleigh's backyard, but psychotically organized. Row by row there were hanging bee suits arranged by size, honey-extracting equipment, pail heaters, five- and ten-gallon jugs. There were unassembled parts for making hives: foundations, supering tops, frames.

And the jackpot. Stacks of boxes. Some so visibly branded the marking could be seen from the doorway. Even Stein's untrained eye recognized a dozen different etched, embossed, or painted markers.

"Those are mine that he stole from me last month," Hollister exclaimed, and made a beeline for his stolen equipment. Stein did not immediately see any of Karma Moonblossom's familiar brand. Wilson snapped his cell phone open and raised a finger for silence.

"Yeah, this is me. Listen. Take down these coordinates." He rattled off latitudes and longitudes in degrees and minutes and was pleased at the response of the person on the other end. "That's right. That's exactly the spot. Call them in to our friend the reporter at the *Fresno Bee*. The one we can trust. You know who I mean. Then call Sheriff Slodaney."

Hollister whispered to Stein, "He doesn't have to tell the sheriff how to get here. Granger is his brother-in-law."

"The ranger's name is Granger? *Ranger* Granger? Really?"

***

When Game Warden Granger emerged into the clearing and saw the warship alighted in his pasture his first response was the power play. He charged at Wilson, threatening horrendous retribution for their trespass. In less than a jiu-jitsu second, the unfortunate ranger was whirled around, inverted head to ground, handcuffed into a full Nelson, set down into a cross-legged squat against the trunk of a white oak tree, and gagged with duct tape.

Wilson allowed him to dwell with that experience for the full forty minutes until the cordon of vehicles lumbered up the narrow road. The TV truck and local radio got there first. Not long after they had established their positions, the law arrived in the persons of county Sheriff Wilfred Slodaney and Highway Patrol Captain Anthony Caravaggio, traveling under full siren and sail. Wilson ceremoniously unfettered the now-humbled miscreant and shoved him forward. "There's your man, Sheriff."

"I understand you two are acquainted," Stein volunteered, to be helpful.

Caravaggio smiled at Stein in contemplation of grand retribution to come. "We are going to tangle, boy."

"How can you say that? We're on the same side."

"Not even when Satan needs an overcoat."

Sheriff Slodaney went through the charade of propriety, pointed a Dreyfusian finger at Wilson's attack craft and accusing it of being parked illegally. Phrases like "warrant" and "illegal search and seizure" tumbled from his mouth.

Stein stepped into the fray with his old flamboyance. Nobody knew how to play to the media like he did. He extended his arm toward the warehouse like Moses over the Red Sea. "Ladies and gentlemen of the free press, you can see without stepping over the threshold of private property that there is a treasure trove here of stolen property."

"And who's to say it's stolen?" Slodaney challenged.

"I see all my stuff right there in front," a small voice said. It was Hollister's.

"You sold me those boxes," said Ranger Granger.

"You lifted them in the night."

"Seems we have a clear case of he said she said," Slodaney shrugged. "And with no evidence of wrongdoing, there's nothing more I can do." He turned to go back to his car.

A shot rang out. Everyone hit the deck and drew. Spade Wilson stood in the center of the clearing like Rambo, Granger's shotgun cradled in his muscular arms. He dispossessed Granger of his halo of geese and ceremoniously tossed them at the lawmen. "There's your evidence of wrongdoing," he said.

Stein bowed down to Wilson and genuflected. "I love you."

Stein could barely contain his glee at the prospect of watching two men in law enforcement uniforms arrest a third. He flashed Caravaggio a joyful peace sign. How amazing for this miracle to happen. The guilty had been punished. Karmic justice had prevailed. He felt so fucking young and alive, he could die.

Chapter Eight

Hail the conquering hero!

It had been ages since Stein had been paraded metaphorically through the streets of Rome, crowned with the olive crest, garlanded with rose petals. He liked to affect an aura of offhand indifference to the adulation, but he needed the adulation in order to affect his indifference to it. And here it would be. Yes, he relished the prospect of Millicent Pope-Lassiter shaking her head in submission, saying *Okay you crusty old bastard, you did it again.*

Hollister had volunteered to drive the Kia the two hundred miles back to the rental place while Spade Wilson airlifted Stein to Sig Kroll's repair shop in under an hour. There, more good news awaited him. The automobile surgeon had done a meticulous three-way organ transplant on Stein's Camry for a remarkably nonexorbitant price. It ran better than it ever had, and at barely past the stroke of three Stein strolled into Millicent Pope-Lassiter's office like Marco Polo bearing gifts of silk and penne pasta.

As Shmooie the Buddhist used to say when he was alive, euphoria fades fast. Millicent Pope-Lassiter appeared neither charmed nor amused nor pleased to see him. She did not pull down her bodice, thrust her still magnificent breasts at him, and invite him to partake. Stein was sure she was doing the baseball thing, when a rookie hits his first major league home run and the team acts completely blasé when he returns to the bench. Then a few minutes later they all pound him on the back and welcome him to the team. There was no back pounding here. No patting on the rump. She glanced up from her desk at a spot somewhere between Stein and the door, exhaled a lungful of exasperation and went back to her paperwork.

"What?" Stein proclaimed.

"You're a housecat who's dropped a diseased pigeon on the doorstep and thinks it's a gift."

"You sent me to do a job and I did it."

"No. I sent you to do one thing and you did something else."

"Things were wrong and I made them right."

"No. Things were one thing and you made them something else."

"I got several of Karma Moonblossom's bee boxes back."

"Well, won't that look great on your college resume."

"I did everything you asked me to do and more! What is the problem?"

"And therein you have answered your own question. From here on you shall consider your working relationship with Lassiter and Frank terminated."

The whole ride down to the subterranean garage and the walk to his car, Stein expected the Candid Camera crew to jump out of the shadows, for the ruse to be confessed, to be taken back up the elevator where champagne and caviar would now be in abundance. They did not. Nor were they waiting for him at Lila's when he parked in front of her house and displayed his Visitor's Monthly Parking permit on his dash.

"Dad!" Angie's voice rang out. It was amazing the recuperative powers contained in that one sung syllable. She flew out to greet him and tugged him by the forearm in through the arched doorway and slate vestibule in over the living room's plush Persian rug past the glassy dining room into the kitchen, where Mercedes was making sardine and pepper omelets. At each juncture Stein expected her to stop, having found the perfect, private spot to tell him how proud she was of her old man. But she continued out through the kitchen door to the patio, and stopped breathless in her tracks.

"Look what me and Matthew found!"

They had attached the found bones to a seven-foot mounting board and stood the skeleton upright. The saws and hammers and putty guns that had been used for the job were still strewn about.

Stein had to restrain himself from raising his voice. "You were told to clean this up," he said.

"Dad, I know. But look what we *found*!"

"I am interested in your learning to listen to me and to Lila when you are explicitly told—"

"We'll clean it. Dad, she knows. She said it's okay."

Matthew, wearing funky khakis and a sleeveless sweatshirt, came out from the pool house. "Hey, Mr. Stein. Pretty amazing, huh. Did she tell you?"

"I haven't told him yet."

There is probably no phrase that can freeze the blood of the father more than that one. So when they announced to Stein that they had discovered a murder, he was so relieved that he gushed, "Thank God." Still, he called for a private conference and conducted Angie back inside to the kitchen.

"What is going on with you?" he demanded.

"What do you mean?"

"Deliberately countermanding my orders." He heard how absurd he sounded but couldn't stop.

"Countermanding?"

"Cavorting around with this Matthew. We know nothing about him."

"I'm countermanding and cavorting? He's your girlfriend's stepson."

"All this"—he groped for the word and found it—"unsupervised contact."

"Thank you, Warden Dad."

"You are sixteen years old. I do not want—"

"Dad." Her voice was laced with pain at having to reveal the obvious. "He's gay."

The revelation hit him like a glass door in the face. So he tried to sound matter-of-fact. "Oh."

"Can we let him back into the house his father bought now? It's getting kind of weird."

"I'm just trying to be protective."

"Protecting me from somebody who doesn't want me. Thanks."

Stein glanced out at the boy, his long supple musculature moving so easily as he completed the cleanup of the patio. Stein now radiated magnanimous empathy.

Lila returned. Hairdressed, legs waxed, nails and facial at Nordstrom's. She looked stupendous and whispered coyly in Stein's ear that she had another beauty surprise for him that he'd discover later that night if he played his cards right.

Matt popped his head in the kitchen and asked what was for dinner.

"Mercedes, what am I making for dinner?" Lila called.

It was Chicken Marsala with a mango and goat cheese salad and homemade bread. Stein kissed Lila on the cheek. "Honey, you've really outdone yourself. A hard day at the beauty salon and still time to make dinner. What a woman."

Matthew had freed himself from filial indenture, telling his mother he was headed back to Berkeley. The four of them held a spirited discussion around Lila's dinner table about who the corpse might have been, all of them interrupting and laughing like a real family. Because the paleontologist had told them the tusk was around seventy-five years old, Angie and Matt reasoned that if it was really a murder weapon there might be a story about an unsolved killing in the newspaper archives, and the plan was floated to go downtown in the morning to the *LA Times*.

Angie and Matthew were excited at the prospect of investigating. It killed Stein to puncture the balloon, but tomorrow was change-over day, when Angie returned to Hillary.

"No," Angie reminded him. "I told you Mom's going to the Caribbean for five days. She got a commercial."

"You never told me that. When did this happen?"

"I don't know. I guess while you were away. God, don't look so devastated. If you don't want me here I can stay at Mom's by myself."

"That isn't what I want and you know it. I'm annoyed because Mom and I have had this conversation a thousand times that she and I should talk directly. It's not your job to be the adult."

She patted her father's fevered brow. "Yes, Daddy. Mom's a bitch."

"That's not what I meant." But maybe it kind of was.

***

Lila was already in bed when Stein came into their room. Very unsubtly he had waited around until the two teenagers departed to their separate quarters. He didn't want to tell her, but he didn't like Lila's bed. It was too high. Mounting it was like climbing onto a pedestal. He couldn't just lean back and plop himself down. He liked plopping more than he liked climbing. To plop into this bed you had to do the Fosbury Flop or else the mattress would hit you mid-spine. But Stein had to be careful about complaining. He knew she would replace it—and that would have implied a major agreement he was not ready to make.

He was too distracted for sex. When he rolled out of bed the third time for no reason, Lila had had it.

"Do you want me to tell him he can't stay here?"

"No, of course not." Meaning *Yes, but I know it's impossible.* "Anyway, he's gay, right?"

Lila laughed robustly. "I didn't think so."

Five expressions crossed Stein's face in quick succession. Lila grabbed his arm. "Stein. You have a bright girl there with a head on her shoulders, whom you've instilled with a good, healthy self-respect.

"My friends have daughters who've done it in bathrooms of clubs, in cars of course, at parties in the hot tub with boys they didn't care about. You're not going to stand in the way of the strongest force in the universe. I'm not saying it's going to happen. But if it did, he's a nice boy. It's a safe place."

She threw the covers back, revealing the clingy satin night thing she was wearing, "You're a fifty-one-year-old man with a receding hairline and a paunch. A beautiful woman is inviting you into her bed. Do you think it can possibly get any better for you?"

The curve of her torso made space for him, coaxed him into surrender, which he fought against and then gave in. So he did not hear the two muffled voices from the room at the end of the hall:

"You told your father I was gay?"

"He believed it."

"Of course he believed it. I didn't know that you knew."

"Very cute."

"Seriously. How did you know?"

***

The negotiation around seating arrangements in the Camry the following morning made an amusing little gavotte. If Lila had come it would have been two and two. But she had to meet Richard, her deceased husband's best friend, who popped into LA every few months and was the principal trustee for the estate. Angie held the passenger side door open and pushed the front seat forward so that Matt could get in. Stein's alarm sensor foresaw them both getting into the back seat as their subtle protest for Stein's imposing himself on their private adventure.

Stein pre-empted the move by placing a restraining hand on Matt's shoulder as he bent his six-foot frame to duck into the back. "Actually, Matt would probably be more comfortable up front."

Angie took the displacement with outrage. "I'm being relegated to the back?"

"Not *relegated*. Matt has long legs."

"Tell me about it," she murmured.

It was a spirited drive. Stein related with great gusto the saga of busting Ranger Granger. Matt propped his elbow on the backrest so that he made an equilateral triangle between Stein and Angie. Every effortless gesture of his came to rest in a magazine cover pose. He was completely taken with Stein's escapade and asked questions. Stein found it impossible not to like the kid. He had a sweet disposition and did not force you to earn every parceled moment of concord, as Angie did. He was like a sun whose only verb was to shine, and he did so on anything he encountered.

Downtown Los Angeles jutted out before them like a skyline of baby teeth. A few shiny objects but nothing with any bite. A movie set. Frontage with no backage. The foreplay of a lover because he's read he's supposed to. The one sentimental exception for Stein was the *Los Angeles Times* building. He negotiated a few arbitrarily designated one-way streets and approached the building from the angle seen in Superman, where it doubled for the *Daily Planet* building. He looked around expectantly for Angie's burst of recognition. But of course she had never seen the TV show. She was leaning forward with her chin nestled in the crook between Matt's neck and left shoulder. It gave Stein a little pang of desire to have a partner in crime. Someone he could have a history with.

The elevator took them from the underground parking lot to the third floor. "We need a cover story," Stein said as they got out.

"Dad. Do not." She recognized the warning signs, the Peter Paniacal bounce in his stride, the impish look that he still thought people found contagious.

Matt innocently asked why they needed a cover story.

"Oh, God. Please do not indulge him."

"You don't just walk into the *LA Times* and announce you're investigating an unsolved murder. You need a little subtle misdirection." He skated in front of Angie to the information desk, where Miss Gibson's desk plate identified her as Senior Research Archivist. Her face looked like parchment from which the print had faded, and where the stories it held hadn't been that interesting in the first place.

Before they could say anything else, Stein presented Angie and Matt as foreign exchange students, she from Denmark, he from Hungary, doing a research project on American history. Angie rolled her eyes halfway to San Diego.

"This is why other countries are so far ahead of us," Miss Gibson declared. "Try to find an American student who cares about history. All they care about is video games and getting high."

"Not these kids. They're particularly interested in Los Angeles in the 1920s."

"It's gratifying to see a teacher so involved in his students' work."

"Well, I'm . . . glad to gratify you."

"Dad," Angie sang in falsetto.

They were directed to a cluster of tables where ancient Moviolas were mounted. Shortly thereafter a young man with a bow tie and a short-sleeved white shirt strode out of the storage bin carrying three smallish boxes. "Your microfiche," he said, and dropped the boxes on the table as if they were porn he was being forced to disseminate.

Stein called after him in his wake, wondering how they expected a person to know how to operate the machine. Stein turned to the kids to echo his outrage. They were already loading their rolls.

Matt showed Stein how easy it was, and they all began to scroll through a decade of archived *Los Angeles Times*. With each rotation of the crank handle, first one of them, then another exclaimed cries of amazement.

"There's an ad for tincture of cocaine to calm the nerves and focus the mind."

"Roast beef. Thirty-nine cents a pound."

"The world's first motel opened in San Louis Obispo."

The tempo slowed as they became encased in the hypnotic narratives. The vivid pictorial displays and the bold writing style presented 1920s Los Angeles as a gun-slinging, land-grabbing, con-artist Wild West show. All of it was triggered by the internal combustion engine, and the realization that the wet goopy stuff they were throwing away was a fuck of a lot more valuable than the tar they were mining for.

LA was an oil boomtown. There were astonishing pictures of derricks packed together as far as the eye could see. Down main streets. In front yards. Alongside churches. Tour buses rolled in, disgorging out-of-town suckers into the grasp of hucksters pitching real estate schemes, scam artists selling shares of nonexistent oil companies, pitchmen offering lunch with Barbara Stanwyck and full sets of Encyclopedia Britannica.

The rich got richer and the poor waited for their luck to change. Silver Rolls-Royces drove past people pushing empty wheelbarrows. Epic barroom brawls erupted—one covered three city blocks. There were knife fights. Gun fights. There was one sensational story about a farmer from Iowa who had bought a parcel of acreage and drilled eleven wells, all of them dry holes. He got the bright idea to drill diagonally into the next parcel, where the sons of bitches had seventeen working rigs pumping hundreds of barrels every day. There had been a gun battle, a court battle, and a huge oil fire that raged for six days.

An hour later, the three explorers left the archive room dazed and more confused. "Forget about one unsolved murder," Matthew marveled. "What about a hundred?" But they had found nothing about an unsolved tusking or anything that seemed even tangentially related. Still, Stein proclaimed the venture great fun and the kind of thing the three of them should do again. Only Angie remained unsatisfied. She had a new plan. They had to go through the property records and see who had previously owned the land under Lila's house, and then through the obituaries to see which of them had died close to the time the tusk was buried.

"All of that stuff would be in the Hall of Records." Stein made it sound like a bit of an ordeal, which Angie was quick to absolve him of enduring.

"If you're not into it you don't have to stick around. We can get back."

"Okay. But you know where the Hall of Records is, right?"

"I would assume it's all around here, right? Wouldn't that make the most logical sense?"

***

They drove away from downtown, passing through painful melanomas of used car lots and junkyards, with Angie grousing from the back seat that you'd think they would have the County Recorder's office and the Hall of Records near *something* else.

"Where the hell *are* we?" A victimized road sign gave her the answer. "NO WALK? We're in the city of No Walk?"

"Norwalk," Stein clarified.

Every tributary of society drained into the Hall of Records. There were formally dressed wedding parties in advanced stages of pregnancy. There were people looking for the office dispensing Fictitious Business Licenses. Grade-school classes were on excursion tours. Lawyers in sweat-stained seersucker suits chased down lawyers with bad haircuts. Bereaved families filed death certificates.

The elevator cranked and gnashed them up to the fifth floor where the room with the materials they needed was overseen by a woman wearing a caftan and a pair of long, silver Incan earrings that chimed like timbales when she moved. Angie jumped ahead of any antics her father might be contemplating.

"We want to find out who lived at a certain address in the 1920s," Angie said. "You want to do a title search?" the clerk interpreted.

"If that's what you call it."

"I need to have your deed number."

"My what?"

"The number on your deed. You want to do a title search, you need to have your deed number." The timbales gave her voice a dancing rhythm.

"Are you saying we can't do a title search without a deed number?"

"I could find it if you have the lot number."

"Are you kidding me? Who in their right minds knows their lot number?" She turned to Matthew for help.

"I know her address," he said.

"Address will work," the clerk said.

Angie went apoplectic. "Why didn't you ask for the address in the first place?"

"I do it the way the county tells me."

Her earrings cha-chinged as she led them through a labyrinth of floor-to-ceiling open shelves stacked with Dickensian-sized, ancient ledger books. She lifted a tome from a shelf and set it down on a small table for them. "These are public records. Don't spill anything on them."

"What am I going to spill?"

It was enlightening to discover how much private information was available in the public records for anyone to see. Birth date, address, phone number, military history, weddings, divorces, property ownership, bankruptcies. Lila's Beverly Hills address was easily accessed once they figured out the organizing principles that guided the bookkeeping system. It was pretty cool. There were maps of the original land grants from the King of Spain back when it was El Pueblo de la Reina de Los Angeles and land was parceled out to friends and nobles in vast haciendas:

"The Alcalde de Los Angeles cedes the land from the asphalt pits for the distance a speedy horse can run in five minutes in the direction of the ocean into which the sun sets; and in breadth, half the distance to the hills lying north and south."

Stein was quietly impressed at the size of the most recent tax valuation of Lila's property. He knew it was worth plenty. So it would not look like *he* was making a land grab, he had hoped the value would be less than seven figures. It was north.

Matthew's jaw was clenched. It took Stein a moment to realize the boy was fighting back tears. He looked down and saw the book open to a photocopy of the deed of purchase executed by Walter T. Cooperman. Matthew's father's name was typed out in block letters, and above it was his signature. An act performed with his living hand while it was an appendage of his living body.

The biography of the property unfolded page by page in a cavalcade of changing ownership: through purchase and sale, death and bequeathal, division and subdivision. Leagues changed to acres. Acres changed to parcels. What would one day become Lila's address at 351 South La Cuesta Drive, Beverly Hills 90212 was lost in bankruptcy, taken over by the bank of Los Angeles, leased to Meridian Oil Exploration, awarded to Ascension Cataluna in a settlement dating back to a thirty-year-old dispute that had gone against Cataluna in the lower court, and then overturned on appeal. It was purchased from Ascension "Sunny" Cataluna on February 13 of 1926 by J. J. Bancroft for the sum of one thousand dollars.

Angie sat back with her eyes wide, waiting for Matthew and her father to join her at the same stunning conclusion. "The guy we dug up was one of these two people. J. J. Bancroft or Ascension Cataluna."

"Or the mailman," said Stein. "Or the guy reading the gas meter. Or anybody who happened to have been on the property."

A plan hatched in the devious portion of Angie's mindscape. She listened for the sound of the timbales, estimated their distance, then furtively told Matt to sneeze.

"What?"

"Give me a good one."

Her fingers were poised on the top of the page containing the title deed, ready to rip it out. Stein saw what was about to happen and lunged to prevent it, too late. Under cover of Matt's diversionary sound, Angie ripped the document from the ledger. Except not quite. A corner of the page remained attached like the last gum strand holding a baby tooth.

A clarion voice emanated from just around the row of shelves, with its accompanying ch-ching of earrings. "What is all the commotion?"

Angie sneezed herself, a high pitched *CHOOO*, hastily rolled up the amputated document and rammed it down Matthew's surfer shorts. She slammed the ledger shut just as the caftan-clad clerk filled their frame.

"What is all the noise?"

"Asthma," Angie complained. "All the dust."

The clerk turned to the adult for verification.

"Something really ought to be done about it," Stein said. "It's a million-dollar lawsuit waiting to happen. And who do you think they'll lay off to pay for it?"

He herded the kids single file to the elevators, keeping Matt's enhanced posterior concealed from observation. They burst out of the elevator looking as normal as the Marx Brothers. Matt feigned a stiff-legged limp along the way across the mall to a bench far from other possible prying eyes, then did a little comic riff at not being able to dislodge the parchment from his shorts.

"It's wedged against a massive obstacle."

"You keep your ego in your shorts?"

"Okay, okay." Stein waltzed between them. "I'll take that."

Matthew handed him the rolled-up stolen document. "I wonder if I could ask you, sir, why do you think your daughter induced me to commit a felony?"

"The question is why did you do it."

"She's very persuasive."

"Well, that's true."

Angie had taken the document out of her father's hands and unrolled it on a wooden bench that bordered a rectangular display of small privet hedges. "I wanted to look at it without that woman hovering over . . . Oh, my God!" One corner of the page, perhaps because of the perspiration on Matthew's thigh, had curled and the top ply of the parchment had separated. She pulled the corners very carefully, and they continued to cleave. There was print on both layers, as though the ink had bled through. With one brittle end pinched between two fingers of each hand, she separated the delicate layers of skin into two distinct entities.

Upon initial scrutiny both documents were identical. "The copy must have gotten stuck to the original," was the diagnosis. All the information was the exact same. J. J. Bancroft the purchaser, Ascunsion "Sunny" Cataluna the seller. Price, one thousand dollars. Date, February 13, 1926. It was Matthew who caught the tiny aberration and asked if the date on the top was a thirteen or an eighteen.

Angie whisked it out of his hands and held it to the sun. "Oh, my God," she shrieked. "Oh, my God. You're right." Her fingers trembled.

"I just asked a question."

"The date has been doctored. The eight was changed to a three."

And now they noticed the larger difference. The parameters of the property lines were different. On the original the diagram of the parcel described a small little pocket of land. But on the second one, a long, narrow swath was delineated.

"The parcel goes from mid-city to the ocean. The entire Wilshire Corridor! One of these bastards stole the most expensive piece of property in America not owned by the Catholic Church."

"Angie, I don't think so." Stein had to laugh at her. It felt odd to be the voice of reason. But she was blasting through all the yellow lights as though they were green. Angie whirled to Matt to break the deadlock. He refused to take sides.

"What are you, the Swiss ambassador?" she railed at him. "Somebody kills somebody and gets rich and that doesn't bother you?" She cauterized Matt with a withering look and turned on her heel. "Death certificates are on the third floor. Anyone want to bet I'll find one dated February 13, 1926, for Ascunsion Cataluna or J. J. Bancroft?" Matthew started to walk with her but she froze him. "Skeptics remain here." She never looked back.

"Strong-willed girl," said Matt.

"Tell me about it," said Stein.

Twenty minutes later she returned at a slower pace bearing a perplexed look. "There's no death certificate for either one of them. No Bancroft. No Cataluna."

"What about lunch?" Stein suggested.

"Go if you need to."

"Actually, I wouldn't mind a little something," Matt confessed. "I'm kind of starving."

"Oh. On that you have an opinion."

***

Back through town and up the heart of the Miracle Mile, Angie continued to obsess that the body they found had to be either J. J. Bancroft or Sunny Cataluna, until Matt declared that he was going to take a stand and declare that the dead man was Cataluna.

"And pray tell where does this supposition come from?"

"One of them seems to have done pretty well." Matt gestured toward the glass and steel edifice they were passing, above whose entranceway the name Bancroft was spelled out in twenty-foot-high letters.

"Then we've got it. Bancroft killed him."

"Excellent. Case closed!" Stein thumped his hand against the wheel with finality. Simultaneously he saw a sign out of the corner of his eye, and veered to the right into the Valet Parking lane of La Chine Belle.

"Here?" Angie's voice rode in a glissando of distaste.

La Chine Belle was the pretentious darling of the foodie set, where the menus changed every day according to the head chef's artistic whims and the prices were written out in words: *Broiled Peruvian Antelope Heart served in a reduction of wasp wings garnished with taproot of free-range cilantro . . . Seventy-Seven dollars.*

The husband of one of Lila's trust fund girlfriends was part owner. When someone had posted bogus bad reviews on the Internet, Lila had suggested that Stein might help. Stein knew squat about the web but he was conversant with jealousy, greed, and small-minded vindictiveness. It took all of eleven seconds to nail the cyberperp who, surprise surprise, turned out to be the jilted lover of one of the sous chefs. As recompense from a grateful ownership, Stein had been given an "anytime" invitation, and as it happened to have caught his eye, this seemed to be the time.

When the proprietor, Claude Cezanne, was told Stein was lunching there, he led a parade of personnel to the table: the head chef and three sous all in their crisp whites, the salad chef, the meat and game aficionado, the sommelier, and of course *le créateur des desserts.* Cezanne sported a French name, an Italian suit, a German haircut, a Caribbean tan, and Beverly Hills teeth. A pageant of gratitude was lavished upon Stein. Complimentary specialties, the best wine. When at last the entourage withdrew, Stein found Angie fixing him with a long, intent Jack Benny stare, and with impeccable timing asked, "What was *that?*"

"People like me. What can I say?"

Angie gasped. Her face fell into fire alarm mode. The source of her concern approached their table. Though *approached* inadequately described the force with which Angie's mother, Stein's ex-wife Hillary, bore down upon them. Everyone who knew them knew of the infamous "no actions deleterious to the well-being of the child" clause she had included in their joint custody agreement. She dangled it over his head like the sword of Damocles as a way of controlling his behavior.

"Harry?" Her voice rolled like distant warning thunder.

"Hillary?" Stein's was more of a reality check. He was frequently bamboozled in restaurants, mistaking a mirror's reflection for another room.

If he was perplexed at seeing Hillary, she was livid at seeing him. "This is the *major vacation plan* you hold our daughter hostage for?"

"Me? You're the one who's out of the country."

"Angie told me you were going to Maui."

"She told me *you* were going to the Caribbean."

All eyes turned to Angie like that moment in a Lucy comedy.

"This is getting a little heavy for me," Matt said, and excused himself to the coffee bar.

"I think I better make sure Matt is okay," Angie said, and attempted to make a sitcom escape.

"You better stay right where you," Stein ordained.

"Let her go," Hillary said. Her tone had become conciliatory.

Angie gathered up her purse, which she had clumsily dropped alongside Stein's chair, and whispered for him not to say anything about the murder.

"I should have seen it coming," Hillary said. "It's clear that she prefers being with you to me."

"It has very little to do with me, you can be sure." Stein glanced in the direction of Matt's departure.

"He's gay," Hillary said, thriving on what she always believed to be her superior inside information. But then her combative posture dissolved. "This is our fault, Harry. We have failed as divorced parents as badly as we failed as married ones."

"I wouldn't go that far."

"Look at her. She lies. She manipulates. It's all a product of what we've done to her."

He could see tears forming. "Hill. I don't like what she did any more than you do. But on the other hand, a little lying and manipulation is a pretty small price to pay, considering some other stories I'm sure we've both heard."

"Of course you can afford to flaunt your generosity now that you're the desired parent."

"Oh, for God's sake, Hillary. Nobody's flaunting anything. This is your custody week. You should take her."

"I suppose when you get married you'll be filing for sole custody."

"Who said anything about married?"

"Are you telling me you and Lila won't be getting married?" Hillary was like a child reprieved from certain dismay. "You don't think you'll be staying there?"

"I didn't say that. I just don't know what my plans are."

"Well, that's better than being certain you're going to get married."

Hillary took a sip of Harry's white wine. "I'm sorry. Do you mind?" she asked.

"No, it's fine."

She studied the glass for a moment after setting it down on the damask tablecloth. Her index finger traced a line down the cool condensation on the graceful curve of its perimeter. "There were things I could have done while we were married, things I *should* have done, that could have helped. A lot of what happened between us was my fault, Harry. I let you do all the heavy lifting."

Jesus, he thought. *Where is this coming from?*

"I've been seeing somebody," Hillary confided.

"Yes, I've heard you've been fairly active in that arena."

"I don't mean dating. I mean as in under the treatment of."

"You're seeing a shrink?"

"Don't you think it's about time?" It was the first time in years he had heard her laugh. "There can't be one winner in a relationship," she went on. "I thought there could be. I thought it had to be me. Because if it wasn't me then it would have to be you. I mistook your understanding for weakness. I apologize for that."

"There's no need . . ."

"Maybe you've moved on, Harry. And that's good. It's probably what I need to do." She kissed him on the cheek, her lips lingering for that one tiny extra beat, by which a woman means to convey to a man either you can have me . . . or you just missed your chance forever.

***

The encounter with Hillary left Stein unsettled. Feeling her undefended vulnerability reminded him of the girl Hillary had been, out of the surf at Santorini, topless, with a ring of seaweed and coral around her neck, her beauty as bright as a sun captured inside the sun.

Lila's car was in the driveway. Stein pulled in behind it and tooted the horn to be sure she was home and there would be an orderly transition of supervision. Stein pointed to his watch as Matt and Angie climbed out and made a vague pantomime gesture meant to convey to her that he'd be back soon. When Angie asked where he was going, he made some vague semi-verbal grunt about some things he had to do.

***

When he needed to be Stein again, not anybody's father or lover or friend or redeemer, he always came back here to the former Chez Stein. He wondered what his former neighbors wondered about him. The occupants of the other four units were all a generation younger. The girl next door was new; he still hadn't met her though he knew a lot about her. The gay couple, Ryan and Ramón, used the back door mostly, where the garages were, so he hardly saw them. The married couple diagonally across was a little bright-eyed and Mormony for his taste. They had matching Audis with sequential personal license plates that read ZESTY 1 and ZESTY 2. The only person he really knew there was Penelope Kim, and she was still away.

Sex with her could always be as matter-of-fact as a milkshake and sacred at the same time. She was an original. She had kayaked down the Amazon, witnessed torture by the Khmer Rouge, been the secret lover of the founders of three religions. All these experiences had given her an air of sad knowingness. She was a sheer piece of silk whose only defense was transparency and the power to disappear.

He let himself inside his old place and closed the door behind him. Nothing had changed since the last time he had been here. Nothing moves in a house except what is moved by the people living there. There were still odd pieces of furniture. A magazine rack in the middle of the floor without the rocking chair that had once been alongside it. Stein felt like he was returning to a desiccated chrysalis or looking at the ruins of Pompeii. Its life had exhaled, retracted from home to four rooms. The envelope he was hoping would not arrive until next month had been delivered. It had a bold red border around its entire perimeter, and in large bold letters, the words RESPOND WITHIN TEN DAYS. He knew what legal document was contained within. His landlord had refused Stein's offer to go month-to-month. This was an order to renew the annual lease or vacate.

Two films ran side by side in Stein's interior Cineplex. In *Living with Lila*, his life was happily enmeshed with a woman who actually loved him, who saw him for exactly who he was and accepted it all. A trusted friend, a loyal partner, a discreet confidant, a co-parent whom Angie was crazy about, and beyond that, the safety net of financial stability, not that he would ever use it, but it was there.

In *Life without Lila*, he lived here. Watson's collar hung on a nail above the front door. These were his holes in the walls. There was the chance of the girl next door. Or of women he had yet to meet.

A third possibility interposed itself, triggered by the oddly haunting exchange he had just had with Hillary. What was that about? Did she want to get back with him? Could all the king's horses and all the king's men put Humpty Dumpty back together again? He could hear Angie's "*No*" thundering through the mountainside.

He understood it would pull the rug out from under her a second time, undermine all the stability she had carefully rebuilt by balancing herself astride two unsecured platforms. On the other hand, what if her posture were an act? Angie was so good at hiding her true feelings, it was possible that deep down the thing she most longed for was her parents' reconciliation. Wasn't that the secret dream of every divorced kid? He closed his eyes for a moment and pictured life with Hillary. But no. Fool me once, shame on . . . somebody. Fool me twice, shame on somebody else. However that saying went.

There was one course of action. It was sitting up there like a big fat piñata of an obvious answer. Two people in the world knew him and loved him in spite of it. They were the nucleus of his life. Period. Lila was one of them. He needed to make that nuclear wall a solid thing. He took the apartment lease in hand, and in a ceremonial act as metaphorical and life changing as when he had stomped on the wine glass or tossed the shovelful of dirt on Stein senior's coffin, he tore the lease asunder. He signed the INTENT TO VACATE form. He took the picture of him in bed with John and Yoko off the wall, left his keys behind him, and drove back to Lila's with the intention of asking her to marry him.

It wouldn't even be an ask. He would drop it into a conversation about some other activities they were planning. As in, "Yeah and probably that week we should find the time to get married. You don't want anything big, right? We'll go to city hall." He would add those last two sentences because she would think he was kidding at first, and he wanted her to get that he was serious and he meant it. It would give her a chance to register the rapture of Stein's saying what she never thought he would say. Followed immediately by the stark horror that this might actually become her life, this possibility that she wanted too much to believe could really happen and had made the compensating lowering of expectations to reduce the pain of disappointment. And then to finally say okay in the same offhand tone that he had asked. As an important but not gigantically important part of their upcoming itinerary.

The closer Stein got to Beverly Hills, the more he attuned himself to be alert for signs of retreat. He did not want to imprison himself to a spontaneous romantic whim. But quite the opposite occurred. The closer he got, the more enthusiastic and calm he felt, and pleased in a profound way that he had made the right decision. Lila was engrossed in a spirited conversation with Mercedes when Stein came home. Lila saw the smile on his face but had no idea of its significance. She remembered there been a phone call for him and handed him the message she had taken down.

"Good news?" she asked.

The message was from Jarlene Moody. When Stein called her back, the news she had was not good news. Not good news at all.

Chapter Nine

Apologue

My mother was a queen and I am a queen. I was nurtured in a queen's chamber. Catered to. Cleansed. Fed a steady diet of royal jelly. One of my sisters was born in a royal chamber, too. Our destiny was to meet. Oh, yes. We met. And she is no more. Her will was weak. Her body snapped under mine. The battle was ghastly and short. Only my mother the queen now stands in the way of my destiny. I seek her out. She knows why I have come. I place my young, fertile body against the aging brittle shell of hers. There is room for only one of us. She tests my will and I hurl her down. I would do what is needed but allow her to choose exile. She signals her followers. They leave in tens, in thousands. I will never see her again. The past is gone. There is only the future.

The scent of my pheromones becomes the new tone key of the hive. It is my colony. My entourage will anticipate and attend to my every need. My sole purpose will be to become an object of desire. There will be an evening, warm and gentle, when I will make my virgin flight into the world. The air will be dizzy with fragrance, none more erotic than my own. He will find me. He will be drawn to me out of the air. He will descend upon me in flight. When I have taken from him every cell he has to give he will fall away and I will be taken by another. He will encircle me, beating his frantic wings. He must have me. Yes, I will say to him, yes and yes. And when he is done there is another who must have me or die. And he will have me or die. A dozen males will have me. And when I return to the colony the future is within me. I will never again return to the outside.

I will lay eggs. Filling every chamber with my legacy. My genes. My pitch. Legions of incomplete females and stingerless males. From the moment they break through the wax, their lives will be a succession of services to me all the days of their lives. They will clean the nursery. They will tend the brood. They will construct new comb to store honey for the winter. Their wings will beat in unison and keep the colony at perfect temperature. They will search for nectar and pollen that will feed us. They will explore for miles. They will return with unerring accuracy. They will ride on currents of light and fluctuations of heat and magnetism, scent and ultra violet. They will guard against invaders. They will fight for me to the death. Tens of thousands may die that I shall live. So it must be. I am the future. I am the life. I am the heartbeat. I am the essence. I will lay two hundred thousand eggs this summer and the next and the next. Among them shall be the one who will be destined to supplant me. If she lives.

The queen is dead. Long live the queen.

Chapter Ten

In the short time Stein had been away from the Central Valley an amazing transformation had taken place. The entire landscape was now awash in glimmering white. Those bare trees, the black, branchy hallucinations of war dead that Stein had driven through just a week ago, were now all in blossom. Cinderella had molted her rags and dressed for the ball. She was illuminant. Bejeweled. And there was a scent in the air: not instantly intoxicating like lilacs, but quietly pervasive. Above the sight and above the scent was an incessant, steady hum, as though earth had a room tone. Stein kept looking up for the power line transformers. But there were no transformers. The hum was the bees. Fourteen trillion of them, he had been told. *Trillion.* More than half the bee population of the entire country had been shipped to this two-hundred-square-mile quadrant to perform the largest man-made pollination event on the planet.

As staunchly as Stein disdained air-conditioning, he made sure his windows were up. Lila had not been thrilled with Stein's leaving the day before Valentine's Day. Despite her wanting to indulge his anticommercial attitude, she was an old-fashioned girl at heart and this would have been their first Valentine's Day together. Still, she held her tongue and insisted he take her car.

Given the rushed and overwrought circumstances and the need for his hasty departure that very next morning, Stein had postponed the discussion of marriage to a time when they could give it its proper clear-cut moment. The needle on the REGRET–RELIEF graph tilted more in the direction of relief, he could not help noticing.

He fumbled with his left hand for the electronic window switch. He never knew where the hell it was. He pressed the control lever for the door locks instead. The loud metallic clomp startled him and he quickly toggled the switch to undo whatever he had done. His fingers searched like four blind worms to be sure that there was no air space between the glass and the top of the window frame. The car was going eighty. At this velocity, if one little bee got sucked into that vortex it would get shot at him, stinger first, like a pygmy blowgun and put his eye out.

He could not dissolve the image of Aloysius Frank Monahan lying flat on that metal slab, the look of terror embedded so deeply into his face that even Jarlene Moody's reconstructive skills could not erase it. Stein knew exactly what thoughts had etched that look into the driver's countenance. It was his mind screaming at him: *All our life we knew this was exactly how we would die and here it is happening and there is nothing we can do about it.*

When that bee had crawled into Stein's ear years ago, it left an indelible prophetic message on his brain that his death would come at the hands of bees. And so he had avoided them. The Holocaust images that had always plagued him were seeing his people walking docilely into boxcars to their own death. Yet here he was doing the same, only faster. Some inexplicable compulsion was propelling him at eighty miles per hour into the dream of his own death, the greatest concentration of bees in the Western world. He was General Custer leading the Light Brigade at Gallipoli. He had to be out of his fucking mind.

He would come out of this dead or no longer afraid of bees. Jarlene Moody's voice echoed through his head: "Fear of death is often the cause of death."

***

Jarlene opened the door at the first knock and looked disoriented to see Stein. She too had changed. She looked her age now. Smaller and stooped. "He was shaving and he just blacked out. He found himself on the bathroom floor. Bleeding. With no idea how he got there."

Stein thought of Sig Kroll telling him about planned obsolescence. *If your battery's guaranteed till Christmas don't expect it to crank on New Year's Eve.*

"Who's out there?" Moody's reedy voice oboed from the adjoining room.

"No one. The doctor will be here in a minute."

"Is it Stein?"

Stein waited deferentially until she yielded permission for him to go in.

"Just, you know, don't kill him, if you can possibly help it."

Stein entered slowly. Renn was tilted back in a reclining chair. He wore a robe. Underneath the robe he wore a shirt and a necktie. That was a good sign. The twin-pronged rubber oxygen tube stuck in Renn's nostrils like the Greek letter Pi. That was not a good sign.

"I'm surprised you came," Renn said.

"I happened to be in the neighborhood."

Renn's attempt to laugh sounded like clogged plumbing. He took some deep breaths out of the oxygen tube and stabilized himself. "Luckily we always keep a canister."

Stein didn't know what Renn's battery life was so he jumped right in to the *Final Jeopardy!* question: What was this deal Hollister made with Henny Spector to rent out depleted bee colonies? Renn struggled to sit up higher. Stein leaned in to help but Renn angrily waved help away. The effort threw him into a paroxysm of wheezing, which was followed by a sharp rap at the front door. Before Renn could answer, Dr. Cartesian strode into the room with an air of imperial command. He was tall with a craggy, architectural face. His curt nod of the head at Stein left no doubt of its meaning.

"He was just about to tell me something I came up here to find out."

"Mr. Stein, please," Jarlene insisted. She stood at the kitchen door urging him to leave her husband be. She had set out a glass of iced tea for him on the thick wooden kitchen table. All the years of good upbringing don't get washed away by disaster—they're instilled as the way to meet disaster.

"Thank you," he said. He sipped it slowly to play for time.

"Sweetener?"

"No, it's perfect."

"I wish you hadn't come."

"You called me."

"I mean the first time. You've opened such a kettle of fish. Oh, I don't even know if I meant that. I can't blame you for what's been happening."

"I'm swimming in mothballs, here, Mrs. Moody. What is happening?"

"Doc was grooming Hollister to take over all his colonies."

"I could see that."

"He taught him better than to do what he did."

"If you could just explain to me a little bit more about what Hollister did—"

Another voice summoned her by name. Dr. Cartesian swung in through the entrance and ordered her to mash up a banana.

Jarlene sprang to action. Her fingers, now having purpose, flew to their task and enabled her to speak without looking at Stein. "Hollister took a deal with Henry Spector for a hundred and seventy-five dollars for weak four-frame colonies while everyone else is getting one fifty for healthy eight-frame boxes."

Stein grasped her wrist for a moment. Her bones felt hollow as a songbird's. Her skin was remarkably smooth. Not baby smooth, but the last layer of filo. "Could you just explain to me why somebody would rent depleted colonies?"

"Ask Hollister," she said. "Maybe he can explain it to you."

She gathered herself to give her ailing husband the vision of a strong, hopeful woman coming through the doorway.

***

Stein got completely bollixed trying to replicate the route that Hollister's wife Ruth Ann had driven the night of the beekeepers' convention. Landmarks he might have passed at night were of no use in daylight. Farmland stretched in every direction. Not all of it was planted with almond groves; some was still given over to the traditional agricultural staples: cotton, asparagus, livestock—the latter causing it to reek to high heaven.

The vertical road came to a road that went horizontal. Stein looked to the right. To the right there was farmland. He looked to the left. To the left was farmland. Ah, but in the distance he noted an absurd familiar object. With barely a breeze blowing, the bright colored buntings that were meant to convey the excitement of owning a condo here hung like wallflowers at a prom. Stein parked behind the only other vehicle, Ruth Ann's Bronco pickup. There were still no takers, no lookiloos, no prospective buyers or renters at the site of Hilltop Vista, save one unsavory-looking person lurking on the third faux flagstone step to the entrance. He was coyote thin with a scraggly four-day growth, wearing a Western-style shirt that had probably been white at one time, or anyway, whiter. His teeth looked like a long-abandoned movie marquee, a few letters missing, the others hanging on lopsided.

Ruth Ann had seen Stein arrive from the window of the model apartment, and when he came in arose from behind her desk as though she were meeting a prospective client. Her business getup was a 1950s Radcliff look. Hair in a ponytail. Freckles and glasses. Plaid skirt, blazer, and loafers.

"Pretend to be a buyer," she said through a pasted smile. She shook his hand with professional gusto and made the scripted introduction to the amenities of Hilltop Vista. She asked, in a voice just a little too loud, how large his family was so she could select the unit that would best suit his needs. "Five," she echoed with gusto. "Well, aren't you the fertility clinic." She ran her index finger down the ledger of available properties, selected a key from the wall-hanging hooks and escorted Stein out along the exterior breezeway toward unit number seventeen and conducted him inside.

Unlike the model they had just come from, this space was unfurnished. The walls were bare, the floor rough concrete. "Picture it with a nice green shag carpet wall-to-wall," she said. "It'll warm the place up immeasurably."

"Ruth Ann, I don't think the room is bugged."

She looked around as a cautionary measure. "Did you see anyone outside?"

"Just a refugee from *The Grapes of Wrath*."

"That's my boss. He owns the place."

"No."

"The man is a visionary."

"You're shitting me."

"Of course I'm shitting you," she whispered conspiratorially. "He's a pig farmer. He leases the manure-reeking piece of slag you just drove past. How could you believe me?"

"I tend to believe people I like."

"Big mistake. They're the ones you have to look out for."

"I mean this in the nicest way, Ruth Ann, but does your husband have any idea who he's married to?"

"Does anyone?

It could have been accidental that her body was inches from his. But when she did not move away it became clear that the proximity was with intent. "Hollister is a sweet boy, and I love him to death. But there's something about an older man."

"Ruth Ann . . ." Stein took a long, careful step back.

"Don't be afraid. I know exactly what I'm doing."

"That's what frightens the hell out of me." He retreated another step.

Her voice twinkled with humor. The moment popped back into reality. "Don't agonize. You never had a shot. I had to see how committed you were to getting Hollister out of trouble."

Stein marveled at this little hellion. "Suppose I had gone along?"

"I meant a good deal of what I said," she purred.

"Really?"

"No!" Her laugh reverberated. "Give a girl some credit." Then quick as quicksilver she was down to business. She wanted Stein to understand that Hollister had not initiated the deal. He had not haggled. He had been approached with a proposition and agreed to it. "Is it weird that someone wants to pay above market price for below market quality?" she asked and answered, "Yes, it is. Is it the weirdest thing I've heard all week? No, it is not."

"You're just your own little catechism, aren't you?"

"Did I leave anything vital out?"

"How about, was it the right thing to do?" Stein asked.

"Do you turn yourself in every time you speed? When your meter is expired and you didn't get a ticket do you throw money in for the time you used? Do you see what I mean? Morality is a fluid substance."

"I need to talk to Hollister. Do you know where I can find him?

Ruth Ann glanced at her watch and was surprised at the time. "He should be in court." Striding with purpose to the parking area she indicated the white Lexus parked behind her pickup.

"Yours?" she asked.

He nodded a provisional yes.

"Improvement."

***

The Calvin Coolidge Courthouse was a granite edifice built in the 1930s. Consistent with its namesake, it was flinty, puritanical, and spare. The original air-conditioning system was still in place, meaning paper fans. When a faucet leaked in one of the restrooms it was repaired with a partially used washer, the ethos being to extract the last molecule of utility from a resource. Those same prohibitions against squander, subsidy, and favoritism were not so fastidiously enforced by the officials the public elected to administer justice in the Calvin Coolidge Courthouse.

The gallery was built to hold two hundred people. Today there was one spectator, so it was not difficult to pinpoint Hollister Greenway. The case was called and the sheriff brought the accused to the dock. Sheriff Slodaney was all brush cut and ironed lapels. He looked like a soloist in the Treblinka Boy Choir. The low opinion that Spade Wilson had earlier rendered was seconded almost verbatim by Ruth Ann, that if he didn't have a badge, he'd have a number. Now as the accused removed his hat and faced the court Stein understood why Hollister was here. It was Ranger Granger's trial.

Justice Benjamin Crowder's day job was coaching football at the junior high. But he had standards, and was a stickler for their being maintained. When he saw the defendant toothpicking a chunk of bacon lodged between two molars he took umbrage.

"I don't recall seeing bacon on my jail's breakfast menu."

"Please the court," Slodaney responded, "what with the over-crowding in the jails, and with the approval of the County DA, the prisoner was remanded to house arrest."

"Your office approved this?" The question was directed to the ADA, Bonnie Banks. A graduate of Case Western's excellent law program, she served today as the state's prosecutor.

"Of course they *approved* it," Ruth Ann hissed in Stein's ear. "They're dating."

"Who?"

"Ranger Granger and the assistant DA."

"Good God. Don't let them have children."

ADA Banks forthrightly reported that due to lack of concrete evidence the charges had been reduced from felony possession of stolen property to misdemeanor goose hunting out of season. Barely had those words cleared her lips when Judge Crowder asked how the defendant pleaded. Ranger Granger's response came simultaneously to the question being put to him, and within a heartbeat Judge Crowder had levied a fine of fifty dollars and had his gavel poised to pound the case closed.

"Hold on there, Chief." Stein Errol Flynned himself over the waist-high balustrade and miraculously struck the landing. "There was enough 'concrete evidence' in that warehouse to pave a highway."

Judge Crowder's gavel froze in mid-air. He demanded to know who this man was.

"Friend of the court. *Amicus jurispendium*," Stein improvised. The dazed and puzzled looks on the grown-ups made him feel like he was twenty-two again. "I was there at the warehouse. *In hoc signo vinces*," he averred, pointing his fingers at his eyes.

Crowder pounded his gavel demanding order and decreed that until such time as a man is proven guilty, all the stolen merchandise in his warehouse shall be presumed his.

Stein practically levitated. "You just called it stolen merchandise!"

Crowder beckoned the court stenographer, a rail-thin woman with bunned-up hair, to read back the statement.

"Starting where, your honor?"

"From where I didn't say stolen."

Stein used the diversion to sidle over to where Ruth Ann was now seated alongside Hollister. "I shouldn't be fighting for you, you ungrateful son of a bitch. You broke Renn Moody's heart."

"Renn Moody thinks he knows everything there is to know about bees," Hollister sulked. "Maybe I can teach him a few things."

Ruth Ann didn't like what she was hearing. "What's going on in that head of yours, Billy Bob?"

The judicial huddle broke. Judge Crowder, in calm and tremulous tones, overruled his previous edict and in a benevolent voice that was meant to carry the very essence of justice in its timbre, added, "While there is no suggestion of deliberate wrongdoing on the part of the defendant, men in public service need to hold themselves to a higher standard of behavior than even the letter of the law requires. For even the hint of impropriety taints us as surely as impropriety itself."

The sheriff tapped his wristwatch for him to get on with it.

"And so," Judge Crowder intoned, "it is ordered that Ranger Timothy M. Granger will pay restitution to claimant Hollister Greenway for the amount of honey lost, estimated in the amount of eighty-seven dollars, and that the three contested bee boxes for which Mr. Greenway has demonstrated ownership, shall be returned to him."

Hollister elevated from his seat. "Did you say three? There were a hundred other boxes that he swiped from Doc Moody that Doc was going to give to me."

"That's hearsay and you can't prove that," Sheriff Slodaney crooned. "And what would you do with a hundred empty boxes? Renn Moody's not going to super you a hundred new colonies."

"What I do with them is my business." The triumvirate around the rostrum grinned like they knew full well what his "business" was. Granger especially. "At a hundred seventy-five dollars apiece, looks like it'll be my business now. Me and Henny Spector's."

"You can't do that," Hollister railed. "He made the deal with me!"

"Oh, it's dood," Ranger Granger taunted.

The gavel had fallen. The victors vacated with their spoils. Stein was confused. Did he hear Hollister suggest he was renting *empty* boxes? Ruth Ann was irate that her husband was dealing with Henny Spector.

"I'm doing this for you," he bellowed.

Something had changed in Hollister's makeup. Proximity to money had liberated a side of his personality. The last thing Stein heard before the Greenways went down the staircase and out of earshot was Hollister telling Ruth Ann that he'd work with whomever he damn pleased, and that from now on he would do the talking. And he didn't want her calling him Billy Bob any more. And was that clear? Stein didn't hear her answer but when he looked down from the second-floor window, he saw Ruth Ann getting into the Bronco alone and driving off, while Hollister walked up the street in the other direction toward a yellow Corvair convertible. The top was down. Ranger Granger and Sheriff Slodaney were leaning down on the driver's side door talking to the man in the car. Hollister strode up to them like a rogue elephant. He pointed his finger at the lawmen while appearing more deferential to the man in the car.

It was heartwarming for Stein to see that even in a tiny town in a peripheral industry, greed and corruption were as prevalent as they were in the high-profile snake pits of finance and politics. Whatever was said to Hollister left him infuriated. The man in the car shook hands with the two lawmen and made a U-turn. His car sported a gaudy hood ornament of a fighting hen.

Stein stood at the window for some time: a still-life illustration of Newton's Law that states a body at rest tends to remain at rest unless acted upon by an outside force. His mind was unfocused as he ambled down the uncarpeted hallway. The door to the adjacent courtroom was open. He glanced in, barely registering what he saw. If he had been more tuned in he might have stopped for a closer look. The people were dressed in tailored business suits, salon haircuts, and five-hundred-dollar shoes.

Stein had no idea he had glimpsed a meeting that would change the face of California, that a secret deal had been struck between the secretary of the interior, the chairmen of three local water districts, two congressmen, and a team of corporate lawyers. One of them was slightly built, babyfaced, sandy haired. Something about the momentary snapshot of his face stayed locked on the back of Stein's retina for an extra half second, giving him the impression of intense déjà vu, as if he had known the man.

Chapter Eleven

A long, black hearse was parked out front of Renn and Jarlene Moody's. Stein restrained himself from leaping out of his car and bursting through their front door. He collected himself, prepared for hysterics, and knocked. He was unprepared for the way the event had transformed Jarlene Moody. The weight of anxiety had evaporated from her body. She looked two decades younger. She invited Stein to come in as though she were hosting a cotillion.

"What's happened?" Stein ventured.

"Bananas!"

He would have assumed she meant she was going bananas, but she exhibited no evident signs of derangement.

"Bananas?" Stein repeated.

"His potassium level was low. He needed bananas."

Her energy swept them both into the adjacent funerary. There, to Stein's astonishment, the miraculously recovered Renn Moody was directing workers to remove from the storage freezer, not his own corpse, but the body of Aloysius Frank Monahan. Moody motioned for the lads rolling the gurney to hold up a second. He nodded discretely to his right. "I'll need a signature on the transfer document."

The widow, in classic black, stepped out from between her two fatherless children, a boy of nine, a girl of seven. She rubbed the toe tag of the deceased between her thumb and forefingers like it was a talisman, and asserted that she was Mrs. Aloysius Monahan. Her head was wrapped in a dark kerchief and she wore sunglasses. She reminded Stein of someone he couldn't place. From the other side of the coffin, also flanked by her two young children, though in her case the older child was the girl, a second woman in widow's weeds advanced. Like the first woman, she too was small, blond, pert. She brandished the toe tag on the deceased's other foot and asserted that she was Mrs. Frank Monahan.

Stein had never seen a double toe-tag before. Each set of widows and children regarded their counterparts with cobra-shrouded eyes. One of them, he guessed Mrs. Frank, wanted her husband buried in their family plot in LaGrange, North Dakota. Mrs. Aloysius demanded he be buried where they lived in Mendocino. They dueled for propriety, each speaking only to Renn, though they stood elbow to elbow. One of them claimed primacy on the grounds of hers being the first marriage. The other countered, "Because you knew we were engaged and you tricked him into getting you pregnant."

"A trick you have emulated . . . illegitimately."

"My children are not illegitimate," the wounded wife screamed. They were a spark away from conflagration. Renn tried to restore some decorum. He reminded the ladies they only had one body. Both women stood their ground. Stein stepped out of the doorway and whispered something in Renn's ear. Renn considered the thought and not having a better idea himself, repeated the suggestion to the widows. They gazed coldly at each other, then nodded in agreement.

"All right, then," said Renn. "Come back in an hour. My wife will hand-paint an urn for each of you. And you will each honor your husband's wishes in the most fitting way."

The two families jockeyed for position at the door and exited in a clatter. Moody saluted Stein. "Very Solomonaic."

"You told the widows to come back in an hour. You can't do what you need to do in an hour."

Renn shrugged. "They don't know that."

"You're just going to fill their urns with . . . what?"

"It's all just carbon."

"I'm glad to see your sense of humor's back. You know your boy Hollister is involved with someone named Henny Spector?"

"That boy's gonna give me ulcers."

"He's got him renting out depleted colonies and empty bee boxes. I'd like someone to explain the economics of that to me."

"Spector is a man I'd like to see professionally. In my profession, if you take my meaning."

"Would it help if I talked to him?"

"Wear gloves and a surgical mask."

"Where would I find him?"

"Under any rock."

"Could you be a little more specific?"

"Under any slimy rock."

There was a ruckus outside. The double doors burst open. The two widows, so recently archrivals, now stood shoulder-to-shoulder united by a common enemy, a woman who was yet a third iteration of their same physical type.

Moody called in to his wife, "Jarlene, would you make that three urns?" He nodded invitingly to the new arrival. Her dress was blue, not black. She was wearing neither sunglasses nor a black kerchief, revealing her crimped blond hair and hard blue eyes. She was the woman the other two had reminded Stein of.

"I presume you are Mrs. Monahan the third?" Moody bowed.

"No. I believe Mr. Stein could have told you that."

"Hello, Mrs. Peering."

"You know this woman?" Renn asked.

"Not as well as I thought. What in the world are you doing here?"

"I was the last person who saw him. The last woman he held in his arms. The woman whose scent was on him when he died. That counts for something."

"It counts for you being a little slut." Aloysius Monahan's widow burned her with a withering look. Though Stein wasn't sure—the widow could have been Frank's.

"I wish I had remorse for what I did but I don't," Barbara Peering said.

Stein had a soft spot for her, he didn't know why. He reminded her that she hadn't done anything wrong. She had just been sitting there when Frank had pulled her up from the booth and made her dance with him.

"Thank you, Mr. Stein. But . . . that was not the first encounter we had."

"Excuse me?" His voice came in on high C.

"At the previous rest stop . . ."

"Oh, don't tell me." Stein sagged into a chair.

"We were getting back to the car after one of my husband's timed five-minute 'bodily functions breaks,' as he likes to call them. You know how you can sense you're being looked at? There was a truck parked alongside us. He was in the cab. The *way* he was looking. It felt like all my clothes had burned off. And I didn't care. I wanted to be seen. I wanted him to see me. My husband . . ." She sighed and in the expulsion of air was carried the history of their marriage. "Frank stayed right behind us for two hundred miles. I turned the side view mirror so we could see each other's faces. And he could read my lips."

"He cannot read lips," one of the widows scoffed.

"He could read mine."

She said that she had climaxed three times while dancing with him at the café. And that she was pretty sure he had climaxed too. She said he had invited her to ride with him. To leave her family behind. She went to the ladies room to calm herself, to settle her heartbeat, maybe to write a note to her family. She opened the dollhouse-sized window to get some air. Leaning her elbows on the gritty windowsill with its veins of cracked uplifts of old paint, her gaze, at first vacant, was drawn to a furtive motion. She saw a man ducking away from the back of Frank's truck.

In the moment there had been far too much going on for her to give it a second thought. She did not realize until the news started coming out that the accident had been caused by an unsettled load and not by a bee sting, that she had witnessed sabotage. The man she had seen had loosened the ties securing Frank's load. Even now, when she closed her eyes she could still see that man scuttling away to the edge of the parking lot, half shrouded by a row of hedges. She had not been able to see the whole car he got into—only in through the front window, where clear as day, the woman who sat waiting for him was . . . she turned dramatically to the right, then to the left. "One of you."

"That's a goddamn lie," one of the widows screamed. "Take that back!"

"Ladies, please. Let's keep the body count down to one, shall we?" Renn asked Barbara Peering if she got a good look at the man. Sadly, she admitted, she had not. But when the car had backed into a Y to peel out of the parking lot, she had noticed an odd hood ornament on the front of the car.

***

It was a guilty pleasure, he knew. But Stein loved driving Lila's Lexus. There was something, goddamn it, to having money. Not that Lila was rolling in it. She was the least well off of all her trust fund girlfriends. She worked three mornings per week as a teacher's aide and reading assistant. Not because she had to. Her husband left her pretty well off. The house was close to being paid for. The mortgage payments came out of the trust. She had Mercedes the housekeeper and Lexus the coupe. She probably would have to cash in some of the Microsoft stock that was owned by the trust to cover the unexpected upkeep, but she'd talk to Richard about that. As annoying as all that might be, she had the awareness to know that most people would trade their problems for hers in a moment. How Stein fit into this picture, he still didn't quite figure. For either of them.

The Moodys had given him the names of three likely places to find Henny Spector. He was heading toward the first, trying to come up with a game plan to disengage Hollister from Spector's clutches. But he couldn't get his mind off Frank Monahan. Two wives and a backup. The man had some mojo working. And cute little Barbara Peering. Ready to throw everything away for a ride on the wild side. As clueless as Ned Peering was about the inner life of the woman he married, in Stein's heart he wanted her to stay with her husband; even if she'd had the chance to run off with Monahan, he wanted her to stay with Ned. It blew his mind to realize that when he was younger he would have rooted for the upheaval, and that now he had slid to the side of stability.

He was thrust from the mental sauna of self-examination by a sharp bump at the rear end of the car. He was startled to see a big-ass SUV on his tail. A glance at his speedometer confirmed that he had been dawdling, down to a dreamy forty-five. He toed the pedal and in seconds was cruising at sixty. Doing sixty in his Camry on this road would have been an adrenaline ride but in this baby it was a walk in the park. He glanced up to confirm that he'd put distance between himself and the other vehicle. The sonofabitch still lurked centimeters from his bumper.

Stein threw both arms up in the classic what-the-fuck gesture. He could play jet fighter pilot too. He eased off the pedal to make the SUV slow down and then gunned it. A wide receiver's stop-and-go pattern. By that analogy, the SUV was a two-hundred-thirty-pound cornerback with the speed of a free safety and the hitting power of a linebacker. Stein could not shake him. The fucker nudged him again.

Stein floored the Lexus into overdrive. He was practically thrown back in his seat. The response was instantaneous. The car went from solid to liquid and liquid to gas. It erupted right under him and threw him into Mach I. He was frightened he wouldn't be able to handle the speed and flexed his ankle off the gas, allowing the transmission to shift out of low and into fifth. The damn SUV was still tongue-licking his tailpipe.

He tried to see who the hell was driving but of course the windows were tinted. There was nothing in front or behind him that would offer any protection. No cluster of homes. No gas station, no general store. Ahead there was a driveway and turnout. He pulled over abruptly, went into a controlled ninety-degree skid, churned up a whole hell of a lot of dust and jumped out of the car to confront the driver of the SUV, who had stopped within five feet of him. Even as Stein slammed the car door behind him, strode under a full head of righteous indignation, he knew this was among the stupidest things he had ever done in his life. He had the gigantic impulse to give it a big *Ooops*, to whirl around, leap into his car and head back from whence he had come.

Any lingering optimism that he had overestimated the level of danger he was dissipated with the emergence of the driver. He was a five-foot-nine-inch cinderblock of a man with a face like a pumpkin that had been smashed in and then frozen solid.

"You."

His voice was a combination roar and snarl. Stein had never been to Siberia, but he was certain that the gamey, goaty, cheesy aroma that swelled from under the man's silk shirt was an emanation of his tundrous homeland. The long slender Tanto blade that he shoved in front of Stein's face was probably Chechnyan. The point of the knife was embedded into the rump of a lustrous orange-colored fruit.

"What called that?" he demanded.

Stein reasoned that the man wanted to know the English word for the fruit. It was a fairly aggressive strategy of asking for information but under the circumstances he put judgments aside and informed him in English it was called an orange.

With a flick of the wrist, ghastly and elegant in its economy, the man propelled the orange from the tip of the blade, and used gravity to halve the fruit into two perfect hemispheres as deftly as if he'd cut the throat of his wife's lover.

"Look that," he challenged Stein. "What see?"

"It's a beautiful piece of fruit."

The man jabbed the point of his knife against each of several small, solid gray pips. It was easy to see them being the eyes of a torturee. "What call those?"

"Pits, I guess. Right?"

Stein's choice of terminology was not satisfactory.

"Is for make grow," the man growled.

"Seeds. Right, of course. Seeds."

"Seeds. Yes. This piece of shit you call piece of fruit was to be *seedless* mandarin. Look seedless to you?" He pressed one of the fragrant sections close to Stein's face. In his enthusiasm he squeezed too hard and a spray of juice bathed Stein's shirt and face. "You know why is seeds?" the man thundered. "Seeds is make from bees! Bees must to stay out of orange groves." He swept his knife in a swift backhand arc that left no doubt of its message. He turned his disdainful look toward Stein, tossed him the fruit. "Bees you keep?"

"Me? No."

"No. Too soft. What you are, car salesman?" He threw a disdainful look at the Lexus. "Piece of shit Japanese." He got back into his own vehicle and left Stein at the side of the road. The scent bearing up out of the freshly cut orange filled his senses. Stein shoved the quartered section into his mouth and savored the taste all the way down. Seeds notwithstanding, it was one tasty piece of fruit.

***

Given all that had happened to him, Stein was due the modest stroke of luck that Henny Spector was at the first of the three places Renn Moody had suggested. A cluster of motorcycles was parked out front of a dive with a sign that said GOOD EATS. Stein left Lila's car out front, the only Lexus parked among the Harleys and Ford pickups and the one yellow Corvair convertible.

There was not the slightest doubt in Stein's mind that Henny Spector was the man he was looking at. The chicken insignia on his denim jacket was a clue. One of his eyes was looking behind to see who was chasing him and the other was scanning ahead for the next person he could cheat, another clue. What cinched it was that somebody had yelled across the room, "Hey, Henny!" and Henny had answered.

From the table that Stein strategically chose at the end of the bar he was able to observe the man operate—passing through the crowded barroom in a seemingly patternless route. Yet at regular intervals he stopped at or was stopped by small clusters of people. A honeybee in a field of clover. The encounters were brief. Generally Henny spoke. Generally people listened or nodded. Sometimes one of the others might speak. Henny would listen. And invariably money would change hands in transactions that were not likely to find their way onto IRS 1040s.

Stein's plan, if such a word could be applied to the vague strategy he had begun to formulate, was to find a casual way of engaging in conversation with Henny. From there, he was pretty sure he'd find the way to ease Hollister out of Henny's grasp. Though he still couldn't fathom why anybody would buy or lease empty or depleted hives. Somebody had to be making money. That, he knew, was the end game. He couldn't see through to the "how."

At a nearby round table, Henny drained the last inch of foam from his beer mug. Stein took this as a sign he was leaving, and came to readiness for his faux casual encounter. His quarry, however, exited by the other door. Stein applauded himself for having anticipated this possibility and positioning himself alongside a window that looked out to the parking area. He glanced out to see in which direction Henny's yellow Corvair was headed.

Stein delayed following for a few moments, left a twenty on the table, and sashayed unhurriedly out the door leaving no trace of himself behind. (As if anyone were paying the least bit of attention to him.) Outside, he ambled to his car with studied disinterest. There was no need to rush, which would tip his hand. He'd give Henny a few minutes' head start.

However, the Hennymobile had stopped in the road a few dozen yards from the tavern. Stein quickly found a subterfuge, a legitimate reason that he was not getting into his car and driving. There was a persistent spot in the middle of his windshield that needed cleaning. He searched for a cloth. He wiped and buffed and elbow greased. He checked his fluid levels. All the while glancing out of the corner of his eye. At last the Corvair moved. Not frontward but in reverse. It stopped and idled ten feet from where Stein was obsessively wiping.

"I think you got the spot," the driver observed.

"Excuse me?"

"You wanted to talk to me, right?"

Stein feigned guileless disinterest. "What would make you think that?"

Henny tapped his index fingers against the back of his head. "Eyes all over." He threw the Corvair into drive and headed down the road, trailing oil leakage and dark smoke. All Stein could do was follow. Despite everybody's low opinion of Spector, Stein's impression of him was not that bad. He had a sense of humor. Plus he didn't have half the car under him that Stein did, but he hugged the line, took the curves skillfully, didn't ride the brake. Credit where it's due.

Chapter Twelve

Stein half-expected Henny Spector's place to resemble the salvage yard where Butch and Burleigh lived, the crazy twin brothers with the blown-out knees. But no. There was no sculpture garden of propane canisters at Chez Spector, no redneck graveyard of deceased refrigerators. His driveway passed beneath an arbor of manicured citrus trees, some in heady blossom, some bending under the weight of ripe fruit. It led to a ranch-style house, not ostentatiously large, not thoughtlessly suburban, but neat and homey and well kept. The Brahms Violin Concerto was playing on the stereo, which delighted Stein, as it was one of a select few classical pieces he could recognize immediately wherever he came in on it.

"I have many beverages," said Henny. "Have you come as a friend or a foe, so I know what to serve you?"

"I'm good with just the company for right now."

There was a long leather sofa that faced a TV. A photograph—at closer look, a painting—hung on the opposite wall above an oak dining table. It was muscular and kinetic and mystical at the same time, depicting an eighteen-wheel open bed diesel barreling through a storm of white so intense the truck was nearly invisible. Stein was surprised by the title: *Route 99 to Fresno.*

"I didn't know you had blizzards here," he remarked.

"Everyone makes that mistake. It isn't snow. It's garlic paper and butterfly wings. Yeah. Very first time I drove through this valley I got in behind one of those big open-framed delivery trucks hauling a million heads of garlic. Skins were blowing off like the tail of a comet. At that very moment a huge cloud of white butterflies flew from one side of the road to the other." He gestured toward the painting. "I still haven't quite gotten it right."

"You painted this?"

"I know. Liberals hate it when Philistines make art."

A bay window diverticulated out on the far side of the room. A cushioned window seat followed its contours. A music stand was placed artfully to the side. In the stand was a guitar. Stein's friend Winston Van Goze, because he had perfect pitch and great weed, roadied when he needed bread, and had tuned every high-profile guitar in the music biz. With him, Stein had seen them all, and knew that the axe he was looking at was a Martin D-28 probably worth forty grand. His estimate increased tenfold when he noticed the small photograph of the instrument being played by its original owner during a pre–Ed Sullivan show live performance of "Heart-break Hotel."

"That for real?" Stein said.

"Pretty fucking cool, huh?"

"So let me ask you something. Empty bee boxes?"

"You come to the point, don't you?"

"We're both busy men."

"Ah, but you're my guest."

Henny filled a pair of glasses with a murky-looking liquid he poured from a decanter. He proffered one to Stein.

"What is it?"

"Try it."

Stein brought the glass to his lips and stopped. Henny read his thoughts and smiled. "Shall we switch glasses?"

Stein took the dare and toasted to mutual trust. The taste was unfamiliar. Bitter but rescued by a vein of sweetness.

"Do you like it?

"It's interesting. What is it?"

"Pomegranate mixed with banana. Pomegranate's the next big thing. I promise you."

"Let's talk about the current small thing. Hollister Greenway? The kid's in over his head."

"From what?"

"I don't know. From whatever little Ponzi scheme you've got going here."

Henny drained his glass and licked his lips in appreciation. "You fucking his wife? That little Ruth Ann? I bet she's a screamer."

"What kind of question is that?"

"That's the first time I ever saw a hippie take umbrage. Very interesting visual."

"I'm not fucking her, if it's any of your business."

"Pretty much everything that goes on in this valley is some part of my business. Which is why I'm surprised that a man of your historical stature would make two visits to our little neck of the woods and only be interested in small change like Hollister Greenway."

"You thought enough about him to make him a partner."

"Hell, I just ran into him by chance at the feed store. It could have been anybody."

"And what would you want to be playing for?"

"You called the game. You call the stakes."

"You're giving me too much credit. I'd like to keep Hollister out of trouble. And for my own curiosity find out why the owner of an orchard would buy empty boxes."

"Okay. You shall find no more than you ask. Hollister's been arrested. He's in jail."

"You're shitting me."

"I shit you not."

"I just saw him!"

"Justice moves swiftly."

"Don't tell me he tried to kill that ranger."

"Just about as stupid. He tried to liberate his equipment."

"Well, there's a sweet American irony for you. The guy who steals the stuff goes free. The guy it belongs to goes to jail."

Spector shrugged a "that's the way it goes" gesture that infuriated Stein.

"You're going let him sit in jail?"

"What does it have to do with me? He stole because he was greedy and frustrated and impatient. He got caught because he was stupid." He cut Stein off. "No, whatever you were going to say would be wrong. The sixties are over. People get *what* they deserve, not *because* they deserve."

"This isn't very enlightened of me, but I hope you get what you deserve." With that as an exit line Stein headed for the door.

Henny wouldn't give Stein the pleasure of sulking. He accompanied Stein to the door like he was a losing contestant on a quiz show that Henny was hosting. "I hate see anyone go away unhappy," he said. "Do you have half an hour?"

"I don't really. No." He pressed the usual complement of wrong buttons to open Lila's electronic door lock.

"I thought you might like to get Karma Moonblossom's bees for him."

Stein took a long time turning around to face him. "You have Karma Moonblossom's bees?"

Henny made a gesture with his fingers that formed a triangle with a circle inside it.

"Why didn't you tell me that half an hour ago?"

"There you go. Correcting peoples' behavior. Do you want the bees?"

"Of course I want the bees."

"All right then. Let's go."

Stein reacted suspiciously to the word "go."

"Obviously these were special bees. They had to be housed in a special place." Henny lowered the ramp of his truck, and rolled a winch and a forklift onto it.

"Wait a minute. You're not thinking I'm going to take them. *Nonono*. I don't have a truck. And second of all—second doesn't even matter."

"No truck, no prob." Henny hit a remote that opened a gate, behind which was a gaggle of vehicular equipment. Backhoes, mini-tractors, and right out front, a small U-Haul. He glanced at the rear bumper of Lila's Lexus. "Hook you right up. But hey, no skin if you can't walk the talk. I just need to release them."

Stein emitted a wordless sigh.

"These are really Karma Moonblossom's bees?"

"Like you said. We're both busy men. Call, fold, or raise."

Stein opened the passenger door of Henny's truck. "How far away is this place?"

"Not that far."

***

The road followed a branch of the California Aqueduct, carrying water diverted from rivers hundreds of miles away. A few puffs of frayed cotton clouds reflected off the water's tranquil surface. It was a perfect day to bask in sunshine and not even think about carcinoma. Bounding the road on the left, separated by a well-maintained fence, was an unending expanse of what Stein now recognized to be almond groves. The Family Farms, Inc. "Happy Face" logo was emblazoned under mile after mile of NO TRESPASSING signs.

"This is America's disease," Stein said, offering his terminal diagnosis. "Corporate farming."

"Tragic. Next thing you know prices will come down, production will increase, and people will be able to afford to put food on their table."

"I don't want to eat corporate food."

"There is no such thing as a corporate tree. A tree doesn't know it belongs to Family Farms. It belongs to the sun and the earth and the water. To an outsider, and I used to be one, agriculture is all about politics or economics. To the people who live in it, it's about the smell." He stopped and opened his door. The warm baked scents of grass and clover, almond blossom and rich, loamy earth, insects, and their own skin wafted in. "Take a breath. That's God's abundance. What have you done to be helpful today?"

Henny had not stopped here just for the smell. There was a turn-off to an access road that continued into the orchard on the other side of a reinforced gate. The gate bore a sign enumerating many dire consequences of trespassing. Stein looked askance as Henny undid the chain.

"Are you sure about this?"

"That's where the bees are at."

Deeper into the vastness of the orchard they penetrated. The plethora of unending trees standing at uniform height, uniform distances apart, all awash in blossoms was driving Stein snow blind. Direction became meaningless. He could barely tell where the sun was coming from. They jounced over a rut and Stein's head nearly banged against the roof.

"Easy."

Stein did not feel easy. He had a sense they were being followed. But when he looked back he didn't see anyone behind them.

"We all right?"

"Yeah. Why wouldn't we be?"

"I thought you said it wasn't too far. This seems far."

Henny turned the engine off and let the truck glide to a stop. He pulled up the emergency brake and took the keys from the ignition. "You want out?"

"Easy, man. I'm just a rube from New York. All these trees are freaking me out."

Stein could almost watch his answer filter down through a cross-section of Henny's paranoid/schizo psyche—topsoil, gravel, sand, and silt—until it reached his mood control center where it luckily settled into a good slot. He retracted the keys from his shirt pocket, started the truck and they drove down deeper into the explosion of plenitude. Stein wished he could call Lila again and let her know he'd be late. He looked about the cab of Henny's truck for evidence of a phone but there was none.

"Got to pee?"

"No . . ." Though he did, now that Henny mentioned it, have a lot of pressure in the bladder area.

"That's surprising. Pomegranate's a natural stimulant to the kidneys."

They reached a small wooden trestle that spanned a four-foot-wide irrigation stream. It was a wooden walking bridge and clearly would not carry anything near the weight of the truck, even if it were wide enough to accommodate it. "I'll assume we're here," Stein said with authentic camaraderie. But as he unlatched the door, Henny floored the engine and veered off the road. They jounced down the steep embankment. The front end hit the stream like a moose in rut.

"Hang tight," Henny warned. Stein's forehead bashed into the windshield, sending a flash of constellations whirling past him. "I *told* you to hang on."

"Yeah."

The rear wheels routered a pair of gullies into the soft earth as the truck tried to climb up the other side. It caught traction, mountain-goated up the embankment, bucked itself onto the road, shuddered like a golden retriever coming out of a lake, and settled. Stein was dismayed to see an amount of blood from his forehead.

Henny tossed him a rag from the side pocket. "Ain't no thang but a chicken wing." Henny grinned.

The road, such as it was, came abruptly to the end of itself in a pancreas-shaped cul-de-sac. "This is us," Henny announced.

Stein wondered how the hell they were going to get back. He envisioned their driving in reverse through the long wooded lane.

But with a series of confident back and forth maneuvers, Henny got the truck facing around the right way, plucked the key out and pulled up the brake. He tossed Stein a cloth that had not recently been sterilized and sprang into action. He had the tailgate down and wheeled the forklift down into place. He was surprisingly springy for someone who walked like he had multiple bone fractures. A metal trunk had been installed against the back of the cab. Out if it, Henny grabbed a well-used bee suit and tossed it to Stein.

"Suit up!"

Stein took some pride in not appearing a complete novice. He got into the suit with some aplomb. Henny meanwhile rummaged through the trunk, spilling its contents out in an arc all around him. A few blankets, a Coleman stove, a propane lantern, a sleeping bag. "Hmm." Stein heard him grunt. "Well, that's poor planning." Henny's lips were mashed together as he looked down into the now empty recesses of the storage bin. A series of disaster scenarios hurtled past Stein's inner eye like asteroids: No gas. No water. No brake fluid. A storm coming. Trapped here forever.

"Damn. I thought I had two suits."

"It's your suit. I'll just wait in the cab."

"Not a prob, amigo. I'm a professional." He helped Stein's arms into the sleeves, zippered up the front and Velcroed the face netting in place. He wheeled the forklift toward a narrow lane that broke between adjacent citrus trees and bade Stein follow.

"Is that where the bees are?" Stein asked.

"That's where the bees are."

Henny crumpled a square of burlap into a metal canister and lit it up. A small bellows blew smoke out its spout. It seemed a pitiful defense to Stein, safely in his HAZMAT armor and Henny all exposed. "Are you sure you're okay?" Stein asked.

"We're good!" Henry ducked his head under a protruding branch and shouldered his way forward. Stein followed. As he entered the grove, the thought belatedly occurred: *What the fuck am I doing?*

The spot Henny had chosen for the bees' home was idyllic. Stein had never thought too heavily about what would constitute a desirable environment for bees, but this would have to be up there. They were off by themselves in a little glade. There was sunlight. There were wild flowers. The white rectangular boxes sat stacked in two regular columns that made them look like an altar.

In the shank of the afternoon, with the heat of the day rapidly dissipating, the worker bees were returning. The air was alive with motion. Stein was in their flight path. Many landed on the arms of his suit. On his back. On his face mask. He found himself eye-to-abdomen with the underside of a bee, half an inch from his face. The bee eyed Stein hexagonically. She wiped down her antennae, one then the other, then the first again. Stein felt his heart pounding. His chest was ready to rupture. He couldn't breathe. His legs faltered and he backed away. "I can't do this," he gasped. "I have to wait in the truck."

"Are you sure?"

"I should have told you. I'm horribly allergic."

"I never would have guessed that." Henny escorted him magnanimously back to the little patch of moss where the truck was parked. He helped Stein out of the bee suit and then zipped himself into it. He grabbed a Gatorade out of the cooler, shook it up, and tossed him the bottle. "Drink this, you'll feel better."

Stein took a small sip. Then a longer quaff. It was tangy and sweet. Not sugary but rich and loamy. "This is not Gatorade. What is it?"

"It's mead."

Stein didn't think mead existed since the days of Robin Hood and evil Prince John. It crossed his mind momentarily to question why Henny would need the suit now if he didn't before, but if it was available, why shouldn't he wear it? Leaning back against a tree, Stein poured a little mead over his head and felt it run in sensuous droplets down his forehead and into the well of his ear and down his cheek. Its scent alone was intoxicating. A feeling of well-being washed away his anxiety like an animated TV commercial for pain relief. The word mead had a familiar ring to it. Something medieval. Like flagons of ale. It was made out of something weird, right? What was that? It's possible that he heard the buzzing but just tuned it out, or that he was in such a state of relaxed pleasure his mind did not bother to isolate the sound and give it a name. Oh yeah, it was honey. That's what mead was. Fermented honey! He loved the feeling of relief and harmony when you can't think of something and it suddenly hits you.

The first stinger penetrated the left side of his neck. It felt like he had been Tasered. He rocketed forward. The drink splashed the front of his shirt. The next stinger hit his cheek. He slapped at it. He waved his hands crazily as three, four, a dozen cohorts flew around him. A cluster of them were on his shirt where the drink had spilled. It seemed to be attracting them. He yanked at the shirt to get them off. One flew under and stabbed him in the chest alongside his heart. It was like a shot from a thirty-eight. He had to run. Now there were more. They sounded angry. They dove at him.

He got to his feet, stomping and waving at them. He screamed Henny's name. One flew into his mouth. He felt the back of his throat explode in pain where he was stung on the soft esophageal tissue. The scream choked in his throat. He had inhaled the bee into his windpipe. He coughed and screamed and Heimliched himself. The bee carcass catapulted from his throat. Three more got him around his soft doughnut middle. He had to get to the truck. He ran in a blind panic. Grabbed the driver's side door and pulled. It was locked. A whimper of terror emanated from his swollen throat. They were in his hair, stinging his scalp. Piercing into his brain. He smacked his head again and again to disperse them. He ran to the passenger side. That door, too, was locked. When did that happen? He didn't remember locking it.

He was losing consciousness. The day was darkening. He couldn't put thoughts together. He rolled himself onto the flatbed, crunching bees under his weight as he rolled to the storage bin. Rising to his knees, he managed to lift up the lid and topple inside, pulling the door closed with his last strength. He could not breathe. He could not scream. The last image he saw was a veiled figure standing at the edge of the clearing, shrouded by fecund citrus trees. The canister the figure held sent puffs of smoke wafting up all around him, an emissary who had emerged through a crevasse in the earth from hell.

Chapter Thirteen

Angie was pissed that her father had not returned by dinner time. It was a matter of pride that she would never betray any evidence of missing him. She enjoyed affecting indifference at his absence, to the extent of pretending not to notice that he had been gone. She enjoyed having that power. She had always viewed her growing up from a fixed perspective, as her molting away from her parents, blasting into her own glorious orbit, giving off a brilliant incandescence in whose heat and light they might luckily bask. She had never considered that her father might be subject to any conflicting gravitational pull.

Matthew was gone. His mother had discovered his little charade and had summoned him for a command appearance. So Lila and Angie were alone. Lila's voice got high and flitty, as it often did when she was nervous. She swilled down the last quarter glass of red wine and offered to pour one for Angie.

"My dad might not be too happy with your getting me plastered."

"Oh, I'm guessing this wouldn't be your introduction to red wine," Lila trilled. "Finding your pot stash in the heating vent freaked him out."

"He should talk."

"It's different when you're a parent."

"It gives you the right to be a hypocrite?"

Lila had to laugh. "That's exactly what it does. No, not the right—the necessity."

"So where is he?" Angie finally blurted out.

Not that he had considered the mission he was on dangerous, but he saw his parental role as being an external kidney whose job it was to filter life's troubles away from his child. So he had invested Lila with the task of not giving Angie any reason for alarm, to be vague about his whereabouts and the mission that had summoned him.

Prevarication and mendacity were not among Lila's well-developed assets, and had the opposite effect of provoking further questions and doubts, rather than dispelling them. Angie's succession of responses to Lila's evasions began at slightly annoyed: "I'm sorry, did you just say *you don't know?*" Then moved to argumentative: "I'm not *interrogating* you. I am simply attempting to acquire the information of my father's whereabouts. Information you are inexplicably withholding from me." Then to combative: "Do you expect me to believe you actually don't know where he is?" And over the line, to insulting: "If you don't really know he might not consider you important enough to be told."

The last one drove Lila from the table feeling abandoned by all of those to whom she had given love and shelter. It did not take Angie long to regret the outburst. She knew she needed to make it right, but was unschooled at the technique of apology. The experience of watching her parents' arguments and their aftermath had taught her more about one-upmanship than forgiveness. The admission of being wrong was tantamount to abject surrender.

She called her friend Alyssa for advice on how to unmuddle the situation. Alyssa's parents were not divorced, but the running joke was that they should be. Her father was a violin virtuoso and flagrant womanizer; her mother had a voice that could scrape the varnish off a coffee table. She gave Angie good sage advice on what to say to Lila. But unpracticed as she was, Angie was reluctant to risk it without a buffer/translator present who could shepherd Lila around the chasms of her insecurities and who would shoulder Angie away from her snide, superior sarcasm.

She did not sleep well that night, awakening several times to check her cell phone for a message from her father and finding none. She finally nodded off around five and slept deeply until ten. When she came down to the dining room Lila was not alone. Matt was there and a man in his mid-forties, with white hair and lively blue eyes. His suit jacket was off but his tie and dress shirt were crisp.

"Hi," Matt said.

"Hi back at you. I didn't mean to interrupt."

The visitor bore the confident smile of a man used to holding the high card in the hole.

Fearing he was there with bad tidings, Angie blurted out, "Are you with the police?"

"This is my make-believe uncle, Richard," Matt said. "He and my father were best friends."

"This is Angie Stein," said Lila.

Angie was afraid to look at her.

"Ah, the famous Angie Stein," said Richard. He had a resonant voice, a winter tan, and a cordial handshake.

Matt placed his arm around Angie's shoulders to include her in the group. "Uncle Richard just came in from Hawaii. Have you ever been to the north side at Waimeia? The surf is amazing."

"My dad took us sewer surfing in New York sometimes."

Richard was the only one who immediately got her sense of humor. He bent into the pose you'd take in the enclosed space. "Of course you'd have to slalom around the rats and the garbage."

She scrutinized for telltale whispers of body language between Richard and Lila. Matt's demeanor had elevated at Angie's arrival. "You guys don't really need me, right? There's something downtown I really want Angie to see. Would that be okay?"

"Do I not remember correctly that you and I had plans, Matthew?" The severity of his uncle's response surprised Angie. She could see it surprised Matthew too.

"I'm not into all that business stuff."

"It's the *business stuff* that keeps you well provided," Richard reminded him.

"I know."

"Learn to be respectful, Matt."

"He likes to be called Matthew now," Lila couldn't help informing him.

"Matthew," Richard corrected, without taking his eyes from the boy. They did not bore into him, though it was easy to imagine that they could have if turned up a notch. They didn't have to. Matthew knew what his duty was and rose to it.

"Sorry," he said, and with a nod to Angie indicated this took precedence over their plans.

"Okay," Richard said, and gave his nephew an affectionate headlock.

It touched Angie to witness a sincere apology made and accepted. No one abashed. No one victorious. Matt asked if Angie could join them.

"I don't think that's a good idea," said Richard with a serious straight face and just a tiny wink to Angie. "I'll see you in three months. Give my regards to your mother. Now you two go have a good time. But first—" His voice was like a burlesque hook that whirled Matthew around. "Clean up that patio. I don't want to see cans of turpentine, and tools and whatnot strewn around. This is somebody's home, not a museum."

Matthew obediently set to the task. Angie lingered a moment and asked Lila if there was any word from her dad, trying to make the question encompass an apology. Lila jumped at the chance to accept. "You know how hopeless your dad is with technology. You have your cell with you. As soon as I hear from him I'll call you. And you do the same."

Angie was uncharacteristically quiet as she and Matthew gathered up the bones from the patio. The skull was placed in a box and all stowed in the trunk of Matthew's car. He opened the passenger door for her. She allowed it.

"What's the deal with Lila and your uncle Richard?"

"He's a trustee for my father's estate. He handles her finances."

"Mmm hmmm."

"What does *mmm hmmm* mean?"

"Gay men don't see hetero sparks."

"If you can be nice for five seconds I have something I think you'll really want to see." When he got in she was sitting with her hands in her lap and finishing the five count.

"I meant five seconds in my presence."

"You really are testing my limits."

He reached around behind to the backseat, where from amid some diving paraphernalia and an old school surfboard, he pulled up a manila file folder. He handed her a faded, vintage newspaper clipping containing a black and white photo of a pretty young girl in a sequined one-piece bathing suit, twirling twin batons.

She handed it back to him with attitude. "What? You want me to dress like that?"

"Read the caption." He pushed the clipping back at her.

"*Local Lass Lucy Lester Twirls Twin Batons.* Nice alliteration."

"Has anybody ever mentioned that it's hard to be nice to you?"

Angie was struck by how sincerely he meant that. He handed her a second clipping from the folder. In this photo, the same girl was twirling fiery batons standing on the back of an elephant.

Gone was all her disinterest. "Matt! She's riding a circus elephant. Did you see that?"

"Gee, no, I probably gave you that picture just by chance."

She squooshed his cheeks. "Sarcasm doesn't work on your pretty surfer face."

"You might be interested in reading this wedding announcement." He handed her the final document from the folder and watched her mouth drop as she read the notice for the nuptials of Lucy Lester, circus performer, dancer, avant-gardist, to Jesse James Bancroft, oil speculator, financial speculator, real estate speculator.

"Did you notice the date of the wedding?"

"Oh, my God. Matthew! A week after the land deal. How did you get this?"

"And one more." This is the one that staggered her. A tall, dashing Spaniard with the aura of a poetic matador held a beautiful young circus performer aloft in his arms. The caption read: ELEPHANT GIRL AND BARCELONIAN MATADOR TO WED. Angie was in a state of religious ecstasy. "I knew that they were lovers! How did you get this!"

"Friends of my dad are big wheels at the paper."

"You didn't tell me."

"You never ask me anything."

"Of course I do."

"No . . . you have this way of being that anything you don't know is probably not worth knowing."

"You expect me to ask if any of your dad's old friends are big wheels at the *LA Times* who can get pictures of Lucy Lester's wedding?"

"Okay, that was a little specific. But how about, 'Hey Matt, I could use your help'?"

"Okay," she said quietly.

He started the car.

"May I ask where I'm being abducted to?"

He swatted her gently in the nose with a folded copy of the *LA Times*. The article he had circled in Magic Marker was about a ceremony today for the groundbreaking of the new Bancroft Performance Arts Center, hosted by Lucy Bancroft. Angie was not as impressed. "So their granddaughter is dedicating an arts center," she said. "How does that help us solve a murder?"

"Okay, that tone of voice you just used? That's the one I'm talking about."

***

From their vantage point amid the lunchtime crowd at Pershing Square, Angie and Matthew shielded their eyes to get a good view across the plaza to the elevated podium. Yet another politician from an endless array of self-congratulatory speakers praised the bounteous philanthropy of the Bancroft Foundation for its latest contribution to the cultural life of the city. The Bancroft Performance Arts Center was lauded as a multimillion-dollar performance complex replete with two concert halls, museums of art and photography, dance rehearsal studios, and subsidized housing for six hundred young artists.

Angie had passed her point of tolerance six speeches ago. She had figured out the whole sordid mess on the way down: J. J. Bancroft bought a piece of land from Sunny Cataluna, drilled for oil, didn't find any; so he forged a new land deed that took all Sunny's property and killed the man to cover up his thievery. Now she chafed at the hypocrisy that thieves were being celebrated as benefactors because they gave back a few crumbs from the whole loaf they had stolen.

Matt had to laugh at her. "You know who you sound exactly like?"

"Don't even say it."

"But you do. Exactly."

She pointed a menacing finger at him. "Not even in jest!"

He said her father's name anyway.

This mayor's voice was as bland and uninflected as his face. He fawned over the Bancroft Foundation's previous municipal benefactions: The Bancroft Public Library, The Lucy Bancroft Children's Hospital, The Eye and Ear Center. To make the final introduction to Lucy Bancroft, he called to the podium the Abused Children and Orphans Chorale to do their a cappella rendition of "You Are the Wind Beneath My Wings." Given its potentially nauseating sentimentality, the piece was done with some hustle and grit, and got a big ovation. Buoyed by the response, His Honor attempted to ad lib, and described the orphans and battered children as Lucy's favorite charity.

Before he could get the next five words out, Lucy Bancroft herself strode out onto the podium. Until that moment, Angie and Matt were probably the only two people in the crowd who had presumed that the advertised and lauded Lucy Bancroft was the granddaughter of J. J, rather than who she was, the baton-twirling, elephant riding Lucy Lester herself, now aged ninety-three, not the daughter or probably granddaughter of J. J. Bancroft, but his wife of seventy-five years. She was a jolt of heat lightning, all four feet eleven of her, wearing a black dress and two-inch heels, somewhat stiffened by age and weather, but the fire was still there. She came up to the mayor's sternum. "Not a *charity*," she scolded. "Charity is one-sided. I get more from them than they do from me."

"Favorite *cause*, then," he quickly backtracked.

"These children aren't a *cause*, they're *children*. My husband and I could not have our own. So we have taken on all the children."

By now the mayor just wanted to get off stage with one of his testicles still attached. "So, these children, then, are your favorite . . ." He waited desperately for her to supply the right word.

"Human beings."

"Let's hear it for Lucy Bancroft's favorite human beings!"

"Oh, hush," she said, making only the barest attempt to play if off as a jest. She held on to the railing, but not for support. To Angie's eyes, she was supplying support. Tightening welds. Compacting mass. Electricity crackled through her extended arms. Her white hair flowed out behind her. It hadn't yielded up all of its young girl's wildness. She was Eva Peron played by Helen Hayes. There was no one in the crowd whose life she had not touched, and in touching, improved.

Her voice carried undiminished to the back of the throng. "My dear departed friend Diane Arbus loved to photograph freaks because she said they had already suffered their life's trauma and had nothing to hide. My children stand with their scars bared. The world has said to them, 'Look how I can hurt you.' They have stuck out their chins and said, 'See how we have survived.'"

Lucy smiled down at the people in the crowd as if they were all close friends. "Valentine's Day is the Commodore's and my seventy-fifth wedding anniversary."

"Jesus," Angie marveled. "Doesn't anyone die in this town?" She realized an instant later to whom she had said this, and threw her hands up at what an idiot she was.

Lucy indicated the Rolls-Royce touring car that was idling alongside the podium. "A friend of ours is making a little party for us tomorrow night and we're going to be up dancing all night. The Commodore is resting up. After all, he's three months older than I am."

Someone yelled out of the crowd, "Save a slow dance for me, Lucy!"

She bantered back, "Your heart couldn't stand it."

After the roar of laughter, she left them with heartfelt senti-ments. "My husband and I have seen a century of change in Los Angeles, from a sleepy little pueblo to the center of the universe. All art, all culture, all social phenomena start here, flow east and cover the nation. Los Angeles has become the repository of the soul of America. A generation from today, this place where we are now standing will be a mere suburb to the Los Angeles of the future. As someone from my era used to say, 'You ain't seen nuthin' yet.'"

Angie yanked on Matt's arm. "We've got to get down to her and ask if she knew Sunny Cataluna." She eeled her way through the crowd toward the podium. Matt did his best to follow her, apologizing to people he bumped, while Angie seemed oblivious to any obstacles, flowing around them like water. Rock star applause erupted as Lucy descended the platform, eschewing the mayor's offer of a supporting arm. Angie's timing could not have been more perfect, her horizontal axis intersecting precisely with Lucy's vertical. They met at the bottom of the platform.

"Hello, child. What can I do for you?"

Angie was tongue-tied at suddenly being inches from her newfound idol.

Lucy's staff were gently herding her to the car. She was drawn to the intense look of longing in Angie's eyes. "Was there something else?"

Matthew came up right behind Angie. "Ask her!" he prodded.

"How do people find the love of their life and stay married forever?"

"Not that!"

In the last moment before Lucy was ensconced beside her husband, Matthew pushed himself up to the car window and asked in a clear, strong voice, "Mrs. Bancroft, does the name Ascunsion Cataluna mean anything to you?"

A new voice entered the scene. It sounded like oil scalding raw flesh and came from the thin-lipped, praying-mantis-bodied man who leaned forward in the backseat. He was in naval officer's uniform from the Teddy Roosevelt era, white with epaulets and decorations, topped with an admiral's hat.

"Find out who that boy is," the Commodore ordered an unseen obedient. He rapped the ornate handle of his cane against the window. "Lucy," he beckoned.

Angie barely noticed him. Her eyes had sprouted rhizomes into the bared soul of Lucy Bancroft, whose lips formed the shape of the word she had not spoken in seventy-five years.

"Sunny."

***

In the immediate wake of the Commodore's directive to "find out who that boy is," a quick crackling consultation over walkie-talkies among the Commodore's security people revealed no threatening act had been witnessed by any of them that would warrant hot pursuit. Recent unfortunate events were no doubt a factor, where charges of excessive force had arisen out of their overzealous efforts at crowd control. Ms. Lucy's propensity for changing the lives of random street urchins was well known to them, and the consensus was that this was another of those instances. Accordingly, the order was assigned a Priority Level 2 (*Pay some attention to it, but don't go out of your way*). Not quite as trivial as a Level 1 (*Don't interrupt your gin game*) but miles away from a serious Level 5 (*Succeed at all costs*).

The young man had bolted from the scene, not to avoid pursuit, but because he himself was in pursuit of the fleeing young girl who had until moments before been under the thrall of Lucy Bancroft. The agents took a few desultory shots with long lenses of the boy fading more deeply into the crowd until he became indistinguishable, and then lost sight and interest in him.

Had the search been in earnest, the couple would have been found in Matt's Mercedes at the exit of the underground parking lot, where Angie was in a state of creative ecstasy, her mind churning oily smoke like an outboard motor.

"Did you see her face? She was in love with him! I was completely wrong about everything. Bancroft didn't kill Sunny for land, he killed him for Lucy. I bet he was a poet. He read Garcia Lorca to her and played 'La Malagueña' on the guitar."

"Which way do you want me to turn?" Matt interjected. "Cars behind us are getting horny."

"Horny?"

"Honky."

"The Commodore? What kind of uniform was that? Spanish American War? He saw her in the circus, saw her twirling her baton under the lights, flames twirling all around her, colored lights flashing off her costume. He had to have her. He challenged Sunny to a duel."

"Please. Right or left?"

"Sunny was a lover, not a fighter. Their duel was a metaphor of the twentieth century. Effete, chivalrous old Europe, against Gold Rush America, anything goes, win at all costs. Bancroft fought dirty and killed him. I know that's how it happened!"

"Okay, I'm turning left." He did, taking them west, away from downtown.

Her chin dropped to her chest, her eyes closed, her teeth clenched. She drummed the dashboard, then the inside of her thighs. She dug her thumbs into her cheekbones, encircled her forehead with her bridged fingers, until the idea came.

"Okay, here's what we do."

She twisted her body around and reached over the seatback to retrieve the skull that was ensconced in a shoebox on the back seat where it had been placed that morning in obedient submission to Richard's directive. Angie had been a little irked about his assumed territoriality at the time, but now she was pleased to have the object with them.

"You know those people who make dioramas at the Natural History Museum? They make the faces of those prehistoric people seem so completely real. We bring them our skull. We have them put a face to it. The face of Sunny Cataluna. We bring it to the Bancrofts' anniversary party. We shove the thing into the Commodore's face. If he flinches we know he killed him."

"If he *flinches*? You shove a decapitated head in front of him, he'll have a heart attack."

"Which will absolutely prove that we're right. That he stole that land and that became the basis for his entire financial empire. We can bring down the whole corrupt system. Punish the wicked. Redistribute the wealth. Why are you smiling at me like I'm an idiot child? I'm asking for your help. Are any of your father's old friends forensic paleontologists?"

"No," Matt said.

"Do *you* know of any such people?"

"No," Matt said.

"Do you know where their anniversary party is?"

"No."

She slumped back into a concave parenthesis of defeat that she maintained for the next several right and left turns.

Matt drove decisively, impervious to her mood, a response to which she was unaccustomed. She glanced out her window and saw a neighborhood that was unknown to her—old, quasi-industrial/residential.

"Where are we?"

"You said you wanted to see a forensic paleontologist."

"You said you didn't know any."

"I said I didn't know any *yet.*"

***

The interior of the Natural History Museum was old and musty and exciting. The dioramas had always been Angie's favorite. She would become absorbed into the depictions of domestic life, imagining herself living in that world, thinking how she would cope, how people would see her, the simple things she could show them (with her knowledge of the future) would make them smack their heads and call her a goddess.

Matthew carried the shoebox tucked under his arm like a football. He nodded toward a door indented into an adjacent hallway. Its signage read AUTHORIZED PERSONNEL ONLY.

"Your plan is to get us arrested?"

Matt circled his palm over her head. "I hereby authorize you. You are now authorized personnel. And in that capacity you are hereby empowered to authorize me."

Duly authorized, they opened the door and slipped inside. It was like being backstage at a scene shop. There were partially staged dioramas, with models that were discarded or were in progress, painted in the surreal pigments that that didn't exist anywhere in Nature. The walls were lined with shelves of sculpted human faces. No two looked alike. Adults and children, elders and newborns. Generations of families who had never lived, fashioned from an artist's imagination. Their expressions were alive, ready to be placed into situations that engendered those responses of fear, contentment, love.

The working artist's back was bent over her workbench at the far end of the room. She did not look up from her labors. "Can I help you?" She did not make the word "help" sound like an intrusion but a pleasant possibility.

"Did you make these?" Angie asked.

"The boys sometimes throw a Picasso in the midst of everything just to mess with me. Do you see any Picassos?"

"I don't think so."

"Then they're all mine." When she swiveled around to face them, they saw that she was blind. She did not wear dark glasses. Her eyes looked like broken eggshells. She was pretty. Probably in her mid-thirties. Slender. Short dark hair. She wore a lab coat over a long-sleeved striped pullover. Her nametag read DR. MARGARET DITTEMORE. In letters and in Braille.

"I never thought of blind people smiling," Angie said.

"I never thought of sighted people blurting out every random thought that came into their heads."

"It's okay. We're authorized," said Matt.

"Yes, I thought there were two of you."

Matt strode boldly toward her. "We need you to put a face on this."

He placed the skull into her hands. They were like no hands Angie or Matt had ever seen, appendages of a species whose brain and central nervous system had migrated into their fingers. The hands engulfed the skull, touching every molecule of its surface.

"Aquiline nose. Long aristocratic neck. Poetic chin. Probably Spanish aristocracy."

Angie was practically trembling.

"You can tell all that already?" Matt asked.

"My fingers have eyes."

"Could you make the face for us by tomorrow night?"

"Tomorrow night? How about in three weeks?"

"It's an anniversary gift for Lucy Bancroft," said Matt in that quiet voice of his that always managed to penetrate without opposition. His utterance of the Bancroft name changed everything. Dr. Dittemore embraced the skull once again. The Bancrofts had essentially built this lab for her, she said, with the funding they provided the museum. There was nothing she wouldn't do for them. She rolled her chair across the room and placed the skull on a pedestal.

"Are you going to their party?" she asked them as the skull was rotated and digitally photographed from three hundred and sixty angles.

"That's the plan," said Matt, careful not to lie.

"Have you been to the Family Farms Ranch before?"

"You mean . . . where the party is?"

"I heard Barry Brickman's parties are to die for."

The computer beeped, signaling that all the images had been processed. Margaret's attention left the kids and went fully to the apparatus. They watched the images become digested, amalgamated, and projected onto a computer screen. It assumed layers, features, and before their astonished eyes, took on a lifelike face.

"Of course a ten-terabyte database, CGI, and DNA recognition programs help," Dittemore said, "but the human soul can only be seen by another human soul."

Her fingers seemed to grasp and penetrate the screen, to move into the contours of the face, pressure here, elongation there. The subtlest of gestures created an astonishing effect, giving life to this lifelike face. History. Backstory in the eyes, not merely a momentary expression.

"Oh, my God." Angie was about to faint. "He's gorgeous."

"Is that really what he looks like?" Matt asked.

"You're asking the wrong girl," said Margaret.

***

Night had fallen as they drove back to Lila's. Angie checked her cell for messages and snapped it shut. Nothing from her father. Nothing from Lila. The plan was to come back to the museum in the morning for the finished product. They had successfully gleaned that the party would be held at the estate of one of the Bancrofts' fabulously wealthy friends, a fellow philanthropist and captain of industry who, like the Bancrofts, had endowed hospitals and culture centers to the tune of hundreds of millions of dollars.

"You tired?" Matt asked. "I could go over to Pico and bring some food back."

"You were cool back there."

"Yeah . . . blind chicks dig me."

She leaned over and kissed him somewhere around the ear and cheek. He hadn't been to the ocean in days but his skin had absorbed the scent of sea and salt and suntan oil. "You're not gay, are you?" she said.

"I'm going to get the food. We'll talk about this when I get back."

She said okay and went into the house. The lights downstairs were off. A light was on upstairs. There were sounds from the second floor. Gigantic relief that he was back mixed with anger that no one had bothered to call to tell her.

"Dad?" She called tentatively. There was no reply. She started up the staircase. She was at the first curve when the second-floor bathroom door opened. She had a perfect vantage point from below. Lila's tanned and toned body, her hair wet and lustrous, completely naked, padded out of the bathroom. Angie averted her eyes. She did not want to see her father naked. Immediately behind Lila, flicking her naked butt with a towel was not Stein, but Matthew's Uncle Richard.

Angie gasped and bolted from the house unseen, her gagging and choked tears unheard.

Chapter Fourteen

The afterlife was not at all what Stein had expected. He had never believed in the afterlife, so any version of it would have surprised him. But this was disappointing. It confirmed what Shmooie the Buddhist had always said: that whatever you think will happen next, it will always be something else. There were clouds. He could tell that. And he was suspended among them. He could tell that too. He was surprised to realize he still called them clouds, the word by which his mortal brain had been taught to define them. If he had any vision of reincarnation at all, it featured a cosmic car wash where high-pressure hoses scrubbed clean the crevasses of memory, washing out every chunk and gristle of experience from the psyche before it was reinserted into a new body. He should not remember clouds. Or Shmooie the Buddhist. His first response was panic, like when the anesthesia wears off while you're still on the operating table and your body wants to cry out to the doctors, *Put me back under*, but nightmarishly you have no power of speech.

Unless.

Geniuses were people whose reincarnated souls inadvertently retained some past-life knowledge the steam cleaning had missed. He thought it might be a nice change this next time around to have a head start instead of constantly playing catch-up. That glee was quickly tempered by anxiety that having an advantage might create complacency and make him vote Republican. But that might be fun too, he thought, seeing how the other half lived. To wear pressed shirts and have a cute, dutiful wife and obedient children named Ashley and Skipper.

His field of vision was narrow. Acuity wavered from unfocused to blurrier. He attempted to reorient himself but had the sensation of being tethered. This puzzled him. If he no longer had a body, how could he be constrained? That he had retained possession of the power of thought no longer surprised him. But he sensed no dazzling new clarity nor perspective. His mind felt no less limited, no less confined than his body did. And damn it! He felt *pain*.

The sole unifying premise consistent with every version of the afterlife he had ever heard was the cessation of physical pain. How could *nobody* have gotten it right except the Evangelicals, who had predicted a horrific eternal life for nonbelievers like him? He was consumed by a wave of dread where he envisioned an eternity in which every single thing he ever believed was wrong. Where greed was rewarded, ignorance celebrated, generosity exploited, idealism shunned. Wait a minute—that was the world he had just come from.

He heard a voice from a great distance announcing his arrival most likely at a way station where he assumed he was to be processed. "He's here," were the word-like sounds. It gave Stein some reassurance to understand that he was so specifically expected, his name did not have to be mentioned. He knew he was powerless to alter or avert whatever was meant to happen next. Struggle would be futile. What would be the point of trying to rush through eternity? There would always be more of it. It felt sweet to surrender his will. He had to just let it be. That three-word phrase resonated through some hidden recess of memory and took on melody. Oh no, he groaned. *Paul* was the enlightened one? Not John? "Let It Be," yes? "Imagine," no?

What was the joke here? That the afterlife was the same as your regular life but without the friends and gadgets? He had a vision of his gravesite, of Lila watching his coffin being lowered into the earth. He felt her loss at the pit of his stomach. What would it do to her, losing yet another love of her life? Then he thought of Angie.

He dared not imagine the expression on her face, her unbearable pain of loss. Or worse. The sad, knowing shake of her head, signaling that if there was a way to fuck up, her father would find it.

Whoever had been alerted to Stein's imminent arrival now loomed into his field of vision. The features that in life had been called a face looked down at him from a pedestal of what used to be called a body, adorned in what in life had been called clothing. This had to be some sort of transitional place, he rationalized, the same idea behind divers not coming up too fast lest they get the bends or rapture of the deep.

But this particular face and body—slight build; buck teeth; furtive, darting brown eyes; olive skin—belonged to a person Stein had known in high school and had not thought of once in thirty years. Except that he had the crazy déjà vu feeling that he had just seen him. How weird that he of all people would be Stein's welcomer?

"Barry Brickman?" Stein blurted out the words, as if he still had the physical mechanism with which to make utterance.

"Harry Stein," the face answered. "Isn't *this* ironic?"

There's irony in the afterlife, Stein mused. Okay, that was good news.

Over the next several minutes, Stein's operating system came back online in stages, revealing to him that:

A) This was not the afterlife.

B) He was not dead.

C) He was in a helicopter.

D) The tethers he felt attached to his body were intravenous lines feeding him glucose, anti-inflammatories, antibiotics, and saline.

E) He had been found in a remote corner of the Family Farm Ranch; a 911 call had been made by an anonymous guardian angel. He had been airlifted to the ER where a significant volume of apian venom had been extracted from his blood. His system had remarkable resistance, because the dosage could have been lethal, but he had only suffered minimal damage.

And finally, F) that this talking hologram hallucination of Barry Brickman was neither hollow nor hallow, but the actual corporeal, substantive, self-same Barry Brickman he had known in West Fremont High School. Barry Brickman who had been a sycophant, who desperately tried to compete with Stein for laughs, but who was just not funny. The same Barry Brickman who, Stein now learned, owned the helicopter in which they were flying—and the hundred-thousand-plus acres of flourishing almond, pistachio, and citrus groves over which they had been flying, and the helipad upon which they now alighted, nestled like an aerie atop his sixty-seven-room replica of Xanadu.

The lawn was the size of Yankee Stadium. Three concentric circles of exotic flowering plants orbited around a magnificent fountain. A marble statue of Napoleon on horseback commanded one end, facing a life-sized bronze replica of Sylvester Stallone as Rocky on the other. The helipad retracted down through a glass-enclosed elevator and deposited the helicopter gently onto a manicured lawn. A scrum of attendants materialized as the flaps of the aircraft opened. They assisted their employer, who in turn offered a helping hand to Stein. The combination of drugs and a diuretic flushing of Lasix had purged his body of the apian venom and its deleterious effects. He felt his body strength returning.

"What is this place?" asked Stein.

Brickman lowered his eyes, affecting a level of false humility previously only attained by Barbra Streisand. "Welcome to my home," he said. Horses were being unloaded from vans and led past them by hot walkers from Hooters. Blinders and ornamental hoods resembling medieval heraldry were being fitted to them. "I'm throwing a little anniversary party for a few friends," Brickman explained.

Through the fog, Stein was beginning to understand that Brickman had saved his life. "Listen. Barry. Thanks, man."

"It was my pleasure . . . to see you disabled," Brickman quipped. He had the same high-pitched laugh at his own jokes that he did in high school. "But now that we're talking honestly, may I ask why you were trespassing on my land?"

Stein agreed that it was a pertinent question but unfortunately the fog surrounding the answer had not yet cleared.

"It'll come," Brickman assured him and conducted Stein inside through a dining room that looked like the Hall of Hrothgar. In its center was a massive oak table at which boar and flagons of ale might be served to boisterous knights. The décor of the adjacent alcove resembled a 1950s ice cream parlor. Brickman went on like a tour guide; they sat on a banquette around a Formica table. "Remember Rumplemyers? When they went out of business, I bought all their booths. At least I *think* it was after they went out of business." *Laugh laugh*. A waitress in a ruffled pink skirt and a round-necked blouse asked if they'd like a menu or if they knew what they wanted. Brickman gave her a sexy wink and said she knew what he wanted. She laughed and squeezed his arm.

"And you, sir?" she said to Stein.

Stein's memory processor was churning. Missing memory pieces floated down through the snow globe landscape of his mind. They settled into the empty spaces and completed the picture. Stein's last retained image reappeared on his retina: a figure dressed as a spaceman standing stoically at the edge of the glade, smoke rising around his veiled visor, watching the disaster unfold like a vengeful God.

"Henny Spector," Stein croaked.

The girl checked the menu for the name of a sundae she might have missed.

Stein wrapped his face in his hands and watched the scene of his near death play out inside his lids. "Arrest Henny Spector," he said.

Brickman laughed. "That's very funny. You haven't lost your touch."

"I'm serious. Do you know who Henny Spector is?"

"I know *what* he is," said Brickman. "What he is, is dead."

"Henny Spector is *dead*? Is that what you're saying? How is he dead? When?"

A new voice interjected from an adjacent room. "I'm disappointed you didn't ask *who did it*?" The source of that voice, the formidable Captain Anthony Caravaggio, filled the door frame.

"What in the hell is going on here?" Stein asked anyone who would answer. And specifically to Caravaggio, "Why do you care if I asked 'who'?"

"Because 'who' would have told me you knew he was murdered."

"Henny Spector was murdered?"

"You can ease off the amazement," Brickman said. "He believes you." He sounded a little disappointed.

"Did the bees get him?" he asked.

"A spike through the back of the head," said Caravaggio.

"You told me it was a knitting needle," Brickman charged.

"I said it was *like* a knitting needle. A long, thin steel cylinder with a sharp point at one end. Came out right through his eyeball."

"Jesus. Somebody really didn't like him."

"That narrows it down to pretty much everybody," Caravaggio said, just the way a cop would say it.

"Right through the mask?" Stein asked.

Caravaggio gave Stein a long, penetrating stare. "What mask are you talking about?"

"The mask. The head thing." He made a haphazard gesture that was meant to convey what he meant. "He was wearing a bee suit."

Brickman looked darkly at Caravaggio. "You told me he died stark naked."

"He did die stark naked. Anyway that was the way we found him."

"He was wearing a bee suit last time I saw him."

"Maybe you better tell us what the hell you were doing there with him." Caravaggio's order opened a portal through which another meteorite of memory splattered itself over the surface of Stein's brain. His family.

"Barry. I've got to use your phone."

Caravaggio left to check out Stein's story at the morgue. Brickman led Stein to a phone.

***

Mercedes answered, and when she heard Stein's voice, called out, "Miss Leela!"

Lila stood there paralyzed.

The previous night after seeing Lila and Richard, Angie had bolted blindly out of the house. When Matthew returned with sandwiches he found Angie kneeling on the front yard dry heaving. He ran to her. Embraced her shoulders. "What is it? What happened?"

She shuddered his arms off her in a violent spasm.

"Angie, what is it?"

"Let's just say your Aunt Lila and your Uncle Richard are more than kissing cousins."

She expected an explosion of outrage and disgust from Matthew. But his response was low key and thoughtful, resigned and almost nostalgic. It was kind of an open secret that the two of them got together when Richard came to the mainland, maybe once or twice a year. It was no big deal, he said. It had been going on for years. Completely misreading her smile, he thought that his explanation had made it all right.

"I'm really glad we've had this conversation," Angie said. "It shows me that your entire family is fucked. Them for doing it and you for thinking it's no big deal. I never want to have anything to do with any of you." She rooted through her pockets and found the car key she was looking for, pushed his confused and imploring arms aside and strode toward the Camry parked at the curb.

"Angie, what are you doing?"

"I'm going to drive up to where my father is and tell him what a bitch cunt he has for an ex-girlfriend."

"It's the middle of the night. You're in a crazed state."

"Get your brain-diseased hands off me." She backed against the cold dark contours of her father's car.

"Where are you going to drive? You don't know where he is."

"He's at that stupid place he kept talking about. Las Something or other. It's not your problem."

"Look . . . just stay here tonight. Go in the morning, okay?"

"I'm not going back in that house. Ever."

"You can stay at my mother's."

It confused her that Matt could be so completely fucked on one hand and yet care about her. She would not give him the relief of telling him she had already decided she would call her friend Alyssa and stay there.

She got into Stein's Camry and started it up. "Do not follow me," she ordained. "Even if you think it is to protect me."

He nodded a sincere okay. Which she appreciated. "I'll go back to the museum in the morning and pick up the head . . . if you're still into it."

She had forgotten all about Sunny Cataluna's head.

"I could call you when I get it and you can tell me where you are."

"Why are you pretending to be so nice?" She started to drive away. He called her name urgently. She stopped and cranked her window down halfway. He gave her the sandwiches he had bought.

She gave him a grudging smile. It was enough.

Alyssa wasn't home. Angie parked in the driveway and fell asleep until Alyssa got home at around four A.M. from the release party of the new video by Gym Creaux. She seemed remarkably awake and coherent and unwasted after the night of indulgence and revelry she described. "I have a vulture's immune system. We eat road kill and don't catch disease."

Angie needed to borrow some money and a couple of good outfits. Alyssa fished a few twenties from her purse; some change and gum wrappers and an ossified half-eaten ham sandwich; a can of Mace, empty; and keys to someone's apartment, she didn't know whose. She didn't give a shit about getting the money back, but promised Angie bodily harm if she lost her Chanel jacket or her Louboutins.

***

Matthew was upset by his blowup with Angie. He took a long drive, not to follow Angie but to clear his head. He realized that his cavalier acceptance of Lila's ongoing affair with Richard was not exactly how he felt. On the one hand, yeah, it was their business what they did. But still . . .

He did not return until he was sure Richard had gone back to his hotel. Then he did something he'd never done before. He knocked on Lila's bedroom door and asked if he could talk to her. She was not in bed but on it, engulfed in many pillows, a thin robe over her waxed legs, her glasses down on her nose, with two novels open in her lap.

He said it was he who had come in earlier and seen Richard coming out of her room. She closed both her books.

"How long have you known?"

"I don't know. It always just seemed like there were different rules for him."

"That's probably how I think of it too."

"It's probably not how everybody would think about it, though. It wasn't me who came in before. It was Angie."

"Oh, God." Lila pulled the robe tight around her chest. Her eyes went wild. She could barely look at him. "You probably think I'm a horrible person."

"No."

Lila reached out to have him linger a moment. She took a long deep breath and hugged her knees. She knew it wasn't exactly right to use the boy as a confidant, but there he was, and she had drunk one more glass of red wine than usual. "If it were going anyplace permanent with Angie's dad, I'd end it with Richard. But he's not going to marry me. He hasn't given up his bachelor apartment. He's been paying rent on it the whole time he's been living here. He doesn't know I know. I'm sure Angie doesn't know about it."

Her nose was snuffling. Matthew handed her a tissue from the night table.

"Has she told her dad?"

"She's driving up there to find him in the morning."

Her chin dropped to her chest. Matthew hadn't seen her cry since his father died.

***

So when the phone rang that morning and Mercedes told Miss Leela that it was Meestir Estine, relief triumphed over other feelings but only by a narrow margin and only briefly. Lila was standing five feet away from her and waved her hands *No*. "Ask him where he is," she mouthed. And she jabbed her finger toward the speaker button on the phone. Mercedes pressed it so Lila could hear Stein's reply. His voice sounded haggard. He said he was at a place called Family Farms and that things had gotten a little bit strange.

Lila grabbed the phone away from Mercedes. "And that's why you don't call for two days?" All her grief and worry rendered down into rage.

"I was unconscious."

"Stop lying to me."

"I know it sounds crazy. Is Angie there?"

"You haven't spoken to her yet?"

"No."

"You will. I can promise you that."

"Lila, what the hell is going on?"

"Call after you talk to Angie. Her number is programmed into my phone."

"I'm not calling from your car."

A fishing line with a barbed hook tugged at a snagged memory. Her car. Her car. He had left it at Henny Spector's.

Stein got off the phone and found Brickman outside supervising beehives of activity. Work crews were setting up for the big party. Long buffet tables were being dressed with expensive china. A movie screen was being bolted into place on a large stage behind which dozens of music stands were being set. He grasped Barry's shoulders and said, "I need you to do something for me."

"In addition to saving your life?"

"Now *that* was funny!"

***

Both of Brickman's six-car garages were accessible from the central circular hub that he called the cyclotron. Stein and Brickman took a steel and glass capsule down one level and headed into a garage that looked more like a showroom. Six brightly shining classic sports cars sat at the ready. Brickman selected the tan '64 XKE 3.8 Roadster. The interior was plush, perfectly restored. The sound of the engine starting in the confined space was volcanic. Hydraulics spun the car around to face the garage door. Brickman pushed the manual shift into first and wound up the rpms. The door was still closed. Stein grasped the passenger side handhold and caught his breath. They were abruptly whooshed up, straight through the retracted roof. Barry released the clutch before the door sprang open. They hit the pavement going sixty. Stein's gasp of relief sounded embarrassingly like an orgasm.

The car's legroom was amazing. Stein could stretch to his full length. Brickman had decked himself out in a jaunty sports car driver's cap and a pair of tan kid gloves. All he needed was a scarf to be the Great Waldo Pepper. Still, he looked like a kid sneaking his father's car out for a joyride.

"You seem to know where Henny lives?" Stein noticed.

Brickman shrugged. "Lived."

"Do you work with him?"

"My subsidiary companies may have used him. I don't get involved on the micro level."

"What about this pollination season? Right now."

"Who knows?"

"All this land and you don't know?"

Brickman turned up his smooth, open palms. "Do I look like I get my hands dirty?"

Both sides of the road were flanked by his orchards: mile after mile of barbed-wire fence, posed with warnings to would-be trespassers and illegal pickers.

"This is all you?"

"I'm the largest producer of almonds in the state of California, which means in the entire world. I'm the largest producer of pistachios, the largest producer of avocados, the largest producer of pomegranates—I bet that's a surprise. I own the largest chain of movie theaters in North America. The largest chain of gyms."

"I notice a theme here."

The road doglegged abruptly to the right, revealing a building that looked like a predatory animal hunched over a partially devoured carcass. Three chimneys belched smoke.

"What is that thing?" Stein asked.

"Processing plant. All the growers in the valley bring their almonds to me to be shelled. You know what our motto is? 'We Crush Your Nuts.'"

"Cute."

Brickman rotated a dial on the dash. "Seat okay for you? I can heat it."

"I'm good."

"You're going to think I'm bullshitting, but I owe all my success to you."

"Fine. I'll take half."

"Aren't you interested to know why?"

They were approaching a railroad supply train at a forty-five degree angle; a long tapeworm of open gondola cars stood under supply chutes. A thunderous load of oranges tumbled down the sluice into the last car's empty belly. The sluice retracted and the train bore itself forward. The front of the locomotive, a quarter mile in the distance, was a hundred feet from the crossing of the road that Stein and Brickman were approaching. The engine was much closer and beginning to gain speed. It did not take an MRI to see what Brickman was thinking.

"Please don't prove your manhood to me," Stein implored.

"You don't buy a fast car to come in second."

The Jag accelerated to warp speed in seconds. From no chance there was now the possibility of chance. Stein liked their chances better when there was no chance. If there was no chance, Brickman would have to stop and let the train go by. But if there was any chance at all, Brickman was going to take it. He patted Stein's knee. "You're always safe when you're with somebody who has more to lose."

The train, with its long heavy load, would never top forty and it was making less than half that now. The needle on the Jag wavered at three figures. It was going to be close and a tie would be worse than a loss. The Jag hit the track first. The steel snout and single eye of the locomotive loomed gigantic in the side window. The train whistle blasted a screaming Doppler. They shot across the grading, missing impact by molecules.

Brickman downshifted matter-of-factly into their previous conversation. "Aren't you curious how I owe it all to you? I hated you in high school. I used to go home and tear pictures of you. Hold half in each hand and ask you if you thought *that* was funny. Do you remember that time in junior year you ranked me out? It was fifth period in the cafeteria. They had Salisbury Steak that day, which I loved, but they always ran out of it by sixth period lunch so I cut English and I was sitting at your table with Calkins and Delberg and Annunziata's brother and a couple of other people I didn't know. And we got into it, you and me. You don't remember this?"

"Sorry."

"Anyway at one point you said 'Oh, Brickman, why don't you just eat shit and die?' I knew you were going to say that. I was waiting for it. And I nailed you with 'What should I do with your bones?' which was always the winner. But then you came back with 'Make a cage for your mother,' and the whole table cracked up. I had never heard that comeback. I always wondered if you knew it already or just made it up on the spot."

"I can see why you'd want to give that a lot of thought."

"You jest but it's true. The worst was watching the girls flock to you. Watching you make them laugh. Having all that power over them. You weren't that good looking. Then one day I had my epiphany. I realized that the only girls you got were girls who went for guys who were *funny*. None of them were the top girls. The top girls went for the guys with the money. Once I knew that, it became simple. Make money, get laid. And as you can see, I get more ass than a toilet seat at Grand Central Station."

"You get women who want men with *money*," Stein said, thinking he was modifying. Qualifying. Narrowing. Diminishing. But Brickman saw it as a celebration of his life. He challenged Stein. "Did you ever fuck Miranda Mickens?"

"No. Not even close. She went out with college guys."

"What about Barbara Gunnels?"

"Don't I wish."

"I fucked both of them."

"No, you didn't."

"Not then. But after I had money. They weren't sixteen any more but I got them." He leaned to Stein with a conspiratorial grin. "You know who Winona Ryder is?"

"The actress Winona Ryder?"

"I fucked her four nights ago."

"You didn't fuck Winona Ryder."

"Yeah, I did. I mean, I could if I wanted to. She always shows up at my parties. I think she steals ashtrays. Is that possible?"

"As long as we're being honest, there's something I'd like to know."

"Shoot."

"Did you have a deal with Henny Spector to rent depleted bee colonies?"

Brickman's answer was ambiguous in its unsuppressed glee. "People are idiots. That's all I can tell you."

"Wouldn't the idiot be the person *paying* top dollar for depleted colonies?"

Brickman grinned. "This is the beauty of it. It's not me paying. I mean, at first it is but . . . dig it: All of us growers insure our crops. Premiums are based on average yield per acre. I have twelve thousand acres of trees too young to produce. If I rent bees for those acres, on paper it makes those acres look like productive land. So it lowers my OPA."

"Your OPA?"

"Output per acre. And yes, you're right. The few hundred grand it saves me is chump change. But here's where the real fun starts. Some of the investment banks are bundling debt obligations and selling them to high-echelon customers. High-risk, high-yield stuff. Eighteen to twenty-two percent profit overnight. It's about hedging. I buy the instruments that carry the highest risk and then buy insurance against their failure. Are you seeing the beauty?"

"I'm still back at chump change."

"You could get in on this too. All you need is two or three million for seed money. I swear to you, this is the road to riches. My little subsidiary company, which is impossible to trace back to me, makes a bogus insurance claim. The instrument that debt was bundled into, along with a hundred others, goes into default. It just takes one bad piece to sour the whole pie. So I lose the few hundred thousand I used to bet on it. Which, incidentally, is the same money that the insurance company paid me for the other scam. *But,* now I collect my insurance policy on the full face value of the instrument. Which is eight to ten million. That's right. Million."

He grinned up at Stein to see his reaction. "I happen to be insured by Lassiter and Frank. In two years I'll own all their resources."

"Lassiter and Frank, did you say?"

"Once they fall I'll own all the little fish inside of them. And then the fun really starts."

"What more can you possibly want?"

"Whatever there is."

"You want everything?"

"Everything I can get."

"But why?"

"So that I'll have it."

***

Yellow crime scene tape was stretched across the entrance to Henny Spector's place. The whole property was cordoned off. Stein explained as they drew closer that he had left his girlfriend's car there, a 2001 Lexus that had his daughter's cell number programmed into its phone.

"A white Lexus coupe?" Brickman asked.

"I think that's what it's called."

"Like that one?" Brickman indicated a car that was roaring past them, off the unguarded grounds.

Stein whipped around in the seat. "God damn it!"

"I'll take that as a yes?"

Brickman made an unhurried Y-turn and then hit the Saturn rocket thrusters full ahead. Landscape whizzed past the window in a blur. The driver of the Lexus was no slouch either. He whipped through tight turns without a brake light coming on.

Brickman stayed right on his tail. Stein noted that people here were surprisingly good drivers.

"Give him the horn," Stein exhorted.

"You don't think he knows we're behind him?"

Around the next tight S-curve the Lexus was suddenly gone. There was a break in the road, a turnoff into an orchard like the one where Stein and Hollister and Doc Moody had to wait for the kid in the truck. Brickman zoomed past it. Hit the brakes. Spun out into a one-eighty.

"Nicely done."

"Thank you."

A cloud of dust rose up a quarter mile ahead of them from the narrow road between rows of blossoming almond trees. They jounced in mad pursuit. The lane was not a lot wider than the car. They swerved to avoid a cluster of bee boxes.

"Incidentally," Brickman asked, "what's your plan when we catch him?"

"I don't know."

"You ought to think of something. Because he's probably the person who killed Henny Spector."

"Thank him then, I guess."

Gravel sprayed at their windshield as the Lexus blew out of the orchard and onto a paved road. It leaped across the oncoming lane and made a stunning ninety-degree left, drawing the wrathful blast of an air horn from the double trailer that hugged the inside lane.

Brickman was going to try to shoot the gap. But Stein reached his left leg across the boot and rammed his foot onto the brake.

They spun to a stop between two blossoming trees. The truck slowed down vindictively and made them wait. They had to wait for yet another passenger car that was driving behind the truck. The Lexus was gone from sight by now. "Are you happy?" Brickman sniped at him.

"Follow the truck," Stein said quietly.

"Forget the truck. The truck is going to my place. Your Lexus went the other way."

"I don't need the Lexus anymore."

"What about your daughter's phone number?"

"I don't need my daughter's phone number. That car behind the truck was my Camry. The girl behind the wheel was my daughter."

Chapter Fifteen

After a few rounds of *What are you doing here? No, what are you doing here?* Stein came down on her. "You're an underaged, uninsured, unlicensed driver in a stolen car. What in the hell were you thinking?"

"Stolen," Angie scoffed.

"Do you understand if you had had an accident—? If, God forbid, you injured someone? Or worse? Do you realize what a monumentally stupid thing you did?" He could feel blood surging through his brain. "Hand over the keys."

She balked for a second.

"Now."

She handed over a pink keychain.

"What the hell is this?"

"My set."

"Yours?"

"I made a copy in like seventh grade. I've taken it out bunches of times."

He stuffed the keys away. "You still haven't told me what the hell you're doing here."

As a penance, Angie told her father everything. Anyway, a strategically redacted version of everything. She did not mention seeing Lila coming out of the bathroom naked with Richard. In its place she caulked in the gaps with the exciting narrative of what she and Matt had discovered and surmised about J. J. Bancroft's ill-gotten financial empire. How at first she'd been sure that Bancroft murdered Sunny Cataluna out of greed, to get his hands on the oil. But when Matt found the old newspaper documents she realized it was a love triangle and that Bancroft wanted to get his hands on Lucy. And that Matthew was bringing the head of Sunny Cataluna up with him from the forensic paleontologist and they were going to expose Bancroft at the party and bring down the Bancroft empire.

When she finished he just looked at her like someone seeing the Pacific Ocean for the first time.

"Why are you gaping, old man? Your Fixodent is showing."

"Sometimes in spite of raising my blood pressure and decreasing my life expectancy, you blow me away."

"Whatever." Since she had now given him "full disclosure," she demanded the same. Which he gave her. Redacting the minor detail about nearly being murdered. And that the person who had tried to kill him had himself been killed. What he was left with was a limp, "Still trying to figure out that bee wrestling thing."

"That's why you disappear and nobody hears from you?"

"I'm still not used to this cell phone thing."

"And what happened to your face? Are you getting Botox injections?"

Stein ruefully admitted that he had gotten careless out in the field and a bee had stung him. He diverted her with a few salacious tidbits about the truck driver who was stung to death (he left it at that) and his many wives and mistress. He thought she'd enjoy the gossip, but the story made her unaccountably angry. People were fucked, she said, and didn't want to hear any more about it.

Brickman's XKE blew back into the scene. Angie had no idea who he was except that he had nearly driven her off the road, for which she had let loose a tirade of curses, given him the finger, and had been on the verge of opening her shirt and flashing him when her father emerged from the passenger side and called out her name.

"I found your girlfriend's car," Brickman said, vaulting out of his own. "But whoever was driving it was gone, so we still don't know who your guardian angel is."

Angie asked what this person was talking about.

Stein introduced Angie to Barry Brickman. Upon hearing Brickman's name, Angie's demeanor went from briefly confused to overly starstruck. "Not the Barry Brickman who owns Family Farms?" she whispered in awe.

"That's a lot nicer greeting than a middle finger. Thank you."

"Oh, my God. I've been wanting to meet you like forever!"

"You have?"

"You have?" Stein echoed, but with many more question marks.

"For school we have to do reports on self-made millionaires. You're the one I picked."

"I'm stupendously flattered," Brickman said. "Unfortunately for you I'm not a millionaire."

"You're not?" Angie asked.

"You're not?" Stein echoed.

A well-timed pause before he delivered the punch line, "I'm a billionaire."

"Good one," Angie applauded. "You had me."

He was charmed by her sophisticated sense of humor and invited Angie to be a guest at his party.

"Is that the Bancroft's seventy-fifth anniversary party?" Angie asked, with apparent stars in her eyes.

"I see your dad has been filling you in," he said.

Stein had no idea what they were talking about but agreed.

Brickman gave Stein meticulous directions to where Lila's car was situated before leaving them to tend to the thousand party details.

"I like your friend a lot," Angie said.

"How do you know about this party?"

She didn't answer. Stein made a U-turn onto the two-lane and started to drive in the direction Brickman had described. "There's something else," he said. "I had a very strange phone conversation with Lila. Is everything okay with you two?"

Angie muttered something gruff and unintelligible that Stein didn't catch.

"I said Lila's a bitch," she repeated.

He turned sharply toward her. She continued looking straight ahead.

"Where is this coming from?"

She refused further comment.

"Does this have something to do with Matthew?"

"That's it, Dad. You nailed it exactly."

"Did he try—?"

"Do you want to hear every detail of my sex life?"

Stein blanched.

"Then don't ask."

"I don't know what is going on here. But Lila is the woman I have chosen to be with. If the three of us are going to live together we have to get along."

Grim, mirthless laughter permeated Angie's reply. "I promise you, the three of us will not be living together."

"That is a decision I will make. And you will make the best of it."

"You may live in that delusion, old man."

***

Stein slowed down and reconnoitered. All the landmarks that Brickman had vividly described were in place: The stream on the left. The overhanging broken weeping willow tree. The rusted sign for Howser's Grapes. There was only one thing missing. Lila's Lexus.

"Either he gave us the wrong directions or I heard them wrong."

"Or he lied to you."

"About what?"

"About where he saw it? About seeing it at all."

"Why would he lie?" Stein asked.

"Because he's a member of the human race?"

Her cell phone rang. She took a step away and turned her back subtly murmuring into the phone that she did not want to talk to about last night. "Really?" Stein heard her exclaim. And then said it again with even more amazement: "Say that name again? I think that's it. I'll ask him."

She clicked the call end button and approached her father thoughtfully. "That was Matt."

"I gathered that. I thought you two were on the outs."

"We are. But it's sweet that he keeps calling. He just came from the museum. He says the bust of Sunny looks amazing. Bancroft will drop dead when he sees it."

"That should make a big hit with the party guests."

"There was something else, though. He was snooping through his Uncle Richard's business papers this morning and he found—"

"He was snooping through his uncle's business papers?"

"Everybody does it. It's no big deal.

"You snoop through my—?"

"Dad! The point is that his uncle is counsel to a private corporation that is buying up shitloads of land. He wouldn't have noticed except that he recognized the name of the courthouse where all the deals were. It was the same place where you went to the beekeepers' convention."

"In Las Viejas?"

"Don't you find that weird?"

"I find it weird and flattering that you actually listened to something I said."

"I said *Matthew* remembered."

"Okay, that's more believable."

"Your turn. One of the officers of the corporation is J. J. Bancroft. And another one is . . ."

"Is what?"

"Is Matthew's stepmother."

"Lila? She's never told me she was an officer in a corporation."

"Funny the things people keep from each other."

"She doesn't pay much attention to her financial matters. Richard handles all that for her."

She took a deep breath and let that opening pass. "The corporation had a very cute name. Boysenberry Pi. Not P-i-e. P-i."

The severity of her father's reaction to that name startled her. "I know we like to tease each other. And you're better at it than I am. Where did you come up with that name?"

"That was the name he told me."

Stein's mind was spinning. He spoke slowly. "In high school. We had a geometry teacher named Maxine Boysen. She would sit on her desk and cross her legs. . . ." He realized where the story was going and who he was talking to, and stopped.

"Yeah, I get it," Angie said flatly. "Boysenberry Pi."

"The person who made up the name and thought it was the cleverest thing any human had ever said . . . was Barry Brickman. It looks like Bancroft and Brickman, the two richest men in the universe are in cahoots to buy up all the orchard land in the valley."

"Cool."

"No. Not cool."

"I mean cool that we found it out."

"You up for a little search and destroy?" Stein asked.

A long black Lincoln town car shot past them headed in the opposite direction. A pretty, dark-haired young woman looked out the back window.

"Whoa," Angie yelped. "Was that Winona Ryder?"

***

There was not a lot of activity outside the Las Viejas courthouse. A few cars were parked in desultory fashion, a pickup truck or two using the spots for other business and a highway patrol cruiser.

The girl behind the desk was as friendly as a baker passing out samples at a county fair. Stein told her they were looking for records of local land sales to the Boysenberry Pi Corporation. "How far back would you like to go?" she asked. Her answer was unexpectedly bright and knowledgeable, as though she had the entire contents of the archive room memorized.

"Let's start with the past six months."

"And would you like the water bank sale too?"

"Excuse me?" said Stein.

"It just came in a day ago. The sale of the Viejas County water bank to the Boysenberry Pi Corporation. Actually it went first to the Family Farm Corp, then to their subsidiary the Honeybee Farms, and then through them to Boysenberry Pi."

"Yes, we would like to see that as well," Angie said.

"And a map that would show their location," Stein added.

The instant the girl went back into the stacks, Stein whispered in Angie's ear, "It's illegal for a private corporation to own a state resource. Something very, very underhanded is—"

The girl returned with an armload of documents and ushered them to a nearby round table. "Take all the time you need," she said.

Stein set Angie up to begin and excused himself to the men's room. He hadn't gone three steps when a large bully-pulpit voice sang out, "Look who's here. Just the man I've been looking for." Caravaggio's black boots made him look even more gigantic.

"Hey, there," Stein said, as though he were trying to place where he knew him. He gave a surreptitious cut-off signal behind his back to Angie.

Caravaggio placed a restraining mitt on Stein's shoulder. "The coroner's got something to show you from Henny Spector's corpse."

"Henny Spector's corpse? What are you talking about?" He affected utter ignorance.

"The man who tried to kill you." Caravaggio was not enjoying the game of stupid that Stein was playing.

"Kill me?" Stein laughed.

"Excuse me, Officer." Angie came away from the table. "Did you say someone tried to kill this man?"

"You see that, Officer? You're giving this poor girl bad dreams." With subtly exaggerated expressions he was warning Angie to pretend not to know who he was and to find out what she could from those documents.

He waltzed away quickly with Caravaggio before she could ask any more questions, and announced in a loud theatrical voice, "You've got to bring me back here in an hour or all these people will wonder what happened to me at the . . . Las Viejas Coroner's office."

Chapter Sixteen

Angie's cell phone buzzed under the stack of land sale documents she was perusing.

"Where are you?" Matthew's voice lamented.

"Oh, God, I am such an idiot. I forgot to call you."

The attendant gesticulated to Angie with great urgency that cell phones were a no-no.

"I have to go outside. Let me call you right back."

"I've got you," Matthew said. "Are you at the Las Viejas courthouse?"

"How do you know that?"

"This incredibly cool device my uncle gave me. It uses the satellites to track phone calls."

"Sure it does."

The young courthouse clerk swooped across the room like a pterodactyl in training. Angie clutched her stuff to her chest and scurried out of the room. She was breathless when she hit the outside and called Matthew back.

"There's a lot going on here," she said. She wanted to know if he was sure he'd gotten the name of that corporation right.

There was some uncomfortable silence.

"Matt?"

"You've got to stop doing that."

"I don't . . . What do you mean?

"Thinking I'm brain damaged. I didn't get the name of the corporation wrong. It's Boysenberry Pi."

"Okay. Don't get your drawers bunched."

"You do it a lot."

"I'm just saying. All the land deeds here for purchases by Boysenberry Pi Corporation were out between Bakersfield and LA. My dad said their plan was to buy up all the almond groves, so this makes no sense."

"If you need me to be wrong about the name of the corporation for your father's idea to be right, then his idea isn't right."

"I have to get inside, okay? I'm on low battery."

"I see you. I'm here."

"Where?"

A moment later Matt's Mercedes pulled up alongside her. He lowered his window and said hi, breathing deeply into the already heavy air between them. She wasn't ready for any of this. The hurt feelings, the apologizing, the giving a shit, it was all new to her and she didn't like it. Nobody's opinion of her had ever mattered enough to make her consider the possibility of change. She had always felt like the fixed object in space, the star around which dependent planets revolved. She didn't like the loss of that immutability. It made her feel negotiable.

He jumped out of his car and caught up with her. "Where are you running?"

"I was getting a little cold."

"You're getting a little weird is what you're getting."

"What?"

"I only drove two hundred miles to bring you a certain object. I thought maybe you'd like to see it."

Angie turned a succession of colors. "What is the matter with me?"

"I've been asking the same question." It was the way he smiled that did her in. As he opened the trunk Angie saw his face full front. There was an angry, colorful welt above his left eye.

"Matty, what happened to your face?" Her hand flew involuntarily to his injury. Her fingertips alighted soft as butterfly wings.

***

What happened was Matthew had stayed at Lila's that night, despite his mother's displeasure when he called her. He slept fitfully. He'd heard, or imagined he'd heard, Lila crying during the night. Mercedes made him pancakes for breakfast and told him Miss Leela not feeling so good.

He had never before snooped into Lila's private papers. He knew that the trust fund his father had set up kept him and his mother and sister well taken care of, but he had balked at the regular invitations Richard had made to go over his financial prospects with him. Denial, as the saying goes, is not just a river in Egypt.

For the same psychological reasons, Lila had always thrown up her hands at the mention of money management. First her own father, then her late husband, now Richard had handled her affairs. She knew enough about money to be frugal. Certainly by Beverly Hills standards. Matthew had never seen reason to doubt her assertions, but now he just wanted to be sure.

It was sunny in the dining room where the large mahogany credenza stood against the white stucco wall. Matt sat cross-legged on the stained hardwood floor and opened the bottom glass cabinet. The files were stacked in an orderly manner. He took out the most recent one and opened it in his lap. Many of the documents were written in small type, single-spaced and in a language where the words resembled English but the sentence structure resembled wild kudzu vines overgrowing a swamp.

Matt could make out enough to see that Lila and J. J. Bancroft were investors or landholders in several newly purchased lots via the Boysenberry Pi Corporation. He was glad when he heard the footsteps approach. However, it was not Lila who stepped into the room and looked down at the open files splayed all around him. Bright morning sunlight made a blazing prairie fire out of Richard's gray hair. His voice was measured. Serious without threat.

"What is your business with J. J. Bancroft?" he asked.

"Uncle Richard. I thought you had gone to Atlanta."

"I was called back. And so I ask you again. What is your business with J. J. Bancroft?"

"I don't have any business with him," Matthew replied.

Richard presented a photograph taken at Pershing Square the previous afternoon of Matthew at the Bancroft limo, and asked his nephew what he had said to Commodore Bancroft.

"Why would anyone take this picture of me?" was Matt's first question. Followed with even more amazement by, "And why do you have it?"

"I like the way your mind works," Richard said. "Very inquisitive. Very logical. What did you say to Commodore Bancroft?"

"I didn't say anything. Angie wanted to talk to *Mrs.* Bancroft." He said this in no way to deflect guilt, but as testimony to how trivial the encounter had been and how mistaken anybody would have been to think otherwise. He began to carefully replace the items in their folders.

"I'll look after that," Richard said. He noted that a particular envelope, one stamped with caveats of privacy, had not been violated. "Let's go outside."

Richard allowed Matthew to precede him out of the dining room through the kitchen and to the patio. Richard stopped outside the dining room and pulled the rarely used set of double doors closed. He spoke briefly in well-accented Spanish to Mercedes before rejoining Matthew on the patio.

"Sit down," he said to Matt, who had waited for him standing. They occupied a low, backless bench. Matthew faced the house, his back to the pool.

"Did you have something you wanted to say to me?"

"Yes. I do," Matthew said.

"Now would be a good time."

"I think you should cool it with Aunt Lila while she's somebody else's girlfriend."

The boy made Richard smile. "I meant about the documents. But that took a lot of courage to say to me. I respect that. It was manly. It was direct. It was respectful both to me and to Lila, and also to yourself. And to answer you, it may seem untoward. It may indeed be untoward. There is obviously something valuable we both derive. And when she says we're done, that is all she'll have to say. Do you understand?"

Matt let out a hard breath.

"I didn't ask if you were happy. I asked if you understood."

Matt nodded yes, that he understood.

"Good. When I came in a little while ago, I noticed that you were going through private papers."

"Yes," Matt said.

With a sudden motion Richard cracked Matt across the face with his open hand. Matt's neck snapped. His ears rang. It was the first time Richard had ever struck him. The first time Matthew had ever been struck.

"Don't do it again," Richard said. He beckoned Matthew to come closer. He put his arm around the boy and whispered something in his ear. Matt nodded that yeah, he knew. They both went into the dining room. Mercedes had already reordered the papers. "I was wrong for nosing into your and Aunt Lila's business, Uncle Richard. I apologize."

"I need to know what you said to J. J. Bancroft." Richard had not noticed that something had changed in the boy through that moment of impact. The slap in the face had set into place the last missing block of manhood.

"Whatever I said to Bancroft is my business," Matt said. He spoke without haste, without rancor, without disrespect, and without youthful fear. He turned and kept walking.

***

Once the boy was out of the room, Richard made sure the envelope containing the water bank documents had not been compromised. He made a call on his cell; he did not need to identify himself to the receiver. He said that the boy wasn't up to anything that would cause a problem. That he was only there because of the girl in the picture. Given all that, Richard expressed the strong desire to recuse himself from any further involvement.

A rasping voice on the other end reminded him that was not how it worked and to repeat the name of the girl.

"Her name is Angie Stein. S-t-e-i-n. But I'm quite certain there's no cause for concern."

The connection was already broken.

***

Matty? Matthew grinned.

Angie was blushing.

"It's sweet that you care about my eye."

"I didn't say I *cared*, I just asked how it happened."

And then she could tease no more. Matthew had taken a box out of the trunk of his car. And Angie was looking down at the face of Sunny Cataluna. It was beyond anything she'd imagined. There was a soul in his piercing gentle brown eyes. There was pain, there was longing. "He's gorgeous," she whispered. "How could she not fall in love with him?"

"You're welcome," said Matt.

"Thank you," she remembered, and threw her arms around him. "This is going to be so good!"

When they came back into the courthouse the girl behind the desk beckoned to her. She was sorry to report that there were no other registered land sales to Boysenberry Pi Corporation. Angie thanked her and apologized for the cell phone.

"Yeah," the girl said brightly. "I'm surprised he left a message for you with me instead of calling your phone."

"My father called?"

The librarian read off her message pad. "He said he was a little delayed. But everything was cool. And to meet him back at—" She squinted at her writing. "I'm not sure I got this right. I think he was talking in code. The brick house? He said you'd know what that meant." The girl folded the note and handed it to Angie. "Your father sounds like an odd and interesting man," she said. "I see where you get it."

"Freak," said Angie.

***

Stein had made the call to the courthouse from Renn Moody's desk at the morgue, where Officer Caravaggio had conducted him. Jarlene Moody had made an interesting discovery in the course of preparing Henny Spector's body for the coffin. She had been working to adjust the insincere curve of his lips to an expression that projected a more honest demeanor when she noticed that the hole in the back of Henny Spector's skull was not connected to the thrust that punctured his left eyeball.

In excising the puncture, she had encountered an obstacle, an obstruction. When she probed it with her sewing needle and magnifying glass she discovered, and subsequently extracted with her husband's help, a three-inch-long steely talon. The one-thrust theory placed the point of entry at the back of the neck. However, the talon in Henny's eye had its blunt end facing *out*, meaning it had been thrust *into* the eye. And from there it broke through the vitreous gel, gashed the retina, pierced the optic nerve, and penetrated into the frontal lobe of his brain.

The initial point of entry behind the neck had presented a wound of a slightly larger diameter and a proportionally deeper penetration, severing the spinal cord, fracturing two cervical vertebrae and imbedding itself deep into the occipital lobe. No part of that implement had been recovered, though there was residue of microscopic white fibrous material, consistent with Henny's having been attacked from behind while wearing his bee suit, as Stein had alleged.

Renn was abundantly pleased with his wife's finding. He rolled the deadly spike in his hand. It was a good three inches long, perfectly round at its shaft, which was greenish gray, tapering to a long, black lethal tip. Its source became the subject of speculation. Some kind of hawk perhaps? A peregrine falcon? Condor? Eagle? Baboon? No, all those nails had curvatures. This was straight as a golf tee. A porcupine quill? No, this was thicker, harder. A sea urchin?

The instant Stein saw that murderous tip he knew where it had come from. It always recalled the worst day of his life, the afternoon seven years ago when Stein and Hillary had informed Angie they were getting divorced. Angie had bolted out of the house into the untamed back hillside of their home in the Hollywood Hills. They heard the scream a moment later and nearly decapitated each other to reach her first.

The maguey, also called a century plant, grew long, broad shafts three feet in length and slightly curled in the center with jagged edges meant to protect the reservoir of sweet liquid down in its heart, called *agua miel*, honey water. It is the long-horned lethal tip, though, that can pierce to the bone. That spear had penetrated Angie's big toe—and Henny Spector's brain.

Looking down at him, Stein had no trouble visualizing the assassin stealing up from behind and pile-driving the point into the back of Henny's unsuspecting head. He could see Henny struggling to pull the head protector off, his last act in life, and watching the point of a second spear penetrate his eye socket. Perhaps by the same hand, likely by an accomplice.

Stein remembered exactly where he had seen a wall of maguey plants growing. He knew who his guardian angels were and who had murdered Henny Spector. He would take care of that little matter first, then pick up his daughter at Barry Brickman's party and get the hell out of Dodge; leave the beekeeping to the beekeepers and the nuts to the nutters.

Chapter Seventeen

Stein's Camry was no longer in the parking lot, so Angie presumed the fat cop had let her father drive himself to wherever they were going. She had heard him use the word "morgue," but she had let that bounce off the trampoline of her mind, as she did with most matters that concerned the lives of her parents. Matthew opened the passenger door for her as he always did. She had never seen the space-age display activated atop his dashboard, which now laid out a route for them in a series of electronic breadcrumbs.

"It's that satellite thing I told you about. My uncle Richard says this is going to be standard consumer equipment in a couple of years."

"The less I hear about your uncle's equipment the better."

He nodded in agreement. "I talked to him about Lila."

"I see he took it well."

***

The men in the dark Buick sedan following Matt and Angie had professional-grade versions of the primitive technology that Matt's car sported, enabling them to lock on to the vapor trail of exhaust particulates and follow them at an undetectable distance. The electronic file they had studied on Angeline Koufax Stein was virtually empty but for the basics: DOB 5-8-85. M: Hillary Stein (nee Stevens); F: Harry Stein. Her current grades and teachers' reports at The Academy, the upscale private school that Hillary had insisted Angie attend, which Stein referred to as Club Ed. Her medical records, and recent credit card purchases: A sweater at May Company for $37.00. *Catcher in the Rye* at Book Soup.

An asterisk in the file next to the name Harry Stein linked to a far lengthier dossier. He was cross-referenced under Peacenik, Potnik, Pain-In-The Ass-nik. He was described as an advocate of social anarchy. A threat to society. A subversive and miscreant. Many of his legendary antics were chronicled and supported by firsthand accounts or newspaper photos. The parade of transvestites he organized to enter the Marine recruitment station. The Pot-In-Every-Chicken dinner for Nixon's henchmen. The Victory Gardens he planted at Police headquarters. Under the dense litany of events of that era there was a long empty gap down to the current notation:

*NO LONGER CONSIDERED AN ACTIVE THREAT.

***

Matthew's routing device brought them unerringly to the gates of the Brickman estate. There were two guards on each side of the entryway scrupulously checking invites and IDs.

"What's our cover story?" Matthew smiled.

"He kind of sort of invited me."

"Strong."

As they reached the gate, Angie geared up to go into a performance-level explanation of why they should both be admitted. Before she got her first syllable out, the guard waved them through, having received the directive to do so in his earpiece. Angie was more irked at being shut up than pleased at being let in.

"What the hell was that," she groused. "Some security system."

Inside the gate, guides were dressed as carnival clowns. A Raggedy Andy flopped into the path alongside Matt's car, squirted them with a fake seltzer bottle, and welcomed them to "the Carnival of Carnivals." A voice in the tiny speaker hidden inside the half-ping-pong ball clown's ear instructed him to give them party bracelets.

Raggedy Andy fastened a blue plastic bracelet around each of their wrists.

"VIPs," said Angie, quite impressed with herself.

Behind their tinted windows, Agent Cortelyou munched raw carrot sticks and watched Angie and Matt on feeds from closed-circuit security cameras mounted above the gate. As the bracelets were clasped, two new screens activated on their dashboard, transmitting live video feed from the bracelets.

"Gottem," Agent Lefferts spoke into the hidden mic. "Well done."

The valet parking attendant drove Matt's car into the garage. Raggedy Andy executed a clownish bow to Angie and directed them a short distance up the hill where newly arriving guests were boarding the open cars of a model railroad train. Each of the six cars seated two adult human passengers. The white-haired engineer, dressed in classic striped overalls and hat, straddled the locomotive, tooted the whistle and opened the throttle. Angie and Matt dashed hand-in-hand the twenty yards up the hill. Matt in his sport jacket and trousers, Angie in Alyssa's boots and blazer and flowing burgundy cape, looked like a pair of elegant young sophisticates late for a party at Gatsby's. They clambered into the last car.

As the train serpented slowly around the estate, a new micro-environment sprung up around each successive quadrant. Here, two mounted Arthurian knights in full medieval armor thundered across the lea at each other with lances drawn. Around the next bend, a sloop, the Lucky Lucy, carried passengers around a tropic lagoon. Behind that, a three-dimensional replica of contemporary Los Angeles was displayed in perfect detail, with all twenty-six Bancroft Buildings in light.

Across the lawn, a line of trained elephants was dancing, trunk to tail, kicking their back right legs out in pachydermian synchronicity. The train stopped at the top of the mesa where the main house was situated. Two large white circus tents had been erected, each with two hundred white folding chairs. Magicians and jugglers and mimes engaged the guests.

Angie grouched at all the excess. "What I wouldn't give for a small, tactical nuclear device."

"You think you're so noir," Matthew goaded. "You're barely twilight."

"Look who's talking. Mr. sweetness and light."

He suddenly smacked his head. "I'm an idiot."

"Okay, that I buy."

"The thing! Sunny's head! We left it in the car."

They realized they were both empty-handed. "I'll get it," Matt said. "No need for us both of us to go."

"Are you sure?" She wasn't fighting too hard to refuse, since she had spied Ashton Kutcher twenty feet away, writing his name on the forearms of a gaggle of thirteen-year-old girls.

The agents had driven onto the grounds. Their car was parked alongside the gate. Cortelyou took notice of the teens' separation on their surveillance screens but it triggered no alarm.

The girls getting their arms signed were all papery-legged and giggly. Angie felt old at sixteen. She also noticed that their long, bare, skinny arms did not have bracelets at their wrists.

She wondered if her father was here yet and if he was on the VIP list. She assumed that probably he wasn't. She had a little feeling that Brickman was hitting on her. Finding Brickman, she figured, would be her best way of finding her dad. The edifice before her looked like Versailles on acid. There were waist-high poles with red velvet restraining ropes across the entrance not very subtly saying DO NOT ENTER. Or, as Angie's brain interpreted the message: *Angie Stein, please enter.*

Wearing Alyssa's boots made her feel three inches taller and as dangerous as an Israeli commando. She bunched the sleeves of her blazer up around her forearms. One snagged on her bracelet. She tried to loosen it but it was on tight.

Down in the agent's car, all the jiggling was causing a blur on their screen. "Pretty savvy for a couple of kids," Agent Cortelyou had to admit. "Splitting up. Creating interference."

"What are you saying?" Church asked warily. Church had seniority and called the shots, between the two of them anyway. But he knew Cortelyou was smarter.

"I'm not saying anything," Cortelyou said, because he knew what Church was asking and he wasn't going to take the heat for any decision where he couldn't get credit. "I'm just saying."

"Saying what?"

"Nothing. Just that we have a situation where the boy is one place, and the girl is possibly creating a diversion."

"So what are you saying?"

"I'm just saying what I said."

"You're saying we have a situation?"

"Do you hear me saying that?"

"Yes, I think I do." Church carefully probed his partner's reaction.

"I'm just saying what I say. I can't stop a person from thinking what they think," Cortelyou said.

Angie had walked through several rooms without being able to tell what they were used for. They were large. They were bright. They had waxed and polished hardwood floors. The only object in the first room was a rowing machine, fully assembled, and wheeled into a corner near the door. A tall ficus was growing out of the floor of the second room. A large, square chunk of flooring had been excavated from which the tree rose toward a skylight.

"Dad?" she called hopefully. No answer.

Three wooden steps led up to an oak door that opened into a room that was much smaller and crammed full. There were no identifying signs on the door. The room was an old-fashioned library. The walls were book shelved, floor-to-ceiling, filled not with books but with comedy albums. She browsed the titles. People Angie had vaguely or never heard of. Bob Newhart. Mike Nichols and Elaine May. The Two Thousand-Year-Old Man. Weird.

Upon a desk a three-dimensional scale model of a city had been erected as part of a remarkably accurate bird's eye view of the greater Los Angeles megatropolis. At first glance the network of residential communities radiating outward from the cluster of high-rise buildings seemed to be downtown Los Angeles and its satellite suburbs. But upon closer examination, she saw that a new development was tucked between Bakersfield and the mountains. Below it, in the flatlands, was a huge aquifer. The original words had been struck over and replaced with BOYSENBERRY PI WATER BANK.

The door behind her opened. The male voice so startled her that she nearly wet Alyssa's pants. She covered her surprise well at being discovered by Matt's Uncle Richard, as he covered his reaction to finding her.

"There you are," he said quite pleasantly. "Matthew has been looking all over for you."

All she could picture was Richard whacking Matthew across the face.

"I've been calling him. I guess there's bad reception here." She displayed her cell phone as evidence.

"Come, I'll take you to him." Richard gallantly held the door for her; Angie could see where Matthew got his manners. She took one debutanticular step outside, then grabbed the edge of the door and threw it shut behind her. And ran like a maniac.

***

Stein made a slow circle around the morgue parking lot. Caravaggio had departed a good ten minutes before he did, but he didn't know where the big man might be lurking and he didn't want to be seen rushing, or call attention to where he was going. He had not let on to Renn Moody nor to Caravaggio that he recognized the talon extracted from Henny Spector's eye socket. He had seen the stand of maguey plants at the back of Hollister and Ruth Ann's property line the morning Renn and Hollister had supered the new hives. He would put his last two bucks down at the betting window that it was Ruth Ann who had implanted that spike in Henny Spector's brain.

He drove several miles in the wrong direction deliberately before turning around and heading for the Greenway place. He wished he had Lila's car, with Angie's cell phone number programmed into it so that he could find out what she had discovered about the land grabs. He was sure the parcels would border Brickman's current holdings, his acquisitive tentacles gobbling up all that there was to have.

Ruth Ann smiled when she saw him at her front door. "Well," she said with just a wee bit of irony, "to what do owe the honor?"

"Hello, Ruth Ann."

"You're looking very well."

"Compared to any particular way you may have recently seen me?"

"I cannot imagine what you mean."

"It's good to see you, too, Ruth Ann."

"So I would think."

She looked sensational, wearing a long skirt and white blouse that buttoned to the neck. He had thought of her as the goofy second lead—the alto in the musical comedy who has the comedic love story. But now she had metamorphosed into Katherine Hepburn, windblown and strong, a heart that could never be taken from her, only given freely. She scared the crap out of him.

"Is Hollister at home?"

"Hollister is still in jail for trying to steal back those boxes. Would you like to come in?"

"On such a pretty day?"

"Shall we stay out here on the porch?"

The portico was overhung with flowering vines. The bees knew to avoid the milky white stickum of the Cruel Vine and gravitated to the Trumpet Creeper. There were a lot of bees. Given his recent experience, Stein was gun shy. "On second thought, inside is fine," he said.

He didn't remember the scent of lavender being so prevalent. He recalled bacon. He sat at the kitchen table. Outside, through the window, standing silent sentry at the back of the property was the row of maguey plants. The tallest and most rugged had its front sheaf amputated.

"Let me see your hands," Stein spoke softly.

She extended her upturned palms toward him. The soft flesh at the crossing of her fate line and health line looked distressed, almost flayed. She withheld nothing. Yes, she confessed, she had done all the things that Stein imagined. She had stolen up behind Henny Spector as he was engrossed in the act of watching Stein suffer and die. She had driven her spear through the back of his skull, right through the protective canvas covering. And when in the throes of searing pain Spector had pulled his helmet off, she had come around in front of him, straddled his head, and drove the point of the second weapon down into his eye.

Stein was a little frightened and flattered by the ferocity of her attention, and then chagrined to learn that he was only a collateral beneficiary of her act. Her decision to impale Henny Spector had been a response to seeing how completely the man had her husband Hollister under his thrall.

She knew exactly how she would do it. Since moving out west from Boston, where the maguey was nonexistent, they had become the central icon in her mythology. She was fascinated by the tall, willowy shoot erupting like a periscope from the soft center of the plant, sprouting upwards of twenty feet in two weeks' time, its clusters of red flowers blossoming brilliantly as if it had nothing to do with the deadly jungle of dart-pointed sentries armed and dangerous below.

She had fantasized doing damage to certain economics professors at Harvard who had disdained her abilities.

After the courtroom decision where Ranger Granger was allowed to retain his stolen merchandise and Hollister had marched away from her to speak to Henny Spector, Ruth Ann had driven home directly and cut down a pair of long green leaf shafts, rolled them tight and wound heavy tape around them to form spears. Even wearing work gloves, the serrated edges had torn into her flesh. She had driven back to town but Henny was gone by then and there was no sign of Hollister. Like everyone else, she knew of the usual hangouts Henny liked to frequent. She had spotted his car out on Route 187, and then to her surprise, she had seen that Stein was following him. She followed them both to Henny's place, and then out to where Henny had taken them in his truck.

She couldn't believe it when that maniac got his truck to cross that naked wash. She left her car there and followed on foot. It didn't take her long once she got there to understand what he had done. He had moved the boxes thirty feet from where they used to be. Her eyes gleamed at this revelation as if she had just explained the essence of God to an atheist.

"First of all, how could you tell he moved them?"

"Pollen droppings, honey residue. Beaten-down grass. It was pretty obvious."

He recalled what Shmooie the Buddhist always used to say: *If you don't know what you're looking at you can't know what you're seeing.*

"Now tell me why it matters that he moved them."

"Bees have their hive's location imprinted on their homing system accurate to three feet. Spector knew they'd all come back to where they had *been* . . . which is where you were."

As a sportsman, Stein had to appreciate the sophistication of Henny's game plan. He wondered about Ruth Ann. "Was it hard to stab him through the back of the head and kill him?"

"I have a Harvard MBA. That's what we're trained for." She was posing. Of course it bothered her. "Can I speak frankly to you, Stein?"

"You've just confessed to murder. How much more frank can you get?"

"He turned my Billy Bob into a greedy, opportunistic—" She stopped herself. "I can't love him anymore. A man is nothing more than the things he does to get what he wants."

"The world's a hard garden to grow integrity."

"I know it is, Stein. That's why you're alone." She leaned closer like she needed him to know being alone wasn't the only option.

"What makes you think I'm alone?"

"You're a man who wouldn't sell empty hives. No matter how much you wanted something. Am I right?"

"You're asking me a hypothetical question."

"Everything is hypothetical till we do it. Do you know what Hollister is going to do? He told me he's already worked it out with the sheriff. He's going to take over Henny Spector's business. What do you think of that?"

Their bodies were close to touching. Any movement forward and the world would have changed. It might have happened. But the sound of a distant telephone ring dissolved into the room. It had the most annoying ring, more like a death rattle. Stein knew that sound. He tilted his ear to locate the source. There was a side door off the pantry that went out to the inverted L where the driveway went behind the house. There was Lila's Lexus. The driver's side window was open. The phone, in its leather nest, was quacking incessantly.

Stein tumbled inside. He got tangled up in the bee suit that was crumpled on the front seat, the suit no doubt that he had briefly worn before handing it over to Henny. He'd verify a puncture hole in the back of the hood later on. Now he grabbed the phone and simultaneously blurted his daughter's name. The automated voice told him he had missed the call and seven previous calls. He whacked the instrument against his thigh as though his ferocious frustration would dislodge the lost messages.

Ruth Ann was a trifle embarrassed at being found in possession of Lila's car. If Hollister was taking over Henny Spector's business and there was a kickback to Sheriff Slodaney that got Hollister released in time for him to have been the second spear bearer along with Ruth Ann, Stein would deal with that later. At this moment he cared about only one thing. He pressed the phone into Ruth Ann's hand and commanded her to play that last message.

She tapped a few buttons, returned the instrument to him. The voice from the earpiece was the soundtrack of Stein's most dire and recurring nightmare: the one-word wail of anguish that loosened every weld in his stomach.

"*Daddeee.*"

Chapter Eighteen

Alicia's boots were not made for running. Adrenaline plus terror more than compensated. Angie clomp-dashed over the hardwood floor of the rowing machine room and out onto the softer resilient sod of the Great Lawn. She dared to stop for a moment to get her bearings and to see if Richard was on her tail. He was not, and for a moment she feared she might have injured him when she slammed the door behind her. But when she pictured what he had done to Matthew, and his naked butt following Lila out of the bathroom, she stopped giving a shit.

There was a slight vibration in her left arm around where the wristband resided. Perspiration from running and anxiety allowed it to slide more freely. The train was just discharging another stream of arriving partygoers. Angie set her course toward a gaggle of girls dressed in don't-you-wish-you-could-fuck-me togs. She sidled up to one and asked, in the way only hip girls know how to talk to each other, if she'd like to get into the afterparty after the afterparty. She surreptitiously extended her braceletted arm.

"How much?"

"Hundred."

Using a small silver implement one of the other girls had around her neck, the clasp was undone and the bracelet slipped off Angie's wrist and onto the other girl's. The new owner made an impressive show of annoyance when she looked in her little bejeweled purse and found no ready cash. "I'll hit you back later," she assured Angie. She and her entourage laughed on.

***

There was relief in the agents' car when screen number two came back on line. "Okay, we have her," Agent Church broadcast. "Let's move now before she tries something cute." They descended upon their target from all directions and corralled her giving head to a guy who said he was Ashton Kutcher's bodyguard. Much to his displeasure, the girl's aperture was uncoupled from his ready member and she was brought to the house where she was presented triumphantly to Richard.

"Who is this?" Richard demanded.

"Angie Stein."

"No, it is not."

He saw the wristband worn as a bangle on her skinny forearm. "Where did you get this?" he demanded.

She shot back defiantly, "I'm on the list."

***

Angie had ducked for concealment into a convoy of old people. Their muddy migration slowly gelled into a larger critical mass of people congealing around the moat area. A buzz of expectation became palpable. "What's going on?" Angie asked of a formidable gray-haired woman decked out in chemise and fur.

A Broadway-sized stage rose up on hydraulics from behind the moat. On it were sixty members of the Los Angeles Philharmonic in gowns and tuxedos. A seventy-foot movie screen rose up behind them. The orchestra began to play a symphonic suite from *Titanic* as imagery from the movie now filled the screen. A tall, handsome, charismatic figure in a tux stood at a podium. "I thought I was the king of the world," he humbly admitted, "but no. The real royalty are Commodore and Lady Bancroft. Seventy-five years!"

On screen behind him, as the LA Phil played the heartrending *Titanic* love theme, the doomed screen lovers Winslet and DiCaprio were magically replaced by blue-screened images of Lucy and J. J. Bancroft. The audience went into upheavals of ecstasy. And then, seemingly through the screen itself, the bodies of the real living couple emerged. The Commodore was dressed in his full white Admiral Dewey array. Lucy was elegant in a straight floor-length gown.

Angie scanned the crowd for Matthew. She flipped open her cell phone. The LOW BATT sign flashed ominously. She had put it on sleep in order to preserve the energy for her father to call back. She dialed, and the ring sounded like an old person trying to breathe. But Matthew's voice answered.

"Where are you?" Her voice cracked between need and longing. "It's starting. We're going to blow it."

"I'm right where I'm supposed to be. Where are *you*?"

"I don't know how to describe it. Can you see the stage?"

"Look left," Matthew said.

She did. He was there at the edge of the crowd. He found his way to her.

"Do you have it?

He cradled the box that in turn cradled the life-sized sculpted head of Sunny Cataluna.

The *Titanic* projection stopped and the music changed to "The Anniversary Song." Al Jolson's voice crooned the most romantic song of the era and a wave of sentimentality eroded Angie's resolve. Lucy and the Commodore gracefully waltzed. It was Valentine's Day. The Bancrofts had found that one valuable, elusive commodity. They had been in love for seventy-five years. She hoped Matthew would bail her out. "Are we really going to do this?"

"Up to you."

"Thanks a lot."

A phalanx of security was stationed around the moat to head off any bad ideas. Matt grabbed Angie's hand and assessed their obstacles. "We need a diversion."

"I could flash them," Angie suggested.

"I mean a diversion they'd notice."

"Oh, you're so cute."

Dear, as I held you so close in my arms,
Angels were singing a hymn to your charms,
Two hearts gently beating were murmuring low,
"My darling, I love you so."

She looked down into the clear eyes of the noble youth's face in the shoebox.

"Fuck it," she said. "What's the worst that could happen?" They eased their way through the crowd, calmly so as not to draw attention. The couple on stage moved as one person. The music rose to a swell. The Commodore dipped his wife. She seemed to fall out of his arms. Two hundred people drew in a collective gasp. But she rolled into a cartwheel and finished with a split. As the music ended the crowd went berserk. In that moment of madness, Angie dashed up the three-step platform to the stage brandishing the bust of Sunny Cataluna.

"Lucy Lester. Do you mind if I cut in?"

A hypnotic hush befell the crowd. Lucy took the head of her long-lost love from Angie's hands and moved it to her breast. Her voice caught in her throat. "Sunny," she croaked. "My Sunny."

Matthew leapt onstage alongside them. Clutched in his hand like a dagger was the elephant tusk that he had kept inside his sport jacket. "This is what your husband used to kill him, Mrs. Bancroft."

Lucy turned on the Commodore with the fury of a welding torch. "You told me he went back to Barcelona."

"It's a figure of speech," Bancroft rasped. "Like buying the farm or biting the dust. Going back to Barcelona."

"You can go back to Barcelona," she hissed. She dropped her multicarat diamond ring to the floor and left the stage with the image of the *Titanic* behind her crashing into the iceberg and crumbling. Then all hell broke loose. Security agents swarmed the stage. A hood was tucked over Angie's head and she was dragged away kicking and flailing.

"Careful, the girl's nuts," Agent Cortelyou cautioned.

"She will be," his partner said, quite pleased with his double entendre. "When we get her to the nut house."

Matthew was caught up in the crowd surge and swept in the opposite direction away from the stage. "Angie, I'm with you," he yelled in her wake.

A low, firm, familiar voice intoned in his ear, "No, you are not."

He whirled around in a fury to face his elder protector. "Damn it, Uncle Richard. What are you doing?"

"Securing your future."

"That's really cool of you." Matthew's young, supple body was capable of containing many contradictory impulses simultaneously. While he smiled gratefully to Richard and his shoulders dropped their combative pose, he saw peripherally that he'd ended up close to the jousting field. Another of the evening's popular contests was about to commence. Across the field, the white knight mounted his steed for what the PA announcer proclaimed would be the ultimate battle of good versus evil. Alongside Matthew, the dark knight, his helmet plumed in red feather, rose up into his saddle. But the evil one never got fully mounted. With the spectacular force of a salmon leaping a waterfall, Matthew dislodged the dark knight's foot from the stirrup, upended him off the saddle, vaulted up into the seat in his place, grabbed the lance from tumbling jouster's right hand, and urged his mount forward.

Across the field the white knight had already begun his charge, his lance wavering in his right hand despite the knowledge that the bout was an exhibition with its outcome preordained. The charging white steed was nothing to Matthew but a trivial impediment. The object of his quest was at the bottom of the hill. He could see the struggling hooded figure being pushed into the back seat of a dark Buick, which then roared through the gate and turned right onto the one road in and out of the compound.

Matthew had never jousted. He had raced quarter horses and played polo.

In a glance he appraised his opponent. He saw the separation between horse and man. Saw the gaps in the knight's armor. Pictured his lance driving through his opponent's body as a needle goes through still water. He let the man come at him, parried his weak thrust with a flick of his wrist, unseated him from his horse, and with the dazed knight sitting on his armored ass, rode at full speed off the course and in pursuit of the agents' car. The PA corroborated what everyone had seen. Evil had fled the field. Virtue had triumphed.

Matthew urged his willing steed down and across the hillside. They leapt the moat and raced along the edge of the property that bounded the road. He could see the headlights of the agents' car on the other side of the six-foot-high fence. A hundred yards in front of him the property line turned to the right, presenting the barrier of the fence directly in front of him.

When Matthew was six years old he had witnessed an eruption of Mauna Loa. Ever since, he had craved the powerful forces of nature underneath him. He had won a silver medal for luge in the Junior Olympics. He had skydived. But his recurring dream had always been to surf down the lava flow of an active volcano. This was the moment. He leaned over and gave his horse a word of encouragement. It had seen the fence in front of them and its equine eyes had widened to marshmallows, but it relaxed under its confident rider. Still, as it approached the fence at top speed, Matthew felt the horse's impulse to shy. He would not let it lose heart. "Now!" he urged. His mount took flight and vaulted over the fence, hitting the main road at a hard gallop.

Once Angie had been ensconced in the back seat of the agents' car they had unhooded her. She saw her knight-errant appear a mere thirty yards behind the rear window. She impulsively screamed out his name, giving her captors warning. With the sight of the galloping knight in the rearview mirror, Church hit the pedal. The Buick rocketed forward. One great horse driven by a great horseman was no match for the internal combustion of three hundred. The distance between man and machine increased. Matthew never gave up until he reached a crossroads. His horse's chest was panting and heaving. Clouds of steam blew from its nostrils. Matthew looked down the roadways in both directions. There were no trailing red lights visible down either way.

The horse questioned its rider's command to abandon the chase, but obeyed. They began the long, slow, hobbling walk back to where they had started. The bitter taste of defeat rose up into Matthew's throat for the first time in his life. He spat it out. It was not for him.

***

As Matthew commenced his doleful walk back, Stein and Ruth Ann set out for the party in Lila's car. Stein permitted Ruth Ann to drive. She was more skillful and knew the roads so it made sense on that level. Plus he hoped it would shut her up. Maybe it was a delayed physiological reaction to murder, but she had not stopped yapping. It wasn't crazy talk that could be tuned out. She was bright and well read and had passionate views on the disproportionate distribution of wealth and the corruptive power of power. It was like getting a mega dose of himself. He could see why people found that trying.

But Stein's only thought was of his daughter. They had played back her previous phone messages where she had told him that maybe they were wrong about the land grab, since none of the parcels were anywhere near the almond groves. He had dismissed that thought; there was no doubt in his mind what was going on. But the only sound that echoed in his mind was that last one-word cry. He tried speed dialing her again but the result was the same as the past five times he tried. The call went straight to voice mail.

They made the right turn into the security gate within ninety seconds of the dark Buick carrying Angie Stein having made its right turn out of the gate. The Raggedy Andy guard duly noted his name, as the security staff had been alerted to do, and upon assigning his car to another clown valet with instructions to boot it, he deferentially bedecked Ruth Ann's wrist with a VIP bracelet. Before he could do the same for Stein, an alarm went up. There was a disturbance across the Great Lawn. The TV security monitor on the booth showed an errant horseman running amok across the grounds.

Raggedy Andy instructed them to wait there a moment, but Stein had no patience for waiting and he scooted Ruth Ann in front of him, losing themselves in the commotion. The shuttle train was still running. In an effort to keep the partygoers calm, the disturbance was quickly announced to be a part of the night's festivities. Magicians and jugglers roamed the hill. The LA Phil played Beethoven's "Ode to Joy." In front of the orchestra, four striking blond women in black cocktail dresses were doing Rockette kicks to the music, thereby demonstrating it was not their statuesque Swedish bodies nor the thirty-year age differences that their multimillionaire husbands married them for, but their irrepressible creativity.

The train deposited Stein and Ruth Ann at the food court. The theme was cheeses of many nations. The excess got Ruth Ann railing that they spent more on Camembert than most people make in a year. Stein caught sight of the main house and said he was going to try to find their host. He was not unglad to get away.

A man with short gray hair tipped his hat to Ruth Ann and told her he spoke English, French, Italian, Spanish, and Portuguese. She called after Stein, now at a distance, "Thank you! I found somebody who can bore me in five languages."

Stein reached the velvet restraining line outside the mansion. In the wake of Angie's previous incursion, there were security guards not in clown suits now patrolling the perimeter. Stein was told politely that the party was down the other way.

"Would you tell Mr. Brickman that Harry Stein is looking for him?"

"Harry Stein is looking for him? That's funny. Because he's been looking for Harry Stein."

"Do you know if by chance my daughter is here?

"Would that be Angie Stein?"

"Yes!"

A gigantic weight tumbled off Stein's shoulders. They knew her. She was accounted for.

Brickman appeared on the portico. He was wearing a white suit and a Gatsby hat, and welcomed Stein like Caesar. Stein followed a trail that Angie had blazed the hour before, past the rowing machine, in through the comedy room, and into the smaller unmarked crowded office where Richard had found Angie. "I believe this is what you have been looking for," Brickman said, and presented the room to Stein with everything it contained.

"How so?"

"The office of the Boysenberry Pi Land and Water Cooperative."

"Ah! I see."

Stein saw nothing. Except that there was something here to see that he wasn't seeing yet.

One thing he had learned from all the antics and antiestablishment guerrilla warfare of the sixties was that the best way to gain control of the situation is to piss off your opponent. So, very disarmingly, he mentioned how flattered he was that Brickman paid homage to Stein's old bit by naming his corporation Boysenberry Pi.

"That was my bit," Brickman laughed.

"Barry. Come on. We're not in school anymore. You don't have to glom on to other people's material."

"What are you talking about? Boysenberry Pi was mine all the way. You didn't even think it was funny."

"Not everything I make up is A-list material. You're welcome to it if you want it that badly."

Brickman was practically shrieking. "I remember exactly when I thought of it. It was in Bio class. Sophomore year!"

Stein relented with a dismissive wave of the hand. "So what have you been doing here, Barry? Buying up all the good orchard land?"

Now it was Brickman's turn to be smug. "No, my friend. I'm afraid you've been misinformed."

"Is that so."

"If you'd done your homework, you'd know that all the parcels Boysenberry Pi has purchased are . . . here." He indicated a place on a topographical display.

It was the exact locale that Angie had described in her message. "That's desert," Stein said. "Unless I am missing something, almonds don't grow in the desert."

"But cities do." He led Stein's eye to the model city display. A gleaming downtown. Sprawling suburbia. Green lawns. Flowering shrubs.

"I'm growing a city, Harry. Twenty years from now, Greater Greater Los Angeles."

Stein disparaged the entire notion. "The Colorado River is already pillaged to feed LA. Where are you going to get your water?"

"Harry! You should be my straight man." He illuminated the deep blue aquifer. "The Boysenberry Pi Water Cooperative." He turned a dial that simulated a flow of water out of the aquifer to the new city, and replenished its contents from the dammed rivers all through the Central Valley. The technology was so cool it made him giggle.

"You're deluded, Barry. That water basin is a public resource. You can't just expropriate it for your own pleasure."

The dam holding back Brickman's glee burst at the seams. He practically levitated with the rising swell. He flipped open his Rolodex. "You see this, Harry? It has the home numbers of all one hundred senators of the United States. I contributed a hundred thousand dollars to every one of their campaigns. And to their opponents. I was on the committee that picked Al Jansen and Leroy Beckons to be the secretaries of agriculture and interior. I could call them right now and get the results of a state environmental impact study reversed, and thereby divert eight hundred thousand gallons of water away from the Sacramento Valley and to me, to the water bank that I just purchased. In fact, I think I'll do that right now, just for fun.

"Oh, no, wait. *I already did*! The papers were filed yesterday at the Calvin Coolidge Courthouse. Signed, yes, by the very same secretaries of agriculture and interior. Barring any complications, the governor signs them into law tomorrow. It's all about water, Harry. In the Middle East, it's not religion. Well, okay, yeah, it is religion, but it's water. It's not even land. Well, yeah, okay, it's land too. But it's water. What you saw on that map, what you looked at but couldn't see, is the new Los Angeles. Two hundred thousand new homes over the next decade. And you want to know the best part? While I lease the water to my neighbors to irrigate their orchards, the state reimburses me for every gallon. So all the land I've bought . . . is paid for out of state money. Now *that's* what I call funny."

"Here's what I think is funny, Barr. Your 'new city' is two thousand feet *higher* in altitude than your aquifer. Last time I looked, water flows downhill to gravity."

"Look again, Harry. Water flows uphill to money."

Stein was exhausted from fighting and losing a bout he thought was an easy win. He needed to regroup in safer territory. "Your centurions out there seemed to know where my daughter is. I'd like to bring her home."

"I could not be happier to hear you express those sentiments, Harry. The one other asset of Boysenberry Pi not shown on this board, Harry, is—yes, I see you getting upset. And of course you're correct. It would be inconsistent with currently acceptable accounting practices to show your daughter on our balance sheet as an *asset*. She would be more appropriately designated as *collateral*, wouldn't you say? As a kind of security deposit, a kind of a preemptive strike against any rash actions that you still mistakenly believe can obstruct the flow of the inevitable. So yes. As crude and obvious as it sounds, I do have her. And presuming that everyone just relaxes and enjoys the party, she'll very likely be returned to you unscathed at ten o'clock tomorrow morning. Although, Harry, I've got to say, what she did to poor J. J. Bancroft—I don't know if she gets it from you or your ex-wife—but she's shown she's got a real mean streak in her. Can I get you a beer?"

Stein was speechless, which delighted Brickman more than owning the valley.

"The last laugh goes to Barry, not to Harry. Now *that's* funny."

He was beaming, absolutely beaming, until Stein's fist caught him flush in the jaw. It was the first time in Stein's fifty-one years that he ever punched someone in the face as hard as he could. Brickman toppled like a ton of his namesakes. The rush of adrenaline made Stein want to punch someone else. Anyone in his path. He burst out the door and stormed down the hill in a blind, desperate search for his daughter.

Chapter Nineteen

Stein stumbled down the grassy knoll, trying to keep his speed down and not yield flat out to gravity. He nearly tripped over the model railroad tracks. His sport jacket wings flapped out to the sides. Three-quarters of the way down his lungs were squeezing through his rib cage and the blood in his temples was beating out the rhythm: *aneurysm, aneurysm*. An indignant voice assaulted him. "Hi. Do I look familiar?"

"Shit. Ruth Ann." He had forgotten she existed.

"Nice greeting."

"I'm sorry. They have my daughter."

"Who does?"

"Mr. Stein!" A haggard young Don Quixote called out to Stein from under a cluster of overhanging trees just inside the perimeter of the fence. "It's me. Matthew."

"Matthew?"

"I know where they have her, Mr. Stein. I tried to catch them." He gestured apologetically to his ragged Rocinante, tethered to the fence.

Stein tried to calm and reassure the exhausted boy, though he was far from calm and assured himself. "Where is she?"

"I heard them say they were taking her to an insane asylum."

"An insane asylum?"

"Pinecrest," said Ruth Ann, quite knowingly. "It's way down by the coast." Then added, "I'm strictly outpatient."

Stein told them both to wait right there while he went to get the car.

To fill in the awkward silence, Ruth Ann said to Matthew her name was Ruth Ann.

Matthew said, "Matthew."

"My husband is taking over the spurious operations of the man I murdered."

"My stepmother had sex with my uncle who gave me this black eye."

"Glad to meet you."

"You, too."

Stein found his car. Booted. "The fuck," he complained into the hollow exhausty infirmament. He returned to the surface where he had left Matthew and Ruth Ann to find Captain Caravaggio with his left python slung around Matthew's shoulder, leading him toward his squad car.

"Hey. Hey. *Hey*!" Stein became amazingly winded running fifteen strides uphill. "Captain. It's okay. The kid's with me."

Caravaggio turned around to see who was giving the ringing endorsement.

"He's telling the truth," Ruth Ann attested.

Caravaggio looked at her askance. "Who are you?"

"I'm Hollister Greenway's wife."

"There's another stunning testimonial."

"The girl in the courthouse with me," Stein gasped.

"She's my daughter. Brickman and possibly Bancroft and this kid's uncle Richard are holding her hostage."

"We think at Pinecrest," said Ruth Ann.

Stein, with more lung capacity, managed to say that there was a gigantic scam going on. That people were getting paid off big time.

"So that's not just a rumor?

"Hell, no. They're bragging about it."

"Well, that breaks it!" He threw open the doors to the squad car and told them all to get the hell in.

"I see they've offended your morality," Stein observed.

"Goddamn right! Who the hell do they think they are, handing out kickbacks and not to me?"

Ruth Ann called shotgun.

Caravaggio blasted out the gate and careened to the left.

"They went to the right," Matthew said.

"This way gets down to the coast," Caravaggio growled.

"I followed them on horseback."

"The other way goes up into the hills. Pinecrest is on the ocean. Now shut up."

"Okay." They flew around some bends in the road. "I never actually heard them say Pinecrest," Matthew said. "Just that they were talking her to the nut house."

Stein jumped forward in his seat and grabbed Caravaggio's massive shoulder. "Stop the car. They're not taking her to the *nuthouse*. They're taking her to the *nut* house."

Caravaggio knew exactly what Stein meant. He wheeled around the other way. His face became etched in painful thought. "You know who we need to talk to? That friend of yours with the helicopter."

"Why? Do we need an airborne assault?"

"He rents machinery to them. Look, Stein. There's no good way to tell you this. The place they have her stashed . . . They crush eight thousand tons of nuts every day."

"This is why I'm never having kids," said Ruth Ann.

Amid the litter of notes and napkin fragments and government documents in his wallet, Stein found Spade Wilson's business card. "It's late, though. He's not going to be at his office."

"Cell phone technology," Ruth Ann clucked at him. "Get into the twentieth century."

The news was not good. Wilson confirmed Caravaggio's apprehensions that he had leased to Brickman's company the very top of the line TGM Series Super Pressure Trapezium Mill.

"We need to disable the equipment," Caravaggio said.

"What kind of operation are you launching? It sounds like something we pulled off in Tripoli."

"How busy are you tonight?"

"I can get there before you."

***

The "We Crush Your Nuts" building looked even more sinister at night than it had when Brickman had driven Stein past it. Harsh, ultrabright exterior lighting rendered the network of gleaming PVC tubes a garish radioactive white, that slid and bent and curved around each other like external intestines.

Wilson was waiting for them outside the gate of the processing plant. Stein insisted on listening to the description of the mechanisms inside. "Material goes into the jaw crusher between rollers and shovels, and is sent into the grinding chamber. All that's left is powder. From there it's sent into the cyclotron and sucked into the centrifugal blower."

Stein tried to picture somebody's cat in the predicament Wilson was describing, not his daughter.

"The good news is that the intake valve has a diameter of twenty-two centimeters. I assume your daughter is wider than that."

"Yes," Stein said.

"The bad news is that they never removed the two-ton concrete slab pulverizing mechanism from the old days. I doubt they would have left it operational. Plus it's off-season, and all their power may be shut down. But on the other hand, you never know. So I say we go in and take it down."

Matthew sprinted back in from a brief reconnoitering run. The agents' car was nowhere around, he reported, so either they left Angie here unguarded . . . He avoided looking at Stein, "Or she's somewhere else," he said.

"Special Ops in Panama would have knocked the place over already. Let's move."

Caravaggio lodged his frame in front of everybody. "I'm giving the orders here. After me." He advanced to the main door and after shoving his shoulder against it to no avail, allowed Ruth Ann to gently pull it open.

It was dark as a bat's balls inside. The misfit posse stayed tight together and tripped over each other's legs. "Anyone think to bring a flashlight?" Wilson groused.

"This might be a light switch." Ruth Ann began groping the walls with snow angel arms.

"Wait, Ruth Ann. I'm not sure you ought to do that."

Stein grabbed her around the middle and whirled her away. The switch she had brushed blindly upward had not turned the lights on, but it had done something. In total darkness, the entire floor began to vibrate. An electro-mechanical hum rose in pitch from bass up through alto and up to a high scream. And then came the first thundering impact. The walls and floor resounded. Another earthshaking thud followed moments later.

"Turn the goddamn thing off," Caravaggio roared. Stein had managed to shed Ruth Ann's grasping arms. He found a lever against the wall and plunged it.

The house of horrors was instantly bathed in blinding light. Seven huge crushers were rooted into the concrete in a prayer circle— a Stonehenge of polished chrome chambers and steel-bladed tur- bines. But they were not the source of the vibrations that seemed to shake to the very mantle of the earth. No, the switch had activated the medieval technology of the concrete crushers. These were long steel rods connected to a series of megaton concrete slabs that rose and fell in sequence like pistons, their rough undersides designed to pulverize anything on the floor below.

"Hey. Up here." A plaintive voice came from the rafters. Angie was perched amid a system of sluices and chutes, which during harvest would feed tons of almonds from each of seven hoppers to be crushed into dust.

"Angie!" Stein and Matthew in unison called out her name.

"The bottom of this thing is opening!"

"Turn that goddamn switch off," Caravaggio bellowed again. Stein went for the wall switch. So did Ruth Ann. All the lights went out. "Not that one!" The lights came back on. All necks swung up to the hopper where Angie had been stuck. But she was gone.

Without hesitation Matthew scaled the rope ladder to the top like a capuchin. The crow's nest where Angie had been was empty. Its floor had opened up and dropped her down into the supply sluice, a winding spiral slide that in its mellower form delighted kids at playgrounds. He followed her through and slid down a twisting luge course. He accelerated through the curves and quickly caught up to Angie. She had gotten stuck, suspended upside down over the opening where all the shells would cascade.

The toe of her borrowed footwear had wedged itself into the gear wheel, catching an iron gear tooth that operated the piston of one of the crushers. The concrete slab was suspended above her while she hung inverted. Matthew was able to stop himself on the slide, rubbing the skin of his forearms raw.

Ten feet below her Angie saw her father and the fat cop and a black man and a strange woman looking hopefully, desperately up at her. With the gear mechanism stuck, an automatic cutoff switch had severed the electric current driving the mechanism. However, it had not shut down the forces of gravity that were straining to push the stuck gear over Angie's boot, which would then allow the weight of the concrete slab to continue its downward plunge, obstructed only by Angie's frame, dangling from the chute like a baby tooth.

Matthew inverted his body, wriggling himself close to Angie. He made his voice sound remarkably calm. "I'm with you," he said. "I think we're okay."

"I don't feel very okay." She tried to squirm. The gear shuddered and loosened and moved an inch and caught again.

"You want to stay very still, Ange. Very still."

"Okay, but don't call me Ange."

"I see a way out of this, but it means doing something you're not going to like." She braced herself to hear what it was. "I mean you're really going to hate it." He called down below for anyone to hand him up the sharpest cutting instrument they had. It was Spade Wilson who had with him a version of a Tanto knife, similar to the one the Russian had used to slice the seeded mandarin.

Caravaggio boosted Spade Wilson up onto his shoulders. Wilson reached to his full height and Matthew reached down. He felt the instrument being placed into his hand. He carefully rearranged his body, gaining purchase against the smooth, slippery sides of the chute by pressing his legs out against them, and supporting his full body weight. His face reddened with the effort.

"Mr. Stein, you've got to be ready to catch her the second I cut her loose. That stone thing is going to fall as soon as her foot is out of the gear tooth and you've got to grab her out before it does."

Angie looked down at her anxious father. "Daddy, I have to tell you something. Promise you won't be mad."

Stein could barely speak. "I promise, baby."

"I still have another key to your car."

"Angie. I need you to look only at me now," Matthew said.

All the blood had descended to her inverted head and she was getting woozy.

"On the count of three I want you to scream as loud as you can, okay?" He gripped the knife tight in his right hand. He jackknifed his body. His legs were quivering to hold fast. He held the knife to her booted shin. "One . . . two . . ."

Stein couldn't bear it. "What are you going to do to her?"

"*Now.*"

Angie screamed as Matt inserted the knife blade and slit Alyssa's borrowed boot down the side. He yanked her foot out. The boot had been the last thing holding Angie in place, and now she plummeted headfirst into her father's chest. Freed of its impediment, the gear holding the concrete slab instantly rolled over the defooted boot, loosing the mechanism to gravity. The two-ton slab of concrete plunged downward.

Directly under the crushing piston Stein staggered with the weight of impact of his daughter hitting his chest. He was snatched out of the path of the pulverizing slab by the strong, fat arm of Caravaggio, who himself staggered under his momentum toward the smashing site right alongside them, where the next slab was now heading down. The three of them would have been powder—indistinguishable as any chain link of predator, prey, and scavenger in the tar pits—had not the strong ebony hand of Spade Wilson grabbed Caravaggio by the scruff of the neck, anchored by his splayed legs and other hand, and kept them all afloat.

Ruth Ann steadied herself and lent a hand to Angie, pulling her to complete safety, then Stein. Matthew vaulted down from the top of the chute and struck the landing in front of her with that grin. "Hi," he said.

Stein grasped his daughter's shoulders, and Matthew's. He knew what would happen if he tried to speak. His eyes fluttered like a butterfly drying its wings.

Chapter Twenty

The work on Lila's Jacuzzi was completed to perfection. The heater motor hummed. The whirlpool mechanism purred. The last chunk of sod was replaced in the backyard. It glistened green as Ireland. The turquoise tiles at the bottom of the pool shone through clear water. Everything was back to the way it had been before Stein arrived.

He carried the last armload of his things down from Lila's bedroom. He had loaded Angie's stuff on the first trip back to his apartment. Her brush with mortality had not altered her resolve never to set foot in Lila's again. She hadn't told him why. Only that she was content to live with her mother full time if it came to that.

Lila followed Stein outside through the front gate to his car. Old hurts live in healthy tissue and every new loss unscars every old one. Her husband's death from cancer had been unpreventable, but this loss was her fault. Not just doing it but telling Stein about what happened with Richard. She had been sure Angie had told him. She had been trying to apologize, or explain, and in fact had gotten angry with Stein for pretending not to know and making her spell it out to him. It was that part she still felt horrible about. Which put them pretty close to even.

She needed some closure, a set of rules to live by. That would do for now in lieu of hope. "We can still be friends, can't we?" she asked.

"We should probably give it a rest for a while," Stein said, not unkindly.

"I liked Angie a lot, you know."

"She's not dead."

"No," Lila said. "I am."

Mercedes came out of the house and asked Lila what she wanted for lunch.

"I'll make it," Lila said.

"Is okay. I do it."

"No, I need to do more things myself."

"I wish you'd have let Mercedes do Richard for you." Stein managed a little ironic humor.

He turned to go to his car. There was a ticket plastered on his windshield for not having a Beverly Hills permit displayed. The irony of it was perfect.

"Do you think we could have made it?" Lila asked. "I mean, erasing that one thing?"

He didn't want to tell her about the decision he'd made to close up the old duplex and make his future with her.

"Never mind," she said. "Either way I don't want to know."

He blew her a sad little kiss before getting into the car. She watched it go by without reaching for it.

***

Stein could have flown to Sacramento and rented a car, but driving the whole way cleared his head. The Peerings' Range Rover was parked on the driveway of their two-story suburban home, set amid other suburban two-story homes on a suburban two-story street.

Stein nodded a greeting through the front screen door to Ned, who was propped up on his elbows on the floor in the family room, working with Skip to build a birdhouse out of bottle caps. It was Barbara Peering Stein beckoned to join him outside. "Your roses look beautiful," Stein said for all to hear, as he guided her out of family earshot.

"I saw on TV about your daughter and her friend discovering and solving that old murder, Barbara Peering said. "You must be proud of her."

He smiled and nodded that he was.

"If only we could keep them babies. It all goes by so fast."

"I think time is going to slow down for you for a long while, Mrs. Peering."

She caught from his tone that this was not a friendly visit.

"Pretend I'm selling you aluminum siding and let's walk around to the side of the house."

"If you were selling aluminum siding I'd tell you to take a hike."

"Pretend something else then."

While he pointed up at random places on the house and jotted down make-believe numbers, he told her what he knew: that it wasn't the lover of a Monahan widow who loosened the ties on Frank's load. That she did not see anybody in the parking lot running away from the back of his truck.

Her breathing became heavy.

"On the way back to Los Angeles I stopped with my daughter at that roadhouse where your family had the encounter. We sat at the booth where you sat. She went around back to the ladies room. She called me in and showed me something I was not surprised to see. It has a door that opens to the back where they keep the trash bins. From there it's a clear walk to the parking lot. You went out to the truck and loosened the ties. It wasn't the bees that killed him, Mrs. Peering. It was you."

She didn't blink. Stein read the flickers of thoughts that passed behind her eyes.

"It's all true," she said. "And I'm quite certain you understand why, or you'd never have known. He took my children's respect for their father away. That I could not abide." She stopped as they reached the back of the house.

"Monahan had kids. They don't have a father now. And your guy is building a birdhouse out of bottle caps."

"I guess. If you look at it that way."

"How would you look at it?"

She tried to think of another way but resigned herself that he was right. "May I have a few minutes to say goodbye to my family?"

"I'm not taking you in, Mrs. Peering."

"Please, call me Barbara."

"I mean, somebody will. I would think. But not me."

"I see."

He returned, not happily, to his car.

Sabrina Peering appeared at the side of the house, hands cocked sullenly on her hips. "Mommm. Are you going to be out here forever? I have cheerleading."

Stein read Barbara Peering's thoughts. Prison might be a pleasant respite.

Epilogue

When word got out that a private corporation had pulled a back-room deal to expropriate the ownership of a vital public resource, one-third of California's fresh water supply, there were howls of protest. About three howls and a whimper. The investigative reporters, all two of them who had not bartered their writing souls for column space and whose papers had not traded courage for access, wrote the story. They drummed for details. They pricked the points of their pens into the veins of public outrage. They drew no blood.

The massive PR wheels rolled into the ruts already rent into the public's mind. They spun their sweet cotton candy yarns of why corporate stewardship of valuable resources was better for us. Their spin song lulled the somnambulistic into contented dreams where everything comes out just right, where plunder is progress, where gargantuan profit is an unintended by-product of altruism. While just out of sight, lawyers and lobbyists crushed out and bought out the flaccid opposition.

There was a good rain that winter and late spring. Wildflowers grew in abundance. There were bounteous crops of almonds that fall and bumper crops of honey. And so the inevitable day was fore-stalled when the well will run dry at the Havelock orchard at nine in the morning. When Ian Peters' pump coughs out sand and gravel. When Garvey Reed's machinery blows out air and no water, and he takes his shotgun to the adjacent farm, thinking his erstwhile friendly neighbor has usurped his portion, but finds that orchard dry as a dustbowl too. When the summer heat beats down, leaving a top layer of clay that bakes hard and impermeable, so developing fruits shrivel on the vine. When parched roots turn unnaturally upward in search of water and crack through the surface, therein falling prey to legions of marauding insects, to the excretions of stray dogs, and to the surprising mortal enemies of roots; sunlight and air. When the distant music of dogs and children disappear and the last remaining sound is the hot dry wind scraping through branches of dangling carcasses and the fading faraway buzz of dying bees.

About the Author

Hal Ackerman has been on the faculty of the UCLA School of Theater, Film and Television since 1985 and is currently co–area head of the screenwriting program. His book, *Write Screenplays That Sell . . . the Ackerman Way*, is in its third printing, and is the text of choice in a growing number of screenwriting programs around the country.

He has had numerous short stories published in literary journals over the past two years, including *North Dakota Review*, *New Millennium Writings*, *Southeast Review*, *The Pinch*, and *The Yalobusha Review*.

His short story "Roof Garden" won the Warren Adler 2008 award for fiction and his "Alfalfa" was included in the anthology *I Wanna Be Sedated . . . 30 Writers on Parenting Teenagers*. Among the twenty-nine "other writers" were Louise Erdrich, Dave Barry, Anna Quindlen, Roz Chast, and Barbara Kingsolver. "Walk Through" is among *Southeast Review*'s World's Best Short Shorts of 2010.

His nonfiction baseball memoir, "Talk to the Stars," appears in the fifteenth anniversary issue of *Sports Literate*.

His play, *Testosterone: How Prostate Cancer Made a Man of Me*, won the William Saroyan Centennial Prize for drama, enjoyed a successful run in Los Angeles, and is currently touring as a one-man play called *Prick*.